A Rob Wyllie p
First published in Great Britain in
Derbyshire, United Kingdom

Copyright @ Rob Wyllie 2024

The right of Rob Wyllie to be identified as the author of this work has been asserted by him in accordance with the Copyright, Design and Patents Act 1988

All rights reserved. No part of this publication may be reproduced, stored in a retrieval system, or transmitted. in any form or by any means, electronic, mechanical, photocopying, recording or otherwise, without the prior permission of the copyright owner.

All the characters in this book are fictitious and any resemblance to actual persons, living or dead, is purely coincidental.

RobWyllie.com

The Maggie Bainbridge Series

Death After Dinner
The Leonardo Murders
The Aphrodite Suicides
The Ardmore Inheritance
Past Sins
Murder on Salisbury Plain
Presumption of Death
The Loch Lomond Murders
The Royal Mile Murders
Murder on Speyside
Murder in the Cairngorms

Murder in the Cairngorms

Rob Wyllie

Murder in the Cairngorms

Chapter 1

Olivia Cranston gave a detached smile of acknowledgment as an attractive young waitress placed the cocktail and a small dish of mixed nuts on the table. She had been pretty desperate for a drink, after what she now recognised had been one of the most exciting but stressful afternoons of her life. Ordinarily she would have selected a large chardonnay to sooth the nerves, but today was not an ordinary day. Instead, it was a day that surely called for a celebration, even although the formal result of the interview wouldn't emerge until tomorrow at the earliest. But she *knew* she'd got it. You almost always knew, didn't you? *Olivia Cranston, Associate Professor of Macroeconomic Theory, Department of Economics, King's College, Cambridge.* It sounded rather amazing, and she only thirty-one years of age too. Finally, she hoped, she would be able to put the utter dreadfulness of the last ten years behind her, leaving Scotland and all it represented as just a distant memory, fading to an occasional nightmare that she could convince herself had never happened. As for the interview itself, it wasn't the actual proceedings which had caused the almost unbearable stress of the last few days, but the realisation of how much was at stake, and how devastated she would have been had it not gone well.

But it *had* gone well, the panel of four faculty seniors warm and friendly, and exactly as she had expected, as much concerned about Olivia's progressive credentials as her academic record. Which was just as well, given her terrible guilty secret, although ten years on, the truth of *that* was unlikely ever to surface, thank God. As to her application, she was a *woman* of course, so that was always going to be a plus-point. Furthermore, she was blessed with a dark sallow complexion that had been the source of cruel teasing when she was at school but allowed her to tick the *mixed-race* box on the submission form, which, she consoled herself, would almost certainly be found to be true were she to go back through enough generations of her family. Sexuality had not been expressly enquired about on the form - that had surprised her- but a member of the panel had asked if Olivia's family would be moving to Cambridge should her application be successful, and she had answered *of course*, and that her lovely partner Rhona was fully supportive of this exciting career opportunity. Why the hell she had said that she didn't know, other than it being another little snippet of evidence that confirmed what she already knew. That she, Olivia Cranston, was not quite right in the head. The truth was, the beautiful Rhona Fraser might or might not have been supportive of this startling career move, but Rhona had disappeared in this self-same city nearly eight years earlier, disappeared without trace and now presumed dead. It had taken great courage for Olivia to come back here, even for just one day, and it was going to take even more courage to actually live here. But that was a bridge that she would just have to cross.

The early spring sun had sunk a degree or two, the clocks having not long sprung forward, and Olivia suddenly noticed the chill in the air. She shuffled her chair a few inches to get closer to the patio heater, which had the coincident advantage of affording her a better view across the river. The vista was idyllic, the Cam winding slowly through the meadows in front of the impressively architected colleges, in a scene that had barely changed over the centuries. True, in recent years, the University had made considerable efforts to broaden the social diversity of its undergraduate intake, in the process generating howls of protests from the great public schools, who saw easy access to an Oxbridge place as an almost God-given right. But the fact was, she reflected, even if you didn't enter this place as privileged, you were unarguably privileged when you left it. Having Cambridge University on your CV presented you with a key to the Establishment, and it was a gift that would last a lifetime, smoothly opening doors as you effortlessly glided your way through a gilded career, and that was true irrespective of what field of human endeavour you had chosen to pursue. And as it was for graduates, so it was too for senior academics, a Cambridge professorship being in many ways as good as a lottery win in the snobbish and status-obsessed world of academia.

Across the river, and probably no more than forty or fifty feet distant, was another drinking establishment, this one rather more traditional than the trendy wine bar on whose terrace Olivia was enjoying what was her third Margarita. You would probably call it a gastropub, she guessed, if such a term was still in fashion - she wondered if it was - and even at this relatively early hour of six-thirty, it was crowded with diners, clearly visible through an impressive glass-sided conservatory. The clientele presented an interesting mixture sartorial-wise, with a clutch of undergrads in regulation t-shirts and faded jeans, occasionally augmented by a college-logo'd fleece for those who were already feeling the chill. But sprinkled amongst them were those who had selected a more formal attire, mainly couples, and it seemed on first appraisal, mostly of an early-to-mid thirties demographic. She surmised that the St George's Arms was a popular first or second date venue for individuals who had wasted their twenties on some dead-beat and were now hoping for a second chance. The women were all attractive, in pretty dresses and rifling fingers through luxuriant locks whilst gazing alluringly at the floppy-haired men in brown corduroy jackets who sat opposite. The floppy-haired look wasn't quite so fashionable back in her gritty home city, but there had been plenty of floppy-*brained* men who had tried it on with her, only to be disappointed to find that she preferred the company of her own sex. And sheer statistics suggested that not all these pretty women were straight. She herself had known she wasn't since she was a teenager, but in some women, the truth took longer to blossom. Perhaps she would find someone in this academic city, someone who might make the loss of Rhona something she could live with at last.

Glancing at her watch, she wondered if she might just have time to slip in one more cocktail before she made her way to the pub venue that was staging the concert. It had been an amazing stroke of luck to find out that Dan Jackson was playing in the town that night, and with his full band too. Adding to her lucky streak, she had been fortunate to bag one of the last tickets available, given they had been selling like hotcakes as soon as this extra surprise date had been announced. She was a huge fan of contemporary folk music, and Dan was one of its brightest young stars, as well as being seriously hot, attracting a female teenage fan-base that had only the remotest interest in his musical genre. As if on cue, the waitress appeared out of her peripheral vision and shot her a questioning smile, which Olivia fantasised might hold more meaning than just an enquiry as to whether she wanted another drink. Looking the girl straight in the eye, she giggled and slowly raised a finger to signal *just one more*. She was *very* nice, but the girl probably wouldn't be off shift until midnight, so she could very easily catch the gig then come back here afterwards for a nightcap, and perhaps something more besides. Disappointingly, it was a male waiter who returned with her drink, and as the tall glass was laid on the table in front of her, Olivia realised she felt *seriously* drunk. *Seriously*. She liked that word, and what the hell, this was turning out to be a *serious* red-letter day, and if you couldn't get *seriously* pissed on a day like this, then when could you? She picked up her glass and took a long draft, placed it back on the table, then began to reflect on how, quite suddenly, life had become a little less bitter. Reflecting on her current situation, what she found truly remarkable was the effect this new and scary opportunity had had on her normally fragile mental health, or more technically according to that head-doctor she had consulted, her *deep-seated mental-health challenges*. She laughed at that, because the truth was, as she had reflected earlier, she wasn't quite right in the head, and had been that way since that shattering event of eight years ago, the event that had defined every moment of her life since. Yes, it was an old-fashioned way to describe her mental state, but no other description quite fitted her situation. *She wasn't quite right in the head.* Although she hated to focus on it, the fact was that on almost every single day of the last eight years, she had contemplated taking her own life. And it hadn't been just some idle self-pitying fantasy either, but a fully worked-out plan, conceived as a sort of insurance policy should the general rubbishness of her life become too much to bear. She would splash out on two bottles of the most expensive chardonnay she could find and buy a new glistening fine-stemmed glass too. Then she would drive north, up alongside Loch Lomond and through Tyndrum, then head west along the A85, savouring the majestic Highland scenery for the last time. A few miles from Connel, the road and the railway begin to converge, as they hug the shore of beautiful Loch Etive. There, she would park up and then wander over to the side of the railway line, finding a soft grassy bank alongside the fence, where she would have a fine view of the loch. She would open her wine, then relax and enjoy the tangy lemony flavours, although she didn't expect the first bottle to last very long. Opening the second bottle, she would be very aware of the pleasing numbness beginning to set in, enough to deal with any second thoughts she might be having, but not enough to prevent her from going through with her plan. There weren't many trains on that remote line, but those that did operate could generally be relied on to adhere to the published timetable, and besides, in that quiet spot you could hear their approach ages before they sped by, so you would always be ready even if there was a delay. And sure, she would feel a tiny bit sorry for the driver, powerless in his cab as she stepped in front of his train, but let's face it, there was always going to be collateral damage, no matter what method she chose. From her selfish point of view, it would be swift, painless and decisive, which was all you could reasonably ask for.

Of course, thinking that way wasn't normal, she knew that, but it was strangely comforting, although she knew that wasn't normal either. But in recent weeks, thoughts of self-harm had been miraculously if perhaps temporarily banished from her mind, because for the first time in a long time, Olivia had something to live for. A new city, a new start, although the choice of Cambridge was poignant, given what had happened to tragic Rhona. But you couldn't live in the past for ever, you had to move on, and now the future was going to be bloody excellent. Smiling to herself, she glanced at her watch. *Oops, better get going if you don't want to be late girl.* Reaching for her drink, she drained it with one long guzzle. Fumbling for her bag, she leapt to her feet, knocking over her chair in the process as the effects of the alcohol hit her, its steel frame sending out a jarring metallic clatter as it landed on the concrete floor. With a giggle and then a mumbled *sorry* to the occupants of the next table, who had been startled by this unexpected intrusion, she ran unsteadily towards the gate that led to the riverside path. She hadn't really been paying attention during the mile or so walk from King's College to the wine-bar, due to her playing the glorious interview over and over again in her head, and now she couldn't remember when and indeed if she had passed the concert venue. It was called the Cambridge Musician or something like it, she remembered that much, and as the name came to her, she remembered exactly where it was, about a half a mile or so from her present location. She had plenty of time, no need to run, not that she felt exactly capable of doing that in her current wobbly state. Floating along in a pleasant euphoria, she played the interview through in her mind once again, laughing to herself at how inept the panel had been, although wondering just a little how thorough they would be in checking out her back-story. But no, they wouldn't be looking too hard into that. *Yes, our new professor of economics is a mixed-race lesbian woman. First class honours too, from the Adam Smith Business School at Glasgow.* That ticked all their boxes, and Olivia doubted if they could believe their luck.

In less than ten minutes she arrived at the venue, the location given away by the crowd of Jackson fans milling around the entrance, the men almost universally bearded, the women favouring daisy-chain headbands- plastic and thus fake, but visually effective - and long woollen coats. Olivia joined the ramshackle queue and shuffled along until she reached the door, where two buxom girls, dressed in black jeans and *Dan Jackson on Tour* t-shirts, stood with hand-held scanners to check the electronic tickets of the patrons. Seeing the sign for the bar, she hesitated for a moment, then decided against it, following another sign for her seat number, which directed her up a narrow stairwell. As she had known in advance, her seat was near the back, but it was a small venue with no more than a hundred or so seats, and they rose in quite a steep slope from the stage, so she was going to get a great view of the fantastic Dan and his band. The auditorium was already more than half-full, with it being just a few minutes before they gave the *please take your seats* warning announcement. She stayed on her feet and scanned the room, subconsciously seeking out the pretty women amongst the gathering audience, of which, pleasingly, there seemed to be plenty to visually savour.

But then her attention was drawn to a man who had suddenly appeared in her line of sight. He was wearing a suit and scrutinising the tickets of two young women, evidently in an effort to help them find their seats. She looked again, this time more closely. Surely, *surely*, it couldn't be *him*? That was impossible. It looked *so* like him, but it *couldn't* be. *Because he was dead.* Of course it was ten years' on, and nobody looked exactly the same after that passage of time, he would be what, fifty-one, fifty-two now? *But it couldn't be him*, she chided herself. *That man died in the Cairngorm mountains, ten years ago.* So she looked again, recognising the same narrow eyes, the same weak chin, the same monks' patch that now covered more of his head, the baldness bright red and freckled through exposure to the sun. He had never been a particularly good-looking man, but he'd had power back then, a power he'd used shamefully to compensate for his unattractive appearance. But she had found out what he had been up to, how he preyed on female undergraduates, exchanging grades for sex, and she had threatened to expose him to the authorities. Turning the tables, she had made him pay for her silence, trading it for the first-class honours degree that now took a guilty pride of place on her CV.

Shaking from the shock, she took a deep breath to calm herself, then looked for a third time. *No, it couldn't be*. Her mind was still in turmoil after the interview, and she had recklessly consumed four powerful cocktails, and the alcohol would be dulling her cognitive powers but stimulating her imagination at the same time. She was mistaken, of course she was. *Because he was dead.* Momentarily frozen by indecision, she scanned along her row, wondering whether she should leave now before he saw her, or whether she should stay, even perhaps confront him and find out what the *hell* was going on? But if this really *was* him, his presence the product of some unfathomable trickery - and the pure absurdity of the situation almost made her laugh out loud - then *everything* she thought she knew about what had happened on that terrible night ten years ago must be wrong. She sat down abruptly, suddenly paralysed by a creeping fear, her mind a confused mess. *What the hell was happening here?* And then, with a sinking feeling in the pit of her stomach, she thought again about Rhona. Back then, nearly eight years earlier, the disappearance of her darling Rhona Fraser had seemed no more than a cruel tragedy, providing further evidence to her that God did not exist, because if he did, why could he have done this to her? But now, through the disbelief and confusion of this emerging nightmare, a horrible truth began to crystallise in her thoughts. Her mind working overtime, she got unsteadily to her feet then pushed her way past the row of seated patrons to the opposite aisle to where the man stood. A teenage usher slouched with his hands behind his back, temporarily without duties as he waited for the next batch of ticket-holders to emerge from the stairwell. Olivia stretched out a hand and tapped his elbow to attract his attention.

'Excuse me, but could you tell me who that man is please?' she asked, pointing across the auditorium. 'The chap in the suit, talking to these two women.'

'That's Mr Berrycloth,' the boy answered pleasantly. 'Mr Peter Berrycloth. He's our boss.'

Berrycloth? Surely not, Olivia thought, her confusion compounded by this new and utterly bizarre coincidence. *Berrycloth. This was just unbelievable.*

Thinking fast, she rummaged in her bag and randomly pulled out one of the business cards that she had been given at the interview. *Professor Roland J Hart, Department of Economics, King's College, Cambridge.*

'Have you got a pen?' she asked the boy. 'Quickly, please.'

'Yeah sure,' he replied, pulling a ballpoint from an inside pocket of his jacket and handing it to her. She turned over the card and, taking care to ensure it was legible, wrote her message on the back.

'Can you give this to Mr Berrycloth?' she said, handing the boy the card and his pen. 'It's important. But wait until I'm gone, if you don't mind.'

He gave her a puzzled look then shrugged. 'Yeah, like sure.' He took the card and shrugged again. 'I'll wander across now and give him it if you like.'

But there was no answer from Olivia, she having already sprinted up the aisle and out into the stairwell. The boy, of course, *had* to read what she had written. It would have been impossible not to, but nevertheless he gave the back of the card a surreptitious sideways glance, as if worried anyone should see him. There were just six words, written in a neat and precise hand.

I Know Who You Are.

Olivia

Chapter 2

Maggie was greatly looking forward to this morning's upcoming meeting for several reasons. For a start, it was going to be great to be working again with her former full-time associate Jimmy Stewart, who now lived in Braemar from where he ran his outdoor adventure company with his former army mate Stew Edwards. Secondly, the prospective assignment itself was already seriously intriguing, even before she knew any of the details of what they were going to be asked to do. The client, the huge and prestigious Edinburgh & Glasgow Assurance Company, had told her they had been added to their shortlist specifically because of Jimmy's experience of mountain-craft, and furthermore, when she had made a preparatory call to the firm's representative the previous day, she got the distinct impression that the company's shortlist of investigators currently contained only one name, that of her firm Bainbridge Associates. Or should that now be Stewart Associates, she pondered whimsically, given her recent marriage to Jimmy's brother Frank? The question was, why should mountain-craft be so important to this stuffy old insurance firm, whose website informed her had been in existence for almost two hundred years? That was something she was very keen to find out.

Contrary to its name, the insurance company had its headquarters in a large business park on the outskirts of

Stirling, the pretty and historic town which was located roughly half-way between Scotland's two great cities. Generally, in her experience, these parks were bland, featureless and somewhat depressing too, but this one was different, a shiny modern complex of low-rise buildings set in landscaped grounds, and with views of the castle to the east and of the scenic Ochil hills to the north. She parked her Golf in the expansive visitors' carpark and followed the signs to the reception building, where, as she expected, Jimmy was waiting for her. They embraced warmly, then he said, 'Nice place this eh? They must have made some money over the years.'

She laughed. 'Yes, definitely. And somehow, I always think of insurance as a particularly Scottish business. I don't know why. I think it's because it's all sober and serious and about care and caution, you know, protecting yourself against the future and stuff like that. Very much the national characteristic in my opinion. And before you say anything, I mean all of that as a compliment.'

'No offence taken,' he grinned. 'Although I would suggest you've never been out in Glasgow on a Friday night, because I can tell you, there's not much sober and serious going on there, believe me. But I suppose you should know all about that care and caution stuff as a Yorkshire-woman. We've got a lot in common, come to think of it. Although we Scots have got a better sense of humour, that's a fact.'

'You think that do you?' she said, shooting him a wry smile.

'You should know, now that you're married to my brother,' he said affectionately. 'Frank's a laugh-a-minute, or so he thinks.' He paused for a moment. 'How is married life anyway? Delightful I assume?'

She grinned. 'Apart from the fact he won't watch detective dramas, it's perfect. And he persuades me to let Ollie stay up to watch Match of The Day sometimes. Oh, and he thinks he can cook, but he can't. But yes, apart from that, it's wonderful. Anyway, how was the drive down?'

'Perfect. I set off nice and early and stopped for breakfast at a wee cafe near Blairgowrie. Had the full Scottish including, would you believe, black pudding and haggis. It was sensational.'

'You'd better not tell Frank about it, or he'll be making a special journey up there,' she said, smiling. She glanced at her watch. 'Anyway, we'd best get signed in.' They made their introductions to an austere receptionist, who punched their details into a computer then stood and watched, unsmiling, as a printer produced a pair of swipe passes, which she handed to them on completion. 'Wait over there please,' she said, gesturing to a pair of black leather chairs in the corner. 'I'll tell Mr Wilson you're here.'

'Friendly girl,' Maggie whispered, suppressing a laugh as they walked over to the chairs.

'It's all part of the image I expect,' Jimmy replied deadpan. 'Sober and serious.'

A few minutes later, a man emerged from behind two frosted glass doors, which had swished open in response to his approach. In contrast to his reception colleague, he radiated an undisguised *bonhomie* that caused Maggie to give an involuntary smile as he held out his hand in greeting.

'Good morning folks,' the man boomed. 'I'm Charlie Wilson. Head of Life for my sins. And yes, I know, it's a daft title, but that's the corporate world for you.'

She laughed. 'I'm Maggie Bainbridge, and I don't really have a job title. And this is Jimmy Stewart, my colleague.' She guessed he was about her own age, smartly dressed in a shiny grey suit, blue shirt and - unusually these days she thought - wearing a tie, a shiny red silk affair which matched the suit and shirt perfectly. This too was probably part of the corporate image, sure and steady and outwardly at least, resistant to passing fads, sartorial or otherwise.

'I do have one,' Jimmy said, smiling. 'I'm an Associate. Don't know what it means though. But it sounds quite important.'

'Well, we'll be having a bit of a title-fest this morning,' Wilson said. 'Because we're going to be joined by my colleague Tina Holmes. She's Head of Fraud, and no, it doesn't mean she's a crook. Head of fraud investigation is what it should be I suppose. But anyway, follow me. There should be tea and coffee in the room already. And this being Tuesday, I think that means caramel wavers too.' He led them through a bright open-plan office to a glass-walled meeting room.

'You need to swipe yourselves in, individually,' Wilson explained, nodding towards the door with a hint of apology. 'I know it seems a bit big-brother-ish, but it's so we know where our visitors are in case there's a fire. Which there won't be of course,' he added. 'And even if there is, we're well-insured.'

Maggie laughed, as she swiped her card on the reader and followed them into the room. 'I wouldn't expect anything else.'

'Take a seat,' Wilson said, 'and let me get you a drink. Tea, coffee?'

'Coffee please,' she said.

'Same for me,' Jimmy added.

As he was pouring, a woman entered the room. Circling the table, she pulled out a chair then sat down with a brusque *'morning Charlie.'* She was about fifty, Maggie guessed, dressed in a dark grey business suit with a knee-length skirt which she wore over a plain white blouse. Her hair was cropped quite short on top and sides, but had been left long at the back, and was coloured a vivid auburn, the overall effect somehow seeming incongruous for an employee of the venerable Edinburgh & Glasgow Assurance company. She was attractive too, but a little careworn around the eyes, and Maggie wondered, quite without corroborating evidence, whether she might be an ex-police officer, securing a comfortable corporate gig after a stressful career on the coalface of crime.

'This is Tina Holmes, our fraud-meister,' Wilson said. 'And she's kept very busy, believe you me.'

'Hi guys,' she said, a trickle of a smile crossing her lips. 'Good to meet you both.'

'You read a lot about insurance scams,' Maggie said, taking a sip of her coffee. 'Is there still a lot of it about?'

Wilson nodded sagely. 'Yes, it's the oldest crime in the book. Ever since this business was invented there's been dodgy folks burning down their premises when their businesses get into trouble, then claiming on the insurance. But that's Tina's department. She's got the job of catching the bad guys.'

'Afraid so,' Holmes said. 'We had over seventy million pounds-worth of dubious claims last year. It's a lot of money. That's why we take it so seriously.'

'Bloody hell,' Jimmy said. 'That *is* a lot.'

'And is that why you've asked us here?' Maggie asked. 'A dubious claim?'

'It is,' Wilson said slowly. 'But a rather unusual one, and highly sensitive too, which is why Tina has decided to call in some outside expertise to assist her investigation.'

It was interesting that Wilson should put it that way. Was it really Holmes' decision to call in Bainbridge Associates or had it been Wilson, evidently the top dog in the room, who had requested their special expertise but did not want to put his colleague's nose out of joint? She suspected that was the case.

'We'd love to work with your team Tina, of course,' Maggie said, 'and we'll try to add whatever expertise we can.'

'Great,' the woman said, sounding distinctly unenthusiastic.

Wilson nodded at Maggie. 'I read all about your great work on the Lomond Tower case and on that Speyside business too. That's in fact how I found out about Jimmy's mountain expertise, and it just clicked with me that we might be able to use you.' He paused for a moment. 'So, to our matter.

You might have read about the tragic death of Gina McQuarrie?'

'Yes, I read about it,' Maggie said. 'Up in the Cairngorms, wasn't it?'

'Aye, I heard all about it too,' Jimmy said. 'She'd been doing an early spring trek up on Braeriach when the wind whipped up and there was a total white-out. The consensus amongst the mountain rescue guys was that she lost her bearings as she traversed alongside Bhrochain corrie and plunged to her death. Terrible thing altogether.'

'Yes, awful,' Wilson agreed. 'But these terrible accidents seem to happen up there with disturbing regularity. Even to experienced walkers.'

'Yes, it does happen a lot, sadly,' Jimmy said. 'It's often that very experience that persuades someone they'll be okay, when really, they know the forecast is saying they shouldn't go within a million miles of the hill. I mean, this was late April, but you can still get arctic conditions up there, even at that time of the year. And the weather can change in an instant, everybody knows that. They say the conditions on a bad day are as ferocious as anywhere in the world, and I've seen that myself, plenty of times.'

'And Gina's death is a case in point, sadly,' Wilson said. 'Because she was a very seasoned walker by all accounts.

She was brought up locally, in Newtonmore and had been walking in the Cairngorms since she was at school. That's twenty-five years at least. She knew her way around the mountain.'

Jimmy nodded. 'It makes my point, doesn't it? You can't be too careful up there.'

'It seems that way,' the insurance executive agreed. 'Anyway, I guess we'd better let you two in on the secret as to why we've asked you here.'

'Good plan,' Maggie said, grinning.

'Not to put too fine a point on it, there was a policy on Gina's life. A big one.'

'For three million,' his colleague Tina Holmes added. 'Which as Charlie said, is big.'

'But it's not just that which is causing us a little *difficulty* in this matter,' Wilson continued, 'if we can call it that. You see the thing is, the policy was taken out just seven weeks ago. Just four weeks before her unfortunate death.'

'And just *two days* after the non-claim period of twenty-eight days ended,' Holmes said, her tone effortlessly suspicious.

'Right,' Maggie said, the word elongated as she began to recognise the implications of what he was saying. 'That raises some questions I guess?'

'You could say that,' Holmes said wryly.

'To be blunt, we're concerned that Gina McQuarrie may have taken her own life,' Wilson said, sounding uncomfortable. 'Although I'm not sure concerned is exactly the right word, because of course we only have our suspicions, and they might be miles wide of the mark.' He paused again. 'As you can see, the whole thing's *bloody* awkward.'

'We don't pay out for suicides,' Holmes said matter-of-factly. 'But you probably knew that already.'

Maggie nodded uncertainly. 'Yes, I think I probably did. But if she did kill herself, the question is why? I suppose what I'm really asking is, who is the beneficiary? Or is it beneficiaries?'

Wilson shrugged. 'Nothing unusual there. Her husband is the beneficiary if he is still alive at the time of her death, otherwise it's shared between their two children.'

'And she was married to that famous economist guy if I'm not mistaken?'

Wilson nodded. 'That's right. Sir Andrew McQuarrie. As you say, he's a renowned economist. A professor at Glasgow University and always on the telly when they need an expert to comment on economic affairs.'

'Aye, they're a bit of a power couple you might say,' Jimmy said. 'Sorry, *were* a power couple. And not harmed by the fact that she was very photogenic too, if that's not a horribly sexist thing to say,' he added, shooting an apologetic glance in Tina Holmes' direction.

'And you think there might be some question about how she died?' Maggie said. 'Any reason for that?'

'No specific reason,' Wilson said, 'It's just that the circumstances are highly unusual.'

'It's automatic,' Holmes said. 'Our policies and procedures make it mandatory that we do a proper investigation when something out of the ordinary like this pops up.'

'I can understand that,' Maggie said. 'And you say the policy was taken out very recently?'

'There was an existing policy,' Wilson explained. 'But it was massively increased four weeks before she died.'

Maggie continued. 'But when Gina McQuarrie changed the policy in the manner you described, that didn't in itself raise any alarm bells?'

He shrugged again. 'Well, the circumstances were a little unusual, in that the couple took out back-to-back policies, of the same value, at exactly the same time. But no, there was no reason for it to raise any specific alarms. Sir Andrew was only fifty-three at the time they amended their policies and Gina was only forty-eight. Neither had any known medical conditions, so it was fantastic business for us. The new monthly premiums were very juicy, and the actuarial tables were telling us they would both live well into their eighties.'

'But *she* didn't,' Holmes said sourly. 'And the company is looking at a huge financial loss now.'

'Which to be fair, is the very essence of the insurance business,' Wilson said hurriedly. 'Most policies of all type, not just life insurance, aren't claimed against and it's those premiums that pay for the ones that do claim. We measure our risk very carefully to ensure we can meet all our obligations.' He paused for a moment. 'But of course, we do have a duty to our shareholders to make sure all claims are legitimate, no matter how high-profile the claimant.'

Yes, she thought, *this* was the nub of the matter for the revered Edinburgh & Glasgow Assurance Company. Gina McQuarrie was indeed a high-profile figure, the famous violinist revered by all of Scotland's music-lovers, and her husband was a well-known media figure and professor of economics at Glasgow University.

'We can't afford for this to leak,' Holmes said bluntly, and then went on to corroborate what Maggie had been surmising. 'As you can imagine, it wouldn't look good for the company if it was to emerge we were being difficult about paying out on the policy. And we can't piss about timewise either. We've got three, maybe four weeks tops until we either have to stump up, or we tell her husband that we're hanging on to the money pending further enquiries.'

Wilson nodded. 'And if that happens, he might go public. At which point, the brown stuff hits the fan as far as our reputation is concerned, and I'm claiming on my redundancy policy,' he added, his tone humorous although his expression told a different story. 'I mean, you can just see the headlines, can't you? *Skinflint Insurance Giant Hanging onto Gina McQuarrie Cash.*'

Maggie laughed. 'No, I guess that wouldn't be great publicity.'

'That's an understatement if I ever heard one,' he said. 'So, the question is Maggie, will you guys take on the assignment? And can you deliver in the timeline we're working to? And before you say anything, I know it's tight.'

She looked at Jimmy before answering. 'Well, it is a bit different to our normal work, but yes, I guess it's something we could do. Of course, I'll be leaving all the mountaineering stuff to my colleague here, but I think I can be usefully employed looking into the McQuarries' circumstances in the months leading up to Gina's death, to see if that gives any pointers to her state of mind.' She paused for a moment. 'Unless of course that's something your team would want to do Tina?'

Holmes shrugged. 'No, might as well keep it all under one roof. Just as long as you keep us informed on how it's going.'

'Of course,' Maggie said. Turning to her colleague she asked, 'And what about that two-to-three-week timeline Jimmy? Is that do-able?'

He nodded. 'Well aye, it doesn't seem impossible. I'm thinking out loud here, but I guess I'll be trying to retrace Gina's steps up to the scene of the incident and just see what I make of it. I can't really say more than that right now. I need to sit down quietly and just figure out what to do.'

'Sure,' Maggie said, then smiled. 'But I'll take that as a *yes*.'

'That's great news,' Wilson said, giving a thumbs-up. 'If you could let me have an estimate of your fees, I'll get a formal purchase order to you by return. Because we're very keen to get this up and running as soon as possible.'

'And we need you to sign a confidentiality statement before you go,' Holmes added, her tone faintly menacing. 'And just so you know, we'll sue the arse off you if any of this gets out.'

Maggie laughed, and then realised it probably wasn't a joke. 'Yes, totally understood Tina. My lips are sealed, and his are too,' she added, nodding in Jimmy's direction.

'Great, great,' Wilson said enthusiastically. 'Let's shake hands on that and we'll call it a deal, shall we?'

***

'What do you make of that then?' Maggie asked Jimmy as they made their way back to their cars. 'Is it something someone would do? Jump off the side of a mountain if you wanted to end it all?'

He shrugged. 'Might do I suppose. It's hard to get inside the mind of someone who wants to do themselves in, but if you loved the mountains, well yes, you might decide that was a fitting way to end it all. But the thing is, women like Gina McQuarrie don't exactly fit the profile of a suicide, do they? She was successful, at the top of her profession as far as I can make out and loved by thousands. You don't get the impression she was a lady who would go and top herself.'

She nodded. 'True, but you never know what's going on inside someone's head, do you?'

'Or what's going on behind the closed doors of a marriage,' he added. 'Which I guess will be the focus of your bit of the investigation.'

'Exactly,' she said. *'Exactly.'*

Chapter 3

It was now six months since Frank's marriage to Maggie, an event that he continued to look back on with a mixture of ecstatic pleasure and amazement. Almost every day he felt as if he needed to pinch himself, the action necessary to convince himself that it was true, and yes, he was actually *married* to the incredible Maggie Bainbridge. In every respect, his life outside of work was perfect and for that he thanked the heavens, and profusely too. But when it came to the question of his work life, then things hadn't been quite so rosy. The truth was, his career had been in somewhat of a limbo following his move to Scotland the previous year, where he had been investigating the fall-out from some new and half-arsed anti-corruption government initiative. Since then, a couple of cold cases had emerged that had kept him north of the border -and he had enjoyed working on them immensely - but now he realised that the vague sense of impermanence that he felt had a danger of spilling over into his private life too. As far as he could tell, Maggie was loving her new life in Scotland, and her son Ollie had settled well in his new school, despite the ribbing he got about his English accent. But she still had her house in Hampstead, and he had his flat, and from time to time they had discussed if they should move back to London before the boy was old enough to go to high school. Back down south, her little legal investigation firm would get plenty of work, and he could continue his not-so-glittering career with the Metropolitan Police. This dilemma, if it could be described as such, had dominated his thoughts for the past six weeks or so, and he recognised that one day soon, he and Maggie would need to come to some conclusion. And then he'd got the phone call from his gaffer DCI Jill Smart, summoning him to a meeting in London, a meeting which she described as both important and urgent. So the next day, he took the early flight from Glasgow to Heathrow, then grabbed the express train to Paddington, from whence a taxi deposited him at the front door of the meeting venue. *An office block in Whitehall.*

There was a lot of complicated and time-consuming security stuff to go through before he was admitted into the airy reception area, the stuff in question including an automated retina and fingerprints scan and a thorough and invasive body search that took place before he was directed through an airport-style walk-through scanner. The formalities completed, he sat waiting in the atrium until a smartly-dressed young woman appeared carrying a buff file, greeting him warmly but not introducing herself, before instructing him to come with her.

'And what is this place, if you don't mind me asking?' Frank said as he followed her along a wide corridor. 'Or will you have to kill me if you tell me?'

She laughed, which he took as a good sign. 'Not immediately at least. This is Abbeygate House, it's mainly

Home Office. Immigration, homeland security and policing are here. And I think there's an MI5 team, but we lock them away in the basement out of sight.' She smiled at him. 'Oops, I shouldn't have said that. Looks like I will have to kill you after all.'

He grinned. 'Aye, well if you could just wait until after my meeting. I was hoping they might have laid on doughnuts and I'm feeling a bit peckish.'

'There'll be water,' she said, suppressing a smile. 'Anyway, here we are. Please, go through.'

The venue was a conference room, wood-panelled on three sides and the fourth windowed roof-to-ceiling, affording a fine view over the Thames. He assumed they were constructed from one-way glass, blacked out when viewed from outside, and he guessed they would need to be bullet- and-bomb-proof too. He wondered why the architects hadn't just gone for a simple brick wall, but then again, they were in the heart of Whitehall, within touching distance of the iconic House of Commons, and you wouldn't want to just throw up some bland rectangular box that could pass for an out-of-town supermarket. It was a large room, big enough to host thirty or more he calculated, but today there were only four souls in attendance, two of them in police uniform, one of which was Jill Smart, who smiled and stood up to greet him.

'Welcome Frank, and grab a seat,' she said, then turned to address the other attendees. 'Guys, this is my long-time colleague DCI Frank Stewart. As you know, he runs the Met's little cold-case unit, although somehow it has managed to stretch its remit to cover the whole country.'

'Supply and demand Jill,' he said, grinning. 'Thousands of satisfied customers already. I'm even thinking of introducing a wee loyalty scheme. I was going to call it Cop-Card.'

'Yes, very amusing,' she replied, giving a wry grin. 'Anyway, I'll let these good people introduce themselves now. Over to you Katherine I guess?' she added, looking at the woman occupying the chair at the top of the table.

The woman nodded and said, 'Thanks Jill.' He'd seen her on television, where she came across as one of the few politicians who managed to appear vaguely human, which was to her credit in his eyes. She was mid-forties he guessed, quite tall and slim, and wearing a navy dress with a string of white pearls, greying hair held back by a leopard-skin patterned band. 'I'm Katherine Collins, Minister of State for crime and policing.' She paused and smiled. 'And I cover fire too, for some reason. But the first two take up most of my time. And I'm the elected one in the room, one of these here-today-gone-tomorrow politicians you read about all the time. But it's nearly a year until the next election so I'm hoping to be here long enough to get this initiative off the ground.' She said it with a pleasing absence of pomposity, which made Frank warm to her even more, unlike many politicians he had met.

'Good to meet you Katherine,' he said. 'I've seen you on *Question Time* by the way. Very good you are too.'

She laughed. 'It's the modern equivalent of the Coliseum I always think, with the audience and viewers hoping to see us politicians eaten alive. But anyway, let me introduce the rest of my colleagues.' She nodded towards the uniformed man sitting opposite her. 'This is David Ramsbottom, Chief Constable of Lancashire, who's working as my special advisor on this project.'

'Morning sir,' Frank said briskly, getting a half-smile of acknowledgment in return.

'And this is Roger Allen,' Katherine Collins continued. 'Roger is Director General of Policing in the Home Office. That's the most senior role in the department's policing stream. And it's a big job, believe me, not just a big title.'

The man nodded, gave a warm smile but made no comment.

'And I guess Roger will be your ultimate boss,' Collins said, 'that is, if you decide to take on the role that we want to discuss with you.'

Frank gave Jill a searching look. 'What, is this a bloody job interview or what?'

'Not an interview Frank,' Collins cut in. 'Just a proposal. We've been looking at the whole mechanism surrounding historic case investigations and decided it might be improved. And with your experience, we wondered if you might want to go on that journey with us.'

'Let me try and explain,' Chief Constable Ramsbottom interjected, speaking in a slow drawl, his accent unmistakably Lancastrian, his tone unmistakably sour. 'There have been a *handful* of cases which have emerged over the last two or three years which, let's just say, perhaps haven't shown the police service in the best light.'

Frank smiled. It had been more than a handful - more like a deluge, if truth be told. And then something suddenly came back to him. *A culture of cover-up and obstruction.* It was Home Office Minister Katherine Collins herself who had said it, in a consecrating interview in a national broadsheet in which she had decried the efforts of police forces when investigating their past failings. She hadn't excused the Met either, despite the evident success of his own Department 12B, but he wasn't going to hold that against her.

'So, after much discussion,' Ramsbottom continued, 'my colleagues in ACPO have decided we can support the

Minister in her desire to improve systems and procedures in this regard.'

Ah yes, ACPO, Frank thought. The Association of Chief Police Officers, which acted as the trade union for the Brass, and who were as resistant to change as any of the firebrand union organisations had been back in the three-day-week nineteen-seventies.

'Yes, it's great that ACPO are *fully* behind this initiative,' Katherine Collins said, with a note of irony that though almost undetectable, was there nonetheless. 'So, we've decided to set up a new unit, fully independent of the police, and reporting directly into the Home Office. It'll be set up as an Agency, with a Chief Executive Officer and a Board of Governors and it will have its own budget, in the normal way of these things.' She paused for a moment, then grinned. 'Did you know Frank, there are four-hundred and forty-two government agencies already? Someone in Cabinet told me that the other day, and I couldn't believe it. Anyway, this one will be number four-hundred-and-forty-three. We've even got a name for it.'

Roger Allen spoke for the first time. 'We plan to call it the National Independent Cold-Case Investigations Agency. Not terribly imaginative I admit, but I guess it will do what it says on the tin.'

'And we've managed to persuade the Treasury to allocate us a budget too,' Collins added. 'Quite generous by their standards. It should run to a headcount of about twenty or so and pay for a half-decent office in one of the regions.' She paused again, then looked directly at Frank. 'And we'd like you to join the new unit. We have you down for Director of Investigations. On paper, you'll be reporting to the CEO, but in practice you'll be running the show.'

'There's a kind of unwritten rulebook for these quango appointments you see,' Allen explained. 'The bosses have to tick all the right boxes. Oxbridge educated ideally, an establishment figure too, but not a stale white male.' He paused for a moment, then raised a questioning eyebrow in the direction of the minister, evidently seeking permission to continue. 'We've got someone in mind as it happens. Her name is Helen Dunbar. Born in New Zealand and has held all sorts of non-exec positions around Whitehall, including advising our present Prime Minister on his government's diversity policy. She's got two or three other Agency board positions already, but this one will only involve a day or two a month, so she's ideal. Oh yes, and she's a Dame too. In the last New Year's Honours.'

'And obviously not a policeman,' Katherine Collins added. She smiled at the Chief Constable and said, 'Because we don't want you guys marking your own work, do we? That's the whole point after all.'

Ramsbottom gave what looked like a forced smile and said, 'No Katherine, we wouldn't want that.'

'So to your position Frank,' Roger Allen continued. 'It would of course be Civil Service graded.' He glanced down at his notebook. 'Let me see.... yes, at SCS3 level. That's about £105k a year plus benefits. And a car, private health, the normal executive package. But that will all be detailed in your offer letter.'

'What?' Frank said, struggling to comprehend what they were saying to him. 'So would I be leaving the police then?'

Allen nodded. 'Yes, but your service would be frozen, and your defined pension benefits will continue to accrue. So you could return to your police career at any time, should you choose.'

'But that's a bloody huge pay rise,' he protested. 'That can't be right, surely? Because the country's already near-enough bankrupt from what I've read.'

'I'm afraid it won't be one of the big agencies,' Allen said, almost apologetically, 'but that's the going rate according to the current salary scales. And ACPO were very keen that the Director of Investigations role should go to a serving police officer. That's right, isn't it David?' he added, smiling at the Chief Constable. 'In fact, it was something you guys insisted on, in order to get your support. Which of course we were happy to go along with.'

Frank saw Jill shoot him a wry smile, and then he cottoned on. Of course, APCO would have wanted the appointment to be a police officer, but they had been thinking of the job going to one of their own, not some jumped-up DCI-level oik from the Met.

'And we were very keen for the Director of Investigations role to go to an officer with solid experience in this type of affair,' Katherine Collins added. 'And when I mentioned it to DCI Smart when I met her at a woman's networking event we both attended, she mentioned you. And now here we are.'

'So, do I have any choice in this?' Frank asked, giving Jill Smart a searching look.

'Of course,' Collins said. 'But we're very keen for you to take the appointment. And as Roger said, it needn't be a permanent move. In fact, we normally make these appointments on a fixed-term basis in any case.'

'And I could come back to the force afterwards?'

Collins nodded. 'Yes, that's a given. There is one condition though that we need to share with you, before you make up your mind. Something you may not like.'

'Aye, what's that?' he said warily.

'It's the question of location,' she said. 'You see, the PM has committed that no new government agencies will be headquartered in London or the South-East during his time in office. You know, levelling-up and all that kind of thing. It's very important to him.'

'So, the office will have to go to one of the regions,' Allen said. 'Sorry,' he added, managing to sound genuinely regretful.

Frank was silent for a moment then asked, 'And tell me Katherine, does Scotland count as a region too?'

'Of course,' she answered.

He smiled. 'Brilliant. When do I start?'

Chapter 4

The news of Frank's surprise new appointment - conveyed in an excited phone call during which she had had to ask him to slow down about five times so that she could understand what he was saying - had lifted Maggie's already elevated sense of wellbeing to new heights. Now the vexed question of where they would live had neatly resolved itself, and she was glad of that, because in the twelve months they had lived there, she had fallen in love with Scotland in general and the pretty Glasgow suburb of Milngavie in particular. It seemed that Frank would be based up north for at least the next three or four years, and perhaps beyond that if he made a success of his new role - which of course, he would, given his brilliance as a detective. It seemed too that the new role came with a ridiculously elevated salary - his words, not hers - which made the other thing they had been tentatively discussing an even more tantalising possibility. She was forty-four now, which meant if they wanted to try for a baby, they'd better get on with it, because her biological clock didn't have many ticks left in it. A baby would be wonderful, and now they would be able to get by perfectly well for a while on Frank's earnings. It wasn't that she wanted to give up work - heaven forbid - but she knew that at her age, she would have to give nature maximum opportunity to deliver a trouble-free pregnancy, which wasn't likely to be achieved if you were charging around the country chasing fraudsters and adulterers.

But now she had to turn her attention to her latest investigation, which was why she had convened a meeting at Byres Road's Bikini Barista Cafe with her associate Lorilynn Logan. Although, as had been the case for the last few days at least, all they had talked about thus far was babies.

'It would be dead amazing, it really would,' Lori said, sipping from her cappuccino, 'and I would be your number one babysitter. I'm good with wee babies, so I am. My sister's got two of them, less than a year between them. I can change two nappies at once and with my eyes shut. And I don't mind the poonamis either. I actually quite like the smell.'

Maggie laughed. 'Yuk! But yes, I'm sure you'd be brilliant, but Frank and I haven't *quite* decided whether it's right for us yet. And I'm such an old woman now, so that has to be factored in too.'

'Aye, you are, but that doesn't matter so much nowadays. Medical science is amazing. There was a woman in Mexico last year had one at the age of sixty-three or something. In fact, I think she might have had twins or even triplets.'

'So I've still got a few years then,' Maggie said, laughing again. 'But come on young Lori, we've got work to do and we've only got three weeks or so to do it. So no more baby talk for a while.'

'I'd like a baby one day,' Lori said wistfully. 'But I suppose I'd better get a boyfriend first.'

'No more baby talk,' Maggie repeated, suppressing a grin.

The girl sighed. 'Aye okay then. Anyway, I did some reading up on our power couple last night. The husband, that's Sir Andrew, is an economist, whatever that is. But he does seem to be very well-known and successful. Almost famous you would say.'

'Yes he is,' Maggie agreed. 'He's always on the telly. He's a good-looking guy of course, which helps, but they say he's also very good at explaining complicated economic stuff in a way the ordinary person can understand.'

'Aye that's what they say. But poor Mrs McQuarrie, or do we call her Lady McQuarrie, I'm not quite sure,' Lori said. 'Anyway, whatever we call her, she was dead beautiful, so thin and elegant and everything.'

Maggie nodded. 'Yes, Gina was a very talented lady. She was a brilliant violinist and she had a beautiful singing voice too. I clicked on a video yesterday, it was of her performing at a folk festival in Edinburgh last year. And you're right, she was very lovely.'

'She was mentally-keen on hill-walking too,' Lori added. 'I was looking at her Facebook, and every other post is of her on top of some mountain or other. And they live in

Milngavie like you do, did you know that?' she added. 'In a great big house in its own grounds. I found it on google maps, on the satellite view. It looks amazing.'

'Really? That's a coincidence. And if it's such a grand place, it just shows how much money they were making. Not that that's surprising, given how talented they both are. Or should I say *were*.'

Lori shook her head. 'Not necessarily. Maybe one of them inherited it or something.'

'That's always a possibility,' Maggie conceded. 'But no, I think they were doing very well for themselves.' She paused for a moment. 'There were children, weren't there? Two, I think the guy from the insurance company said.'

'Yeah, twins actually. A boy and a girl. There was a picture of them in the Chronicle the other day. That Yash guy that you're mates with wrote an article about the family.'

'What, Yash Patel's onto this?' Maggie said, surprised. 'I wonder why he's sniffing around this?'

'A scandal, presumably,' Lori said. 'That's what drives him.'

Maggie laughed. 'Yes, you're right. But before we start worrying about Mr Patel, shall we piece together what we know about the background of our couple? Because in my experience, that always throws up some interesting information, even if you don't recognise it as such at the time.'

'Well the good thing is, I bet they're both famous enough to have their own Wikipedia entries,' her associate said. She picked up her phone from the table and began to browse. 'Aye, here's his. Andrew Stephen McQuarrie, economist, born Glasgow, Scotland, now aged fifty-three. That's the guy.'

'Brilliant. What does it say about him?'

Lori peered at the screen. 'Went to a private school in the south side but didn't do too brilliantly in his Highers. Then off to Strathclyde Uni to study politics and economics. Only got a lower second-class honours it says...'

'That's nearly a fail,' Maggie interrupted, surprised.

'Is it? I don't know about that stuff, 'Lori said. 'But then after that, he moved to Glasgow University to do lecturing and some post-graduate research. Which is where he came up with something called... hang on...' She furrowed her brow as she read on. '.. *Money Supply and the Link to Inflation - An Algorithmic Theory for Governments.*'

Maggie grimaced. 'What the blazes is that then?'

Lori shrugged. 'No idea, but it's got its own section in his entry, so I guess it must be important. Let me have a wee look.' She swiped down and continued. 'It says.. let me see...' She screwed up her features as she evidently struggled to make sense of what she was reading. 'It says - and I'm just reading this out by the way - it says *the theory was a breakthrough in understanding the causal link between central banks' printing of money and how it affects inflation.* I've no bloody idea what that means,' she added.

'No, I don't either, but it sounds very important,' Maggie said. 'I'm guessing that's probably why he got his knighthood. And how old was he when he came up with this theory? Twenty-five, twenty-six?'

'A bit older, I think. He was working on it for nearly four years before it came out it says. He published it in some academic journal, and it really took off after that apparently. The Governor of the Bank of England called it the biggest breakthrough in economic thinking in more than fifty years, and even the French economic minister said it was brilliant, although best suited to Anglo-Saxon economies, whatever that means.'

'It must be good if the French like it,' Maggie said, laughing. 'And so Andrew McQuarrie's career and reputation took off as a result?'

'Aye, it seems like it,' Lori agreed. 'Which is quite amazing, given he was hopeless at school. Just shows you can be a late developer,' she added. 'Like maybe I'll be.'

'You're already a very clever lady,' Maggie said, 'You've nothing to worry about in that department.'

Lori smiled. 'Thanks boss. Appreciate that.'

'So what about Gina?' Maggie said. 'Does she have a Wikipedia entry too? I assume she does.'

'Aye she does, quite a big one. Let's see...yep, here it is. Gina Berrycloth, born in Maidstone but brought up in a place called Newtonmore. Her parents were English but moved up to Scotland from Kent when she was just a toddler.'

'Berrycloth? That's an unusual name. But yes, I remember seeing signs to the town when we were driving up to Aviemore on our last case. So she's a Highland girl then? Or at least, an adopted one?'

'Yeah, definitely. And she was also Scottish Ladies Downhill ski champion three years in a row, and that was when she was at the Uni.' Lori was silent for a moment then said, 'It doesn't seem fair, does it? I mean, that one person should be given all these amazing talents and be beautiful too. You'd have thought God would spread them around a bit more evenly. You know, leave some good stuff for the rest of us.'

Maggie gave her associate a look, half-curious, half-admiring. 'That's very profound Lori. And I didn't know you were religious. Not that there's anything wrong with that,' she added hastily.

The girl laughed. 'I'm not, not really. But *somebody* must have made the world. I mean, it couldn't have just *happened*, could it have?'

'Well, that's a question that mankind has been trying to answer for aeons,' Maggie said, screwing up her nose. 'And not a subject I expected to be discussing in the Bikini Barista cafe, that's for sure.'

'Yeah, sorry. It's just that it's dead interesting. But aye, I guess we should get back to our case.'

Before they could continue, they were interrupted by the approach of Stevie, amiable proprietor of the cafe, who was also Lori's former boss.

'How's it going folks?' he said with his customary bonhomie. 'Those big brains in good form I hope? Lots of powerful thinking going on? Anyway, can I tempt youse with a wee bit of lunch? I've some nice broccoli and stilton soup today, served with fresh crusty bread and a wee pack of Lurpak. It tastes lovely, even if I say so myself. Peppery, but not too peppery, if you know what I mean.'

Maggie laughed. 'Yep, brains are in great form this morning, particularly young Lori's here. And yes, you can tempt us

Stevie, definitely. Your soup sounds amazing and I'm blooming starving.'

'Aye, me too,' Lori said.

He gave a thumbs-up. 'Two soups, coming up at the speed of light. And I'll dollop in an extra ladleful each, nae bother,' he added, scuttling back towards the kitchen at speed.

'Where were we?' Maggie said. 'Ah yes, after discussing the unfairness of fate plus the origins of mankind, we were looking at Gina McQuarrie's biography.'

Lori picked up her phone again and grinned. 'Yeah, so we were. Anyway, in between all the ski-champion stuff, Gina studied music at Glasgow Uni and then embarked on a career as a violinist. It says here *Gina Berrycloth was one of a group of emerging Scottish talents who lit up the traditional folk scene in the nineties, most notably in the virtuoso duo Flaming Fiddles, which she co-founded with fellow student, the late Rhona Fraser. Their debut album Skye Lament sold more than a hundred thousand copies.* No' bad, eh?'

'That would have been on CD,' Maggie said. 'Those were the days before downloads, which I expect you don't remember. And a CD cost more than fifteen quid at the time, so they weren't cheap. And now you get all the music in the world for free, more or less.'

'My dad's got loads of CDs,' Lori said. 'He's got racks of them all over the house. My mum's always nagging him to get rid of some of them.'

Maggie laughed. 'I've got quite a few too. But goodness, I sound like a right old dinosaur, don't I?'

'Only a wee bit. But I guess Gina and her fiddling pal Rhona must have made a nice wee bit of dosh out of them, don't you think?'

'Yes, very probably,' Maggie said. 'But it described the other woman as the *late* Rhona Fraser. She must have been very young when she died, poor girl. I expect it was cancer or something. A terrible disease.'

'I'm sure it'll tell us. There's a link I can click.'

Maggie nodded. 'But looking at Gina first. What does it say about her personal life? Anything?'

Lori shrugged. 'Not a lot. Just that she married Andrew McQuarrie and that they have two children. Nothing we don't know already. That's all you usually get on Wikipedia. Not much detail. No, most of it is about her music career. And interestingly, it says that Gina gave up recording and performing for quite a few years after the tragic disappearance of her musical partner.'

'The *disappearance*?' Maggie said, surprised. 'So it wasn't illness?'

'Just a minute and I'll click her link,' Lori said. She was silent for a moment as she read through the violinist's Wikipedia article, then said, 'Aye, so it says that after Flaming Fiddles broke up, Rhona played in a traditional Gaelic band, and they had been booked to play at the Cambridge Folk Festival. This is about eight years ago apparently. So anyway, the band travelled down to Cambridge the night before their scheduled appearance and stayed at a hotel out in the suburbs. They were due to have a rehearsal and a sound-check at eleven o'clock the next morning, but Rhona didn't turn up. And she hasn't been seen since.'

'Bloody hell,' Maggie said. 'That *is* a tragedy.'

'Aye it is. And obviously it must have hit Gina really badly, not surprising really. It says it took her years before she would play Skye Lament or any of the other tunes in public. In fact, it says last year was the first time, when they organised a concert in Glasgow as a tribute to Rhona.'

'Maybe that's something to think about, I mean for our case,' Maggie mused. 'Because a tragedy like that can stay with you forever, can't it? Trying to deal with the sense of loss, and then there's always blame, you know, as if somehow you could have done something to prevent it.'

'Aye, but would it make you want to kill yourself?' Lori said, her tone sceptical. 'Gina doesn't seem the type to me.'

'No, perhaps not,' Maggie conceded. As she said it, something struck her. 'So her Flaming Fiddles duo with Rhona had broken up before she disappeared? Does it say why?'

Lori nodded. 'Flaming Fiddles has got its own link too. I'll give it a wee click and see what it says.' Quickly, she scanned her phone then said, 'Seems like Gina wanted to spend more time with her babies, simple as that. It says the split was amicable, and the band didn't actually break up, they just wanted time to do other things and had always expected to get back together in the future.'

Maggie sighed. 'A future that never arrived. How sad.' She paused for a moment, contemplating, then said, 'Well, it's hard to say if Rhona's disappearance is relevant to our case or not, but obviously it's something we need to keep in mind. But in the meantime, I think we just start by speaking to Sir Andrew and see where it leads us.'

***

Back at the office, Maggie allowed herself a quiet moment of reflection. It was absolutely true what Lori had said, that Gina McQuarrie *née* Berrycloth had been dealt an extraordinary array of gifts by the hand of fate. She was beautiful, she was an accomplished athlete, she had amazing musical talent, a talent that she had evidently turned into commercial success too. She had made what looked from the outside at least a good marriage, living with her successful husband and two wonderful children in a fabulous house in one of the city's most desirable suburbs. But as fate could give, it could also take away. First, the tragic disappearance of her musical collaborator Rhona Fraser, presumed dead, and now Gina McQuarrie was herself dead, at the young age of forty-eight. *A terrible accident, or was it?* The insurance company were concerned that she might have taken her own life, without, it had to be said, a shred of evidence to support that concern.

But as Maggie reflected, a woman like Gina McQuarrie could bring out the worst in people as well as the best. There would be plenty of women in her circle who would be fiercely jealous of her accomplishments, and plenty of men - and perhaps some women too - with a burning desire to lure her into their bed, irrespective of her marriage status. Of course, Jimmy's investigative expedition into the Cairngorms, retracing her last fatal steps, might well conclude that her death was indeed a tragic accident.

But somehow, she didn't think it would.

Chapter 5

It was true to say that the events of the last few days had left Frank's head in somewhat of a guddle, although gradually he was beginning to settle, as he turned his attention - reluctantly - to getting the whole shebang up and running. The thing was, there was a horrible pile of tedious admin to get through for that to happen, and admin, most definitely, was not his strongest skill set. It wasn't that he couldn't do it - because he could if he had to, particularly when Jill Smart chased him up for his monthly reports- it was just that he found it all irredeemably tedious. He had, however, been given some temporary assistance, in the form of one Trevor Park, who was some sort of civil service human resources drone. He hadn't actually met this Park guy yet, and wasn't sure that he ever would, given that nobody in the civil service ever seemed to come into an actual physical office these days, such was the endemic nature of the working-from-home movement. To be fair though, Trevor would be helping Frank with the recruitment of his nascent team, and given the frightful amount of paperwork involved in any public sector appointment, he was bloody glad of the assistance. But the fabulous news was of course that he would be based in Glasgow, and he had in fact wondered if there was any reason why his new office couldn't actually be in Milngavie itself - or, when he thought about it some more - in the city's West End, where he could be within walking distance of the modest headquarters of Bainbridge Associates and, more importantly, Stevie's excellent Bikini Barista cafe.

Until all of that was settled though, he would continue to plonk his backside in the salubrious surroundings of New Gorbals police station, just south of the river, and where he was about as welcome as...well, as what? And then one of genius comic Billy Connolly's classics suddenly came to mind. As welcome as a fart in a spacesuit. Yes, they didn't like him at New Gorbals for a whole host of spurious reasons, starting with the fact that when he had left the place fifteen years or so earlier to join the Met, there was the inevitable vibe amongst those left behind that Frank Stewart felt himself too good for his old manor. Then he'd come back, as a Detective Chief Inspector no less, and that hadn't gone down well either with the troglodytes who were still there. No, he reflected, he would be glad to see the back of the joint, and that day couldn't come soon enough. Before then though, there was an important matter to attend to, which was why he was at his favourite table in the basement canteen, sat opposite DC Lexy McDonald.

'I heard on the grapevine about your new job sir,' Lexy was saying whilst squirting a blob of brown sauce on her roll and sausage. 'Congratulations. It sounds amazing. And important too.'

Frank grimaced. 'Bloody hell. So how the hell did that get out? I thought there was only two or three people who knew about it in the whole wide world.'

Lexy shrugged. 'Our union rep was at one of those communications sessions with the Chief Constable the other day, and the boss told them about this new national cold-case thing that's being set up. He said it wasn't something welcomed by ACPO, but they would run with it until it fell flat on its arse. That was the exact words he used apparently.'

'Right,' Frank said, cottoning on. 'There was one of the top brass at my meeting with the government minister. I understand now how it got out.'

'You're hob-nobbing with government ministers now are you sir?' Lexy said. 'Very impressive. I'm surprised you're not here with an entourage of flunkies.'

He gave her a wry look. 'Ha-bloody-ha. Actually, the minister was quite a nice woman, and surprisingly, she seemed to know what she was talking about too. But anyway, we digress.' He paused for a moment. 'Or in fact, we don't. Because it's my new job I want to talk to you about. You see, I'm putting together a small team. No, more than that,' he added, laughing again. 'It's a crack team. And there'll be an opening for a bright detective like you.'

She smiled. 'I'm flattered sir, and of course I've always liked working for you. But I'm enjoying it here too, even although half my colleagues are dickheads, if you'll excuse my French.'

'Only half of them? Standards are obviously rising around here then. But aye Lexy, I hear what you're saying. Technically, it would be a secondment, and so you could go back to your current position at any time. But I think the government wants to give it a fair chance, so I would say we'll have at least three or four years to prove we can make a success of the unit before they pull the plug.'

'And it will all be cold cases, will it?' she asked.

He nodded. 'That's the current remit, aye. But we'll be pretty self-contained. Administratively, it will be outside the police force, so we can have our own technical staff on the team if we want to, a bit of IT and some forensics, stuff like that. Which will be great, in theory. Means we won't have to arse about waiting for forms to be filled in if we need something done pronto.'

She smiled at him, an eyebrow raised. 'And when you say IT and forensics, did you have someone in mind?'

'Do you mean was I thinking about wee Eleanor Campbell?' he said, then laughed. 'God Lexy, can you imagine how that conversation might go? Hi Eleanor, I'd like you to come and work for me. I'll be your actual boss, but it'll all be fine. As much as I would like her on board, I don't see that happening, do you?'

'Couldn't you bribe her with money and a fancy title sir?' Lexy grinned. 'Head of Forensic Investigations, or something like that?'

He laughed again. 'I had thought of that, although I'm a bit ashamed to admit it.' He paused for a moment. 'Look, I know it's something you need to think about carefully Lexy. The fact is, you're going to have a wonderful career and I wouldn't want to do anything to jeopardise it.'

She frowned. 'But I assume I could go through the same promotion path in your new outfit as I would if I stayed here?'

He nodded. 'Aye, at least I think so. Look, they've allocated me an admin fella and I'll talk to him about all of that. But obviously I rate you Lexy, so I'm not going to be an obstacle to you proceeding through the ranks, which is more than can be said for some of the misogynist dinosaurs that call this place home.' He paused again. 'But listen, it's really important that you don't feel I'm pressurising you in any way. I think it'll be interesting work, but it's entirely up to you, and I won't think any less of you if you turn it down.'

She smiled. 'I appreciate that sir, and I will think about it, very seriously.' She paused for a second. 'So, what's the case load like, if you don't mind me asking?'

He chuckled. 'Light, as in non-existent. We've got a name for the agency, and they've done me a nice wee business card, but that's about it at the moment.' He thrust a hand into his pocket, pulled out a card and handed it to her. 'See, that's me.'

She took it from him and gave a mock grimace as she read it. 'Frank Stewart, Director of Investigations?'

He grinned again. 'Aye, it sounds like I'm in the FBI, doesn't it? But I'll just be doing the same old job as always. Once we get some cases, that is.'

'Actually sir,' she said, her tone now businesslike, 'we had something come in a couple of weeks ago that might be a candidate for us. It was a real odd one, but I thought it was quite interesting at the time. My DI wouldn't let me take it any further, which was fair enough to be honest, but it's been nagging away at me ever since.'

'Oh aye?' he said, interested. 'Tell me more.'

She shrugged. 'I don't know if it's anything, but as I said, a couple of weeks ago this guy walked in the front door and said he wanted to report two murders. One happened seven or eight years ago and one was more recently, just three months ago in fact. He was quite excitable, talking at about a thousand words a minute. Wally Jardine was on the desk that day, and you know what he's like sir.'

Frank laughed. 'The friendly welcoming face of Police Scotland. It's a wonder they don't use his girning boat-race in all our recruitment videos.'

'Yes, that would be funny sir,' she said, grinning. 'Anyway, he told Wally that these alleged murders had both taken place in Cambridge.'

Frank raised an eyebrow. 'Cambridge eh? So I suppose our Wally told him that wasn't our patch and that he should sling his hook, or at least catch a wee bus down to East Anglia and report it down there.'

Lexy shook her head. 'Well, no, to be fair to Sergeant Jardine, he didn't. He told the guy to wait where he was, and then he wandered down to our office to see who was in.'

'And he found you.'

'Yep, he did. He told me he had a raving nutter at the front desk who was going on about two murders and also saying it was reading about Gina McQuarrie's death up in the Cairngorms that made him realise something weird was going on.'

'What?' Frank said, astonished. 'Gina McQuarrie? That's a crazy coincidence. Because my Maggie's looking into her death on behalf of an insurance company as we speak.'

She returned his look. 'Gosh, that is a coincidence. But as you'll hear, Gina isn't directly involved in the story, not first-hand at least. So anyway, back to that day. I didn't really want to get involved, but I told Wally I would have a word with the guy since there was no-one else around. I went and fetched him and brought him down here to the canteen in fact.'

'Still excitable? Him I mean, not you.'

Lexy nodded. 'Yep he was, very. So we grabbed a coffee, and I asked him to calm down and tell me all about it.'

'And what was it? Some crackpot conspiracy theory or something like that?'

She gave him a sharp look. 'Nothing like that sir, he was a really nice guy. He's a musician, plays in an Indy rock outfit, the Purple Tigers, They're quite well known, but I'm not sure you would have heard of them.'

He laughed. 'No, not if they're a happening band, I wouldn't have.'

'I don't think they've had any hits or anything like that, so not many people would have heard of them sir,' she said, then paused for a moment before giving a sheepish grin. 'But the guy was very good-looking too sir. In fact, I thought I might arrest him to get his phone number. Actually, he looked a bit like your brother Jimmy. You know, tall, slim, broad-shouldered. Slightly older perhaps, but not much.'

'Oh aye?' he said, giving her a sideways look. 'And did it ever occur to you that my wee brother is just a younger and slightly stretched version of me, although without the rugged good looks?'

She laughed. 'Yes sorry sir. In fact, the guy did look a bit like you come to think of it. From the back at least.'

'Aye, very funny,' Frank said genially. 'So, now that we've established he was a good-looking fella, what was his story?'

'Well sir, one of the claimed victims is his sister, a woman going by the name of Rhona Fraser. He's Finn Fraser by the way, her younger brother.'

Frank gave her a startled look. 'You mean the Rhona Fraser?'

'That's right. Do you know her sir?'

'I know of her. She was a brilliant fiddle player, really big in the traditional folk scene. And God I remember the case now. She just disappeared off the face of the earth, about eight years ago, something like that. It's all coming back to me, and aye, it was in Cambridge right enough where she was last seen.' He paused for a moment. 'So, what was it that made your guy Finn think that Rhona was murdered? Because the local cops would have investigated it thoroughly at the time, but without a body there wouldn't have been much they could have done. I mean, she could have just as easily drowned in the Cam as anything. I'm guessing after all these years there'll have been a formal presumption of death?'

Lexy shrugged. 'I've not had a chance to look at that yet sir. Like you, I'm guessing there has been, but I don't know. But here's the interesting thing. The other alleged victim is a woman called Olivia Cranston, and apparently Rhona Fraser and this Olivia lady had been in a relationship. They had been living together in Glasgow for nearly three years at the time of Rhona's disappearance. And now, almost eight years later, Olivia has vanished in the same city where her partner was last seen. Finn thought that was very odd, and disturbing as well.'

'Aye, I suppose it is odd,' Frank agreed. 'You say this other woman has disappeared too? Three months ago? So how come it took this Finn guy so long to come up with his murder theory?'

Lexy frowned. 'Well it seems like Miss Cranston suffered from quite severe mental health issues, going back many years. And when she went missing, he said her family at first feared the worst.'

'You mean that she'd self-harmed?'

'Exactly sir. Finn said Olivia's family spent weeks and weeks in Cambridge after she disappeared doing their own search, but there was absolutely no trace of her. And then Gina McQuarrie's death hit the headlines and he realised all of this just had to be related in some way.'

Frank gave her a quizzical look. 'How? I don't see it myself.'

Lexy smiled. 'So for that sir, we have to go back more than ten years, to the murder of a girl called Naomi Neilson. Up in the Cairngorms.'

He gave her a blank look. 'Doesn't ring any bells. Mind you, I'd moved to the Met by then so it wouldn't have been on my radar.'

'And I was still at primary school,' Lexy said. 'Or was it nursery?'

'Aye, go on, twist the knife why don't you?' he said, laughing. 'But as I said, it doesn't ring any bells.'

'I did a bit of digging sir. Not in our own files, but just online. The Moray Advertiser's website was very helpful. It was a big story in that neck of the woods as you can imagine.'

He nodded. 'I can imagine. So fill me in, what happened?'

'Well basically sir, twenty-one-year-old Naomi Neilson was found strangled in her hotel bedroom, with a leather trouser-belt pulled tight round her neck. The place was just outside Nethy Bridge, one of these swish four-hundred-pound-a-night country house hotels.'

'A bit out of my league I'm afraid,' Frank said. 'But go on.'

'A party of six had been up in the mountains, doing the big four-thousand feet challenge. That's climbing five peaks over four thousand feet in height in a day. Apparently it's a thing. And before you ask, Cairn Gorm itself is the only one I can pronounce properly. But as I said, apparently it's a thing, this challenge.'

He nodded again. 'Aye, I've vaguely heard of it. I think my brother Jimmy's taken a few nutters up there to tackle it. But not me, I hasten to add.'

She laughed. 'I'm sure you'd do it with your eyes shut sir. But anyway, it turns out that all of the six were in a Glasgow Uni walking club. It was called the Cairngorm Conquerors and it was centred around the university's Economics department. The members were all staff and students or friends, and Finn says that there was an active social scene too. Lots of parties and stuff like that.'

'And who were this six?'

'Right sir, this is where it gets very interesting. So Finn's sister Rhona was one of this expedition, and her lover Olivia was another. Then there was Andrew and Gina McQuarrie, who hadn't been married that long. And then there was the murdered girl, who was an economics undergraduate, and finally a lecturer in the department called Gordon Baird. They'd got back to the hotel about six o'clock after their long walk, and then went for a dinner and a few drinks. Actually, more than a few drinks, according to the newspaper report.'

'So they had an almighty piss-up to celebrate their achievement? Pretty par for the course.'

'I imagine so sir. But then the next morning, Naomi Neilson was found dead. There was speculation at the time that it was some sort of sex game gone wrong.'

Frank laughed. 'That would have gone down a storm with the local Moray rag. A sex scandal up there in the middle of nowhere? That would definitely have been a first. But I think I can see where your boy Finn is coming from. Because if my maths is correct, six people went on that wee walking tour of the Cairngorms and now four of them are dead. That's definitely odd.'

'Yes it is sir. But it's not four that are dead, it's five.'

'What?'

'Yes sir, five. Because Gordon Baird's dead too. In fact, the police eventually decided that he was the murderer, but by that time he'd been found smashed up at the bottom of a corrie up on Braeriach.'

'Bloody hell, this is a crazy tale, isn't it? So by my reckoning, this Andrew McQuarrie character is the only one who's left?'

'That is the case sir, yes. It's a very bizarre situation, don't you think?'

He nodded. 'Aye, you could say that again.' He paused for a moment. 'There's another thing as well. Did you know that Gina and Rhona were in a folk group together? It was called Flaming Fiddles and they were bloody marvellous and very successful too. They did this amazing record called Skye Lament, an absolutely cracking album and it sold by the ton at the time. I think I've still got a CD of it somewhere actually. And the interesting thing is, they only did that one album before they broke up, so that added to its mythical status.'

Lexy smiled. 'You're really into that fiddle and folk stuff aren't you sir? And it seems they all eventually turn into cases for us too.'

He raised an eyebrow. 'Well, to be fair, I think that recent Claymore Warriors business could be classified as exceptional. I'm not sure any of my other favourite bands are harbouring nutcases and murderers, at least not as far as I'm aware.'

'Good to know that sir.' She was silent for a moment then said, 'So what do you think sir? Are Finn's murders worth taking a look at?'

He gave her a non-committal look. 'Well I don't think it's exactly what the Minister was thinking of when she set up the unit. But it's bloody intriguing, there's no denying that.'

Of course, it was true that it probably wasn't the sort of case the Minister had in mind when she was setting up the new cold-case unit. Its primary purpose was for the government to be able to say we're doing something when the latest episode of police ineptitude hit the headlines, whereas in this case, he doubted if the Cambridgeshire force were at fault in any way, other than having failed to find the missing women in both instances. And as he thought about it some more, it struck him that Finn Fraser's case might be an ideal one with which to bed down the new organisation and his new team. Something for them to get their teeth into, but a low-stakes affair where they could fail without causing a big stink.

Decision made, he said. 'You know what Lexy, this case might not be a bad shout to get us up and running. Plenty of intrigue and interest, but not much scope to piss off the brass if we screw up. After all, we don't want to be making enemies before we're even off the ground.' As he said it, he realised that he was being presumptuous with the us. He paused for a moment then said, 'But sorry, I know you'll need some time to think about my wee job offer. I'd love to have you join the team, but remember, there's no pressure. Whatever's best for you. Honestly.'

His parting words to her were sincere, but that didn't prevent him leaving the canteen with his fingers firmly crossed. And then a seraphic smile crossed his lips as he remembered a phrase she had used earlier. We had something come in the other day that might be a candidate for us. No doubt about it, she had definitely said it. For us. Giving a mental click of the heels, he found himself wondering if perhaps this was to be one of these red-letter days that occasionally turned up out of the blue, the type of day when everything you touched turned to gold. Deciding to test the theory to its limits, he fished his phone from his pocket and swiped rapidly down his frequent contacts until he landed on the number of Eleanor Campbell.

Chapter 6

It was Thursday evening, and for the first time in what seemed aeons, the whole gang was back together in their recently-adopted meeting place, the Horseshoe Bar on Glasgow's elegant Great Western Road. For years, when they had lived in London, the Thursday-evening after-work drink at the Old King's Head had been an unmissable ritual, stretching back to the days when she had only just met the wonderful Stewart brothers. Back then, she didn't know she would fall in love with the elder one, then marry him, then find herself longing for them to have a baby together, even at the ridiculous age of forty-four. But that was where she now found herself, and what an amazing journey it had been. There were five of them tonight, Frank, Jimmy, DC Lexy McDonald, Maggie and her new associate Lorilynn Logan, the atmosphere as usual warm and convivial, aided by the lubricating effect of their second drink of the evening.

'So what brings you back to town bruv?' Frank was asking his brother. 'Struggling to cope with the bright lights of downtown Braemar?'

Jimmy laughed. 'Far from it pal, I love it up there. No, I got a call from someone at Edinburgh & Glasgow Assurance, wanting us to organise one of our management team-building events for a group of their senior managers. They want to do the five four-thousands in a day, which is actually ridiculous. But I'm hoping I can talk them round to looking at something a wee bit less ambitious to start with. I've got a big meeting with them tomorrow. Could be a nice contract for me and Stew if we win it.'

'Funnily enough, me and Lexy were just talking about that exact challenge earlier,' Frank said, surprised. 'Apparently, and I'm only quoting my DC here, it's a thing. And a thing you need to be super-fit to do by all accounts.'

'Aye, it *is* a thing,' Jimmy said, 'and yes, you need to be pretty damn fit if you want to complete it safely. Not something an overweight forty-something who's only used to pushing a mouse around a desk can take on without some serious training.'

Frank gave a mock grimace. 'Why are you looking at me like that? I'm fitter than a racing snake, me.'

Maggie, overhearing, laughed and said, 'That statement *might* just benefit from a second opinion.' And then she wrapped an arm around his waist and kissed him on the cheek. 'But you're perfect for me as you are.'

'Get a bloody room you two,' Jimmy said, pulling a face. 'Anyway Frankie-boy, how come the four-thousand in a day challenge is on your radar? Because I guess you're not planning to do it yourself any time soon.'

'There was a murder, in a hotel near Nethy Bridge,' Lexy interjected. 'Ten years ago now, a girl called Naomi Neilson. She had just done the challenge with some friends from a Uni walking club, and they were having a bit of a celebration dinner and an overnight stay. And now nearly everybody who was on that walk is dead. *Five* of them. It's mental. Mental enough to be the first case for Frank's new unit I think.'

'Tell you something else,' Frank added. 'Your Gina McQuarrie was on that walk, and her husband too. In fact, Sir Andrew McQuarrie is the only one of the party of six who's still with us. As Lexy said, it's mental, the whole damn thing.'

'And do you think it's connected in some way?' Lori asked, who had been uncharacteristically quiet thus far. 'I mean, that old murder and Gina's accident?'

Frank shrugged. 'The jury's out on that one as far as I'm concerned Lori. The thing is, I've been thinking about it again, and I know I've always said that three connected events are more likely to be conspiracy than coincidence, but I'm not sure that works when you get up to five. Because *that's* so off-the-wall that it has to be a kind of one-in-a-million occurrence, an outlier if you will. But to be fair, this thing is so crazy, I could well be proved wrong. Although I suspect that when Jimmy does his wee investigation, it'll confirm that Gina's death was nothing more than a tragic accident.'

His brother nodded. 'Aye, probably. But we'll see once I get up there.'

'It didn't say anything about the Neilson murder on Sir Andrew's Wikipedia profile, or on his wife's for that matter,' Maggie said. 'Which is surprising, given they both must have been questioned about it at the time.'

'Wikipedia's self-editing,' Lori said wryly, 'so if anyone did post anything about the murder, the McQuarries could delete it themselves no bother. I'm not saying they *have* ever done that by the way. Just that it's really easy to do.'

'We'll have to take your word for that,' Maggie said. 'But whatever the case, I think we're going to be going on an interesting journey in the next few weeks and months, and make no mistake.'

Smiling, she looked at her watch. 'And we have to go on an interesting journey back to Milngavie to relieve Ollie's babysitter my darling. Come on, drink up.'

'They're going to do some baby-making,' Lori said to Lexy, in a whisper that was just a decibel or two too loud. 'I think they've been doing it every night.'

'Lorilynn Logan,' Maggie exclaimed in mock horror. 'I think we can definitely file that under too much information. *Way* too much information.'

But, embarrassing though it was, the girl wasn't wrong.

***

It had seemed obvious that the first person Maggie and Lori should speak to in the Gina McQuarrie case should be the tragic violinist's husband, the revered economics professor Sir Andrew, so the next day, that's what they did. His place of work, it turned out, was the University's Adam Smith Business School, located in the eponymously-titled building, a substantial construction of quite spectacular ugliness, apparently opened in 1967 but presumably not deliberately intended to resemble an Eastern Bloc housing complex of the same period. As to the man himself, Maggie didn't know much -actually, call that anything -about Smith, other than he was a famous historic figure credited with having more or less invented the modern science of economics, if indeed the subject was worthy to be called that, and had conducted much of his important research at the University. Three hundred years ago, he had written a book called The Wealth of Nations, a work usually described as seminal, although she didn't precisely know what the word meant. Still, the building's challenging appearance meant they didn't have any trouble finding it, located as it was off a lane directly behind picturesque University Gardens, and barely five minutes' walk from the Byres Road offices of Bainbridge Associates. They signed in at reception, then settled themselves in the house-plant-decorated seating area, waiting for their host to collect them.

'You were a lawyer, weren't you Maggie?' Lori said. 'So you must have gone to university I suppose?'

She grimaced. 'I did, yes. To Leeds. I did a law degree. But it was a long time ago now. I hardly remember anything about it.'

Lori grinned. 'Was that because you enjoyed the student lifestyle too much?'

Maggie gave her associate a wry look. 'Yeah, I *wish*. I was a very hard-working student, I'll have you know.' But it was true, she didn't remember much of it at all, and she knew exactly why that was. Three years earlier, she, then Mrs Maggie Brooks, had been the most hated woman in Britain, the selfish barrister who had engineered the acquittal of a teenage terrorist using legal trickery, and that teenager had gone on to kill again. Now, in the aftermath of her life-changing trauma, it was if her conscious mind had performed a massive re-arrangement of her memory banks, archiving the 'before' in some deep recess that could only be accessed with great difficulty. Everything prior to the trauma had disappeared. Her childhood, her school days, her time at Uni, and, above all, her disastrous marriage to

Philip Brooks, all of them had been buried in a murky shapeless blob. She knew they had all happened of course, but the detail was lost. Except for one event, thank God, and that was the birth of her adored son Ollie, the joy of that day as crystal-clear as if it had happened yesterday.

'I'd have liked to have gone to uni, so I would,' Lori said wistfully. 'But I never really got the chance. With looking after my mum and everything. My sister was the same. She was clever too.'

Maggie laughed. 'You're young Lori, there's nothing to stop you going if you want to.'

The girl shrugged. 'Maybe, although I love this job so much, so I wouldn't want to give it up, so soon after I started. But maybe one day I'll do a degree in detecting.' As she spoke, she looked up, evidently spotting the figure approaching them. 'That's him,' she whispered, nodding in the man's direction. Sir Andrew McQuarrie was tall, slim and athletic-looking, wearing pressed blue jeans and a smart light-blue dress shirt, open at the neck. His footwear was a pair of polished brown leather brogues that looked expensive and could well have been hand-made. His reddish hair was slightly thinning and brushed back from his forehead, his face lined but craggily handsome, with what Nashville songwriters liked to describe as a crooked smile. But the good looks couldn't hide the haunted expression he wore, nor disguise the dark circles around his eyes. He directed a sad smile at Maggie, who had stood up and was extending a hand to greet him.

'Hi, I'm Maggie Bainbridge, and this is my associate, Lorilynn Logan. Good to meet you Sir Andrew.'

He shook her hand then did the same for Lori. 'Yes, good to meet you both. We'll just wander up to my office and we can have our little chat. Follow me. And by the way, I prefer just plain Andrew. I only use the Sir when I'm trying to shoehorn my way into a restaurant.' It sounded like a line he had used often, but today it was bereft of the humour it was no doubt intended to convey.

Maggie smiled. 'Very well, I'll try to remember that. But I'll probably end up calling you Sir Andrew for most of the meeting anyway. I'm quite a slow learner.'

He led them along a dull corridor lined with beech-panelled doors, each bearing a name plate, presumably that of the academics who occupied the rooms, rooms in which perhaps the next wonder breakthrough in the alchemy of economics was being conceived. His own office turned out to be impressively large, two walls lined with bookshelves and a large conference table with about a dozen chairs taking centre stage. One wall was given almost entirely to glass, looking out onto a dark tree-shaded courtyard.

'Grab a seat, please, ' he said, gesturing to the opposite side of the table to where he stood, then pulled out a chair and sat down.

'Thanks,' Maggie said. She took a little notebook and ballpoint from her bag and placed it on the table. 'You don't mind if I make a few notes Andrew?'

He gave a half-hearted shrug. 'Feel free.' He rested his elbows on the table, clasped his hands together then lowered his chin onto the outstretched thumbs. 'So,' he began, 'Edinburgh & Glasgow believe Gina killed herself, is that what I'm given to understand?'

Maggie shook her head. 'No, they don't think that. But first of all, I'm *very* very sorry for your loss. It's the most tragic situation and you and your children must be devastated.' She hoped her tone conveyed the genuine sympathy she was feeling for the man and his family.

He shrugged again and sighed. 'It's been an incredibly difficult few weeks of course. But somehow, you just have to carry on, don't you?' *Yes you do*, Maggie thought, although McQuarrie would presumably be unaware that she and her little son Ollie had faced a similar but more gruesome tragedy in their lives.

She hesitated, wondering whether to make any comment. Finally she said, 'I've been through something very similar.

And though it's hard to believe it now, it does get better. Slowly. But it will get better. I can't say if it will for you of course, but it did for me.'

He gave her an appreciative smile. 'Everybody has told me that, but it's good to hear it from someone who's been through it too.' He hesitated. 'It's not for now, but I'd like to hear your story one day. If it's something you share, of course.'

'I don't,' Maggie said, hoping her tone wasn't too abrupt. 'It's one of the ways that *I* cope.' She was silent for a moment then said, 'If you don't mind, I'll just summarise what it is that Edinburgh & Glasgow has asked my firm to do. And I don't expect an ounce of sympathy from you when I say this, but it is horribly awkward for your life insurance company. They don't want to go through this process any more than you do. But it's standard procedure, when there's such a large sum of money involved.'

McQuarrie leaned back in his chair. 'So they called you in to do their dirty work for them.'

She shook her head. 'No, it isn't like that. We were chosen because my associate Jimmy Stewart is a mountain-craft expert. He's an ex-army officer and he runs an outward-bound school in Braemar. He's going to try and retrace Gina's exact steps and work out what happened to her. It's

Jimmy's investigation that'll be forming the main part of our report.'

'But we know what happened to her,' he said quietly. 'She lost her bearings in poor visibility and walked over the edge of the Bhrochain corrie. That was what the mountain rescue team said must have happened and I've no reason to doubt their findings. It was a tragic accident, nothing more, nothing less.'

Maggie hesitated then said, 'Look, we've got to face the elephant in the room, and in fact you've already brought it up yourself. Put bluntly, Edinburgh & Glasgow want to rule out any possibility that your wife took her own life. And that is the angle they're coming from. They're anxious to rule it out. They're not trying to prove she did do it. Totally the opposite.'

'Aye, and Jimmy should be able to prove that nae bother,' Lori said. 'That bit's nothing but a big tick in the box for the insurance company I think. Before they hand over a wee cheque for three million pounds,' she added, wearing an expression of cherubic innocence.

Maggie gave McQuarrie an apologetic smile. 'And that of course is the other elephant in the room. Because it's a very large amount of money by anyone's standards. Andrew, I'd be interested to understand why you and your wife decided on such a high sum. And you only took out the joint policies relatively recently, didn't you? Hardly a month ago.' That was the third elephant in this already-overcrowded room, and the one that, more than anything, had raised the red flags at Sir Andrew and Gina McQuarrie's insurance providers. *Guy takes out huge life policy on wife, wife suddenly dies, guy comes into a fortune.* It had been a reliable plotline in detective fiction ever since the genre started, and an equal concern for life insurance companies since the beginning of their industry too.

'Our twins are at private school, and both of them want to study medicine when they are old enough.' He smiled. 'There's a mountain of expense ahead of us, which of course we don't grudge for a second.' He paused and then sighed, sad-eyed. 'I keep saying *us*, as if Gina is still here. But yes, we do - did - have expensive lives, Gina and I, and so a few weeks ago our financial advisor persuaded us to relook at our life cover, just one thing amongst a bunch of other financial matters that needed tidying up at the time.'

'It's a very expensive policy,' Maggie said.

McQuarrie nodded. 'Well yes, that's true. But it gave us great peace of mind knowing that our children would be well-looked after if anything should happen to either of us. We were both mad keen on outdoor activities, like climbing and walking and skiing too of course. And these activities are not without risk...' His voiced tailed off until it became almost inaudible. 'Which sadly was proven to be all too true in my darling wife's case.'

'That makes perfect sense. And what of your general financial situation? How would you describe that?' Maggie tried to make the question sound casual, as if the answer was of no real consequence. But there were two classical reasons that drove life insurance fraud. One was greed, the other need. And a cool three million would go a long way to helping anyone out of a financial hole, that was for sure.

He smiled. 'Robust. I'm adequately rewarded here in the Chair of Economics, and I have my extensive media work, which is particularly lucrative. And Gina was very comfortable in her own right.' He smiled again, 'In fact, all she really had to do was sit in her favourite chair overlooking our beautiful garden and listen to the *ker-chink* of royalties hitting her bank account.' As he said it, Maggie saw tears well up in his eyes.

'Skye Lament, that was their big hit,' Lori interrupted. 'That's an absolute belter of a tune. And they're using it in a British Airways advert at the moment. It's everywhere.'

'Yes, licensing generates most of the revenue from the back catalogue these days,' McQuarrie said, raising a hand to wipe away the tear that had now trickled down his cheek. 'Look, I'm sorry,' he said, giving a half-smile of apology. 'Now that streaming has taken over from physical album sales,' he added. And of course, that lucrative revenue would continue to flood in for years and years to come, Maggie thought.

She gave a bright smile. 'It does seem your finances are in great shape, which is good.' Now though, she would have to raise what were likely to be the most difficult topics of the morning. She took a breath then asked, 'So tell me Andrew - and forgive me asking this - but how would you describe Gina's general state of mind in the weeks leading up to her terrible accident?'

He looked at her, seemingly surprised at the question. 'Her state of mind? Well, no different to normal I should say. She was busy with the twins' day-to-day stuff, and she was planning her mountain walks and looking forward to them. Yes, just the same. No different.'

'And is there anyone who could corroborate that sir?' Lori said, rather abruptly.

He gave the girl a sharp look. 'And why would you need that?' he said.

Lori shrugged. 'Just routine sir. I think the insurance company would probably want to hear from someone other than her husband.'

He seemed to consider the point then said, 'You can speak to her sister Laura. Gina and her were close. I'll text you her number.'

'That would be excellent,' Maggie said. 'So really, just one more question and then I think we'll be done.' She paused for a moment, then said. 'Forgive me again Andrew, but how would you say your relationship with your wife was, in the weeks and months leading up to her death?'

'Perfectly normal,' he replied testily. 'We were no different from any other married couple. As I said before, we both led busy lives, but yes, it was fine. Why, have you heard something to the contrary? Because you know what journalists are like, always looking to dig up dirt.'

'No no, nothing like that,' Maggie said with an apologetic smile. 'It's simply a question that we're obliged to ask. If you're saying everything was good, then that's what will go into my report.' Although that of course wasn't strictly true. The fact was, they couldn't simply take his word for it, not if they were to do a thorough job, and further corroborating investigations would have to be made.

'Did she have a will?' Lori said, out of the blue.

'Well of course she did,' McQuarrie answered sharply. 'As I said, our affairs were in extremely good order.'

'And did she leave everything to you?'

'The terms of my wife's will is a private affair and only of concern to my family. It has nothing whatsoever to do with the matter you are investigating as far as I can see.'

Maggie intervened, sensing his growing annoyance. 'No, you're absolutely right, your wife's will is none of our business.' But it would still be interesting to learn all about it nonetheless, she thought. Anxious to take the discussion on a different track, she asked, 'Were you worried when you heard about your wife's plan to tackle those tough passes in April, and alone? Because my colleague Jimmy tells me it's one of the most dangerous routes in the entire mountain, at any time of the year never mind in late winter.'

'I had my concerns,' he said. 'But Gina's fitness and strength were exceptional, so she wouldn't have seen it as particularly dangerous. And the fact was, the mountains were her obsession, and it was what she lived for. That and her music of course. She tried to have a day up in the mountains most weeks, but she seldom discussed her detailed plans with me. But she always filed her route with the mountain rescue guys in advance, even if she was only planning a simple hike. She respected these hills, as you must. And she died doing what she loved. That gives me some comfort at least.'

Maggie nodded. 'I'm glad.' After a moment's hesitation she said, 'Andrew, I think we've probably covered most of the things I wanted to ask you about, and hopefully I won't have to trouble you again. There's just one final thing,' she added. 'It would be good to touch base with your financial advisor, just to confirm the circumstances that led to you and your wife taking out your life insurance policies. Because from what you've told us, it was just a sensible bit of family financial planning, and if I can put that in my report, then that'll go a long way towards satisfying Edinburgh & Glasgow.'

He didn't reply for a moment, and she wondered if he was mentally weighing up the pros and cons of agreeing to her request. Finally he said, 'Yes, I suppose that's okay. It's a firm called Johnson & King. They're actually in Milngavie, on Douglas Street. Emma King is one of the partners and she's the person who looks after our family affairs.'

'Yeah, I think I remember seeing their offices. And obviously we'll only be asking her about the life insurance policy,' Maggie said.

He shrugged. 'Emma takes client confidentiality very seriously. Not that we've got anything to hide,' he added. He took an exaggerated glance at his watch and said, 'So, it's been good to meet you both, but I don't think we can take this discussion much further.' He looked at Maggie. 'I trust I've given you everything you need for now?'

She nodded. 'It's been tremendously helpful Andrew. And just so you know, my colleague Jimmy Stewart is planning to set off on his Braeriach expedition in the next five days or so. Once we have his findings, that'll add to today's discussions and go off to Edinburgh & Glasgow, and then hopefully that'll be it, done and dusted.' She stood up and extended a hand in his direction. 'And yes, it's been great to meet you too.'

***

'So, what do you think then?' Maggie asked. They were on University Avenue, wandering down to Byres Road with the intent of calling in at the Bikini Barista cafe before returning to their office.

'He's a bit too smooth for me,' Lori said, having to raise her voice above the background noise of the traffic, 'but he was really sad too, to be fair. Not surprising after what's happened. It's not that I didn't like him, it was just that there was something about him I didn't take to. Although he does look exactly like he does on the telly. Quite handsome, if you like old men.'

'Yes, he is handsome and a bit smooth too,' Maggie agreed, 'but on the other hand, he did seem quite open about things. I didn't get the impression he was lying to us.'

'But *she* was a bit of a selfish cow, don't you think? His wife I mean,' Lori said. 'Because if I had two kids, I wouldn't be risking my life every week trekking all over the Cairngorms on my own.'

Maggie nodded. 'Funnily enough, I thought that too, which got me wondering how Sir Andrew might really have felt about her obsession as he described it. Supportive though he sounded.'

'And that thing he said about journalists always digging up dirt?' Lori said. 'Has there been a story kicking about that we've missed, do you think?'

'Yes, I remember he said that. Let's see if we can find that on Google, shall we?' Maggie picked up her phone and opened the search app. 'How about *Sir Andrew McQuarrie family scandals?* Because where a journalist is involved, a scandal's never far away, is it?'

'Good shout,' her associate said, craning her neck to look at the screen as it began to fill up. 'Anything?'

Maggie scrutinised the results for a couple of seconds, then smiled. 'Right at the top. An article in the Chronicle from three weeks ago, author one Yash Patel.' She clicked to open it then started to read. 'Look, this is very interesting,' she said. *'Rumours are circulating in academia that Sir*

Andrew McQuarrie is about to take up a prestigious position at a leading US university.'

'Not exactly a scandal,' Lori said. 'But it is blooming interesting, like you say. What do you make of it Maggie?'

She shrugged. 'I don't know. Maybe it's something, maybe it's nothing. Although certainly, something to add to our growing list. But let's concentrate on Gina for now. Obviously, we'll need to talk to the financial adviser, but it's her sister I'm really looking forward to catching up with. She might give us a different perspective on our unfortunate victim.'

Lori shrugged. 'Maybe. But I think we'll still find she was a selfish cow.'

Chapter 7

Eleanor Campbell hadn't been available when Frank called, so he'd dropped her a text of suitable vagueness and turned to the next item on his half-formed and unwritten to-do list, that being the recruitment of the corpulent reprobate that went by the name of DC Ronnie French. The detective answered his call on the third ring with a cheery *morning guv,* followed by a loud belch and then a hurried *'scuse me.*

'And good morning to you too Ronnie. What are you up to?' From the background chatter and clinking of cutlery on plates, Frank was pretty sure he knew the answer, if the belch hadn't already given it away.

'I'm just down the greasy spoon right now having a bit of breakfast. I'm run off my feet at the moment, as you know. Cases coming out of my ears, left, right and centre.'

'Aye, of course you are,' Frank said, laughing. 'Anyway Ronnie, how long is it now until you put your feet up and pick up your big fat pension?'

'Forty-one days guv. My missus has stuck a whiteboard on the kitchen wall and is ticking off the days one-by-one with a felt-tipped pen.'

'With dread or with pleasure?'

French laughed. *'Bit of both guv. Bit of both. But she's cutting back her hours too, so I think she's looking forward to having me around more.'*

'I can understand that,' Frank said, lying. 'But listen, remember I mentioned this new department that folks have been talking about? Well, it's turned into reality now, and I've got the balls-aching task of getting it up and running.'

'Is that this fancy new cold-case department then guv?'

'That's it Ronnie. To be honest, it's not much different from our Department 12B, except it comes under the civil service and not the police. Which actually is one of the reasons I wanted to talk to you. You see, my new set-up has been given a pretty generous budget for the first year. So when the lovely Mrs French gets fed up with you cluttering up her kitchen and hogging the daytime TV control, as I'm certain she will, I wondered if you might like to do a wee bit of part-time work for me? It wouldn't be much different to what you do now, except you'd be a civil servant instead of a copper, and the money's quite a bit better too. It'd pay for your West Ham season ticket and maybe your fishing permits as well. A nice little extra earner. You could even take your missus on a nice romantic holiday with the proceeds.'

Frank heard a cackle at the other end of the line. *'Sounds good guv. But would I have to go on one of them diversity and inclusion courses and learn about all them other sorts of pronouns?'*

'Of course, it's the civil service, isn't it? But since you're very much the modern man Frenchie, you won't have any problems passing the exam. You'll sail straight through, no bother at all. You might even get a gold star.'

'Sounds good,' French said again. *'I'll check with the missus, but I already know what she'll say.'*

'What's that?'

'When can you start?'

Frank laughed. 'We'll call that a deal then. But as it happens, I've actually got a new case for you right now, if you can somehow fit it into your busy schedule. It'll be your last before you retire I expect, and if it's still going by then, we'll transfer it over to the new organisation.'

'Great guv,' French said. *'I just need to nip up to the counter and get Terry to do me some extra toast, and then I'll be all ears.'* Frank heard the phone dropping on the table, the background becoming a morass of hard-to-make-out conversation and muffled clattering. But soon, the DC was back and able to take up proceedings from where they left off.

'Sorry about that guv,' he said through a mouthful of toast. *'You were talking about a new case.'*

'Aye, I was. To be honest, it's a bit ill-defined but it still an interesting one to get our teeth into. To cut to the chase, it's two women who disappeared off the face of the earth, last seen in Cambridge. And two women who happened to have been in a relationship.'

'What, you mean like lesbians?'

Frank gave an exasperated sigh. 'Aye, *lesbians* Ronnie. Just remind me to book you twice on that bloody diversity course, will you?'

'Sorry guv,' French said, sounding not the least bit apologetic. *'You know I was only winding you up.'*

'Well *don't*, not if you don't want to cause an international incident in Whitehall, if that's not an oxymoron. Anyway, the two women are called Rhona Fraser and Olivia Cranston. They're both Scottish as it happens, and Rhona disappeared nearly eight years ago and Olivia just a few months back. I want you to get your arse up the M11 and talk to the local cops and see what they've got on the two cases.'

'Are you thinking they've been murdered guv?'

'I'm not thinking anything right now,' Frank said. 'That's what I need you to find out, what happened to them. The objective couldn't be simpler.'

'Fair enough guv,' French said, *'I'll get on to it right away.'*

'Okay Frenchie, I'll put a courtesy call into their Chief Constable's office and tell them to be expecting you. And listen, the local cops had no way of knowing that these two cases might be connected, so go easy on them, all right?'

'You know me guv, I'll be as gentle as a butterfly on a bed of roses.'

Frank grinned. 'Aye, very poetic. Anyway, keep me informed of developments. Over and out.'

***

Given what he knew about the Cambridge missing person cases, Frank didn't think there would be much immediate call for Eleanor Campbell's services, but nonetheless he was anxious to talk to her about the opportunity to join his team. Anxious yes, but not exactly looking forward to it if the truth be told. But then, as he sat contemplating what he was going to say and how exactly he was going to say it, she took the matter out of his hands. With some trepidation, he swiped the screen of his phone to accept her incoming call.

'Eleanor, how's tricks?' he started brightly. 'Lots of interesting techie stuff going on to keep your great mind buzzing?'

'I read your text,' she answered sharply. *'I'm busy, so I can give you like forty seconds.'* The sharpness of her tone bothered him not one bit, it being her default setting.

'Okay, I'll get straight to the point and then I'll get out of your hair before I'm even in it. As I said in my wee message, I've got a new job, running a new cold-case unit, and there's an opportunity for Head of Forensics, covering the whole nine yards. Post-mortems, scene of crime, forensic IT, the lot. You wouldn't have to do it all yourself of course, but you'd be in charge, and you could still be hands-on with the IT stuff if you wanted to be.' He hesitated for a moment, then continued, in an effort to anticipate her likely objections. 'Or, as I suspect, if you don't fancy becoming a manager, I can make you Senior Forensic Consultant. That'll get nearly the same money and the same perks, but without the responsibility. What do you think?'

'And would I be like working for you?' she asked, her tone making it plain she didn't view this as one of the perks he'd been promising.

He hesitated again before answering. 'Well, *technically*, yes. But it would be the same as our current excellent working arrangement. I'd ask you to do something, you'd decide if you wanted to do it or not. I'd make some helpful technical suggestions, you'd ignore them. I'd ask you how long a job would take, and you would say you'll tell me when you're finished. As I said, exactly as now.'

If she had detected his mild sarcasm, which he doubted, she had evidently decided to ignore it.

'And would I still be in the same civil service grade structure?' she said, a question that surprised him, because somehow, he'd never seen Eleanor as particularly interested in that sort of stuff.

'To be honest Eleanor, I'm not sure, but there's a nice man called Trevor Park who's helping me with all this kind of thing. I'll phone him as soon as we're done, and I'm sure you'll have an answer in minutes.'

'And what about location?' she asked. *'Would I have to move back to Maida Vale Labs?'* She paused for a moment then added, *'Because you know I like it in Atlee House.'*

Frank allowed himself a half-smile, as it dawned on him that Eleanor's inexplicable love for the old dump was an angle he hadn't thought of exploiting. 'Well, aye of *course* you can stay in Atlee if you really want to. According to my guy Trevor, my new unit's going to be adopting a hybrid virtual workplace model, which basically means you can plonk your backside anywhere you want. So if you're in love with the old place, you can stay there as long as you like. In fact, you can have the pick of the desks, other than Ronnie French's, which I think he's already bagged.'

'So is Ronnie joining your unit? Because I thought he was like retiring?'

He laughed. 'He is like retiring, but then he's getting raised from the dead and joining us. Only on a part-time basis mind you, but at the speed Ronnie works, it'll be hard to tell the difference.'

'Part time, did you say? So would that be an option for me?'

The question surprised him. 'Well maybe,' he responded guardedly, 'but why do you ask?'

'It's me and Lloyd,' she said in an unmistakably proud tone. *'We're like trying for a baby.'*

Chapter 8

Johnson & King, Financial Advisors (specialising in mortgages and low-cost unsecured loans, according to the by-line below their name) occupied smart shop-front premises on Douglas Street. Maggie had often passed it on her visits into Milngavie's little village centre without it really registering, but now, as she stood outside awaiting the arrival of Lori from the station, she could see that it exuded an understated prosperity. The signwriting above the door was picked out in a classy gold leaf against a dark burgundy background, and the firm's name was engraved in each of the windows too. Her own offices on Byres Road weren't exactly shabby, but they were nothing like this. Precisely on schedule, Lori hove into view, breathless after ascending the mild incline up from the station at pace.

'Morning boss, and sorry, the train was a few minutes late,' she said, wiping a bead of perspiration from her brow.

'But you're not,' Maggie said, smiling. 'So, let's go in and see what Mrs King has to tell us.'

Emma King was about mid-fifties, the absence of a ring on the third finger of her left hand suggesting she was a Miss not a Mrs, although that was never a totally reliable indicator. She was heavily made-up, with greying blonde hair pulled back severely from her forehead, wearing a brown houndstooth-checked suit over a crisp white blouse with an elaborate bow.

'Please, come in, sit down,' she said pleasantly, gesturing to two seats opposite her sleekly-modern desk. 'Would you like a coffee or a tea?'

'Nothing for me,' Maggie said. 'I only live five minutes up the road, and I've had about three already this morning.'

'I'll take a wee coffee please,' Lori said. 'Milk no sugar.'

'We've got a new machine,' King said, smiling. 'It's a bit hi-tech but I know how to press the right buttons, just about.' She wandered over to the elaborate-looking machine, placed a cup under a chrome spout and stabbed a button on the touch screen. 'You see, simple as that.' When it was ready, she picked up the drink and took it back to her desk.

'Thanks,' Lori said. 'I'm Lori by the way. Lori Logan. And this is my boss, Maggie Bainbridge. Just in case you were confused on which one was which.'

'Good to meet you both,' King said. 'So, I think you're here to ask about the McQuarrie family?'

Maggie nodded. 'That's right. Specifically, it's to do with the life insurance policy they took out jointly a few months back. Edinburgh & Glasgow are going through their due process, which includes assuring that Gina McQuarrie's death wasn't by her own hand. I know it's a bit disagreeable, but every insurance company would be doing the same in the circumstances.'

King shook her head. 'Yes, it was a terrible business. And those poor children losing their mother. It's awful.'

'I guess you knew Gina well,' Maggie said. 'It must have hit you very hard.'

The woman nodded. 'I did. I've known her over ten years. In fact, I was her personal advisor several years before I started looking after the family finances.'

'Really? That's interesting.'

'Yes, she came to us when the Skye Lament album took off. These two girls were making serious money, and we were recommended to them.'

'You looked after Rhona too?' Maggie said, surprised.

Emma King nodded. 'I did, poor girl. Our firm advised both women on how they should structure the finances of their band.'

'That was Flaming Fiddles.'

'That's right. We didn't do anything particularly clever. We just set up a limited company with Gina and Rhona as sole directors, and all their royalties and tour earnings flowed into that. Rather than a salary, they took dividends, which is by far the most tax-efficient method. It worked very well for them. It's a standard approach.' The woman paused for a moment. 'What about your firm Maggie? Are you set up as a limited company?'

Maggie gave her an uncertain look. 'No, I'm just sort of self-employed, I think.'

'That's a mistake,' King said. 'You should speak to me afterwards. We can sort out a much more efficient arrangement for you.'

'Maybe I will,' Maggie said, laughing. 'But back to the McQuarries. Just to reassure you Emma, we don't need any details of monetary amounts or anything like that, and of course I know all of that is bound by client confidentiality in any case. All we're trying to do is to get a statement from an independent source as to the state of the family finances at the time they took out the policy, and what motivated them to take it out in the first place.' She hesitated for a second before continuing. 'According to Sir Andrew, it was you that advised they look at their life insurance arrangements, as part of... how did he describe it?'

'Just one thing amongst a bunch of other financial matters that needed tidying up at the time,' Lori supplied. 'That's what he said.'

King drummed her fingers on her desk and gave a sideways glance. 'Well, yes it was a bit like that I suppose.'

'Sorry, I'm not sure I understand,' Maggie said gently.

The woman looked momentarily uncomfortable. 'They wanted to free up some funds. Or to be precise, Sir Andrew did.'

Lori intervened. 'Does that mean they needed cash? Big dollops of it?'

'You could put it that way. Let's just say they wanted to increase their liquidity.'

'Why?' Maggie asked. 'What was the reason behind that?'

King shrugged. 'They didn't tell me. And even if they had done, I couldn't share it with you.'

'Of course not. So how did the new life insurance policy fit in with that?'

'That was Gina's idea,' the woman said.

'Gina's?' Maggie said, surprised. 'Not Sir Andrew's?'

'Yes. She was anxious to make sure her children were properly taken care of should anything happen to either of them.'

'But it was a particularly big policy, wasn't it? Was it you that advised them how much they should insure for?'

'Yes, to a certain extent. Given how much cash they were trying to free up, I assumed they had some ongoing financial commitments that I wasn't aware of. So I suggested the sum that should be insured, yes.'

Maggie looked at her. 'And Emma, did you ever speculate what these commitments might be?'

'No, I didn't,' the woman replied sharply. 'We advise our clients how to manage their money. As long as it's not obviously illegal, we're not concerned with what they do with it.'

'And was this a regular thing, this need for cash?' Lori asked. 'Or is that something you can't tell us?'

'Yes, that's a good point,' Maggie said. 'That would help us understand the general state of their finances. It would be very useful to put into our report'.

'It wasn't a regular thing, no.' King hesitated for a moment then said, 'I'm not sure if I should be telling you this, or even if it's relevant. But there was *one* previous occasion.'

'Go on,' Maggie said, interested.

'Look, this has been troubling me for years.' The woman hesitated again. 'I'm really not sure I can say anything.'

'That's totally understandable,' Maggie said quietly. 'We're really only here to talk about the life insurance policy. But if this is something that's been troubling you for so long, maybe it would help to talk to someone about it. Or not, whatever you prefer.'

There was a long silence, then King said, 'It was just a few months after poor Rhona disappeared. As you can imagine, it left the finances of the group in a kind of limbo. She hadn't been declared dead, that didn't happen until years afterwards, and there was a lot of money just sitting in the band's bank account. But then one day the McQuarries approached me and asked me to arrange the transfer of a substantial sum of the band's money into their personal joint account.' She paused for a moment. 'It made me really uncomfortable at the time.'

'Why was that?' Maggie asked, although she thought she could guess the answer.

'Look, the mechanism was there to make the transfer, because the articles of the company allowed either director to access the bank account. There wasn't a joint signatory arrangement in place, and to be honest, that was an oversight on my part when I set up the account. But it felt as if I was being asked to steal from Rhona, and I wasn't comfortable about that.'

'And *do* you think they were trying to steal from Rhona?' Maggie asked. 'Because that surprises me. Everything I've read suggests that Gina and Rhona were as close as sisters.'

'It wasn't Gina, it was Andrew,' King said quietly. 'He was putting pressure on her, I'm sure of it.'

'But why?' Lori asked. 'Was it just greed?'

'Not greed, need,' the woman answered. 'It seemed they needed money, and they needed it quickly. There was a terrible desperation that I never understood.'

Maggie gave her a puzzled look. 'And this desperation, it was both of them, not just Sir Andrew?'

'Yes. I felt Gina wasn't happy about it, but yes, I think it was both, definitely.'

'Okay,' Maggie said. 'And as far as you're aware, that was the only other occasion when they needed to free up cash? With such urgency I mean.'

The woman nodded. 'I think so, yes. But look, I don't think I should have told you that. Please keep it confidential.'

Maggie smiled. 'It's interesting, but I don't think it's relevant to our matter. We're only concerned about the life insurance policy.' She looked at Lori as if seeking guidance as to what to say next. 'And Emma, I think there's just one final thing I need to ask on that subject - and forgive me if you feel it's something you're unable or unwilling to comment on, because I'll understand.'

The woman gave her a suspicious look. 'Okay, what is it?' she asked.

'My question is, how would you assess the general financial situation of the McQuarries? Were their finances in good shape, or was this what this recent tidying up exercise was trying to address?'

King seemed to visibly relax. 'No, no, their finances were very healthy. As I said, this was simply an exercise to improve their liquidity.'

'And was this one in desperation too?' Lori asked. 'Like that last time.'

For a moment, the financial advisor seemed unsure how to answer, as if this was the first time she had considered the point. Finally she said, 'No, I don't think they were desperate on this occasion.' But to Maggie, it wasn't one hundred percent convincing. She looked at Lori. 'So Miss Logan, are we done?'

Lori nodded. 'Yep, I think so Maggie.'

Maggie smiled and stood up. 'Well thank you Emma, you've been very helpful. I think we've probably got everything we need for now, but if anything else springs to mind, I'll give you a call.'

'Can I ask you what you're going to say in your report?' King asked as she ushered them to the door.

'Well, it doesn't seem as if the McQuarries were under any financial stress,' Maggie replied, 'and you have told us that it was yourself who proposed the value of the life insurance policy. That's what will go into my report.'

***

'So what *are* you going to say in your report?' Lori asked as they made their way along Douglas Street.

'Let's grab a quick coffee and we can talk it through,' Maggie said. 'There's a place on the corner over there, Jack's it's called. And you'll be pleased to know they do a nice bacon roll.'

Lori gave a thumbs up, and a couple of minutes later, they were settled in a table near the window and giving their order to an attentive waitress.

'Right,' Maggie said. 'As Emma was talking, I was doing some rough calculations in my head. Firstly, Gina and Rhona's Skye Lament album has sold hundreds of thousands of copies, according to what Frank told me, and it's still selling to this day, plus there's a healthy income stream from licensing from adverts and such like. Secondly, Sir Andrew must be earning at least eighty grand a year in his position at the University, and he's probably making about the same on top, if not more, from his media work. So between them the couple were probably bringing in, I don't know, maybe three or four hundred thousand pounds a year? That's a lot of money by anybody standards. Enough such that you can do more or less anything you want without having to worry about it.'

'And yet they had to do this liquidity stuff,' Lori said. 'To get their hands on a massive pile of dosh.'

Maggie nodded. 'Exactly. So in answer to your question Lori, I don't think we're ready to write up that report quite yet. We need to find out why the McQuarries – and this happened on two occasions remember – why they had to go to unusual lengths to get their hands on what were presumably very large sums of cash. That's intriguing, given the huge amounts of money they were earning in the first place.'

'Aye, and there was another thing too I thought,' Lori said. 'I might have been wrong, but I thought Emma King gave away without meaning to that there was a tension between the McQuarries. As I said, I might be wrong, but it was as if they were bound together by something, but a bit reluctantly. Maybe it was money, I don't know. But there was definitely something weird going on there I thought.'

Maggie looked at her thoughtfully. 'Yes, I noticed that too. There was definitely something.' She paused for a moment. 'No, I don't think we're going to be in a position to write this bit of the report until we have a better insight into the McQuarrie's relationship.'

'We'll need to speak to the sister?' Lori asked.

Maggie nodded. 'We'll need to speak to the sister.'

Chapter 9

Frank had finally managed to catch up with Trevor Park, the unlucky admin wonk tasked with helping him get his new cold-case unit up and running, and as he had feared, the guy spoke in a blizzard of civil service jargon of which it was only possible to make sense of every third or fourth word. But to be fair to the fella, he seemed keen to help, for example confirming very quickly that Eleanor Campbell could stay on her existing grade structure should she join his team, which had been important to her, presumably because she wanted to be able to slot back into her old job if Frank's new unit went pear-shaped. As far as a headquarters for the new organisation was concerned though, that matter had been unexpectedly taken out of his hands, Park having identified that a floor of a Department of Work & Pensions building on Glasgow's West Nile Street was going spare. Since it had been made clear that for budgetary reasons he had no choice in the matter, Frank had gone to take a look at the place, and it wasn't too bad at all, being certainly a step up from Atlee House in both decor and appointments and, as a bonus, within easy walking distance of the city-centre amenities. It didn't have a name, just a number, but that wasn't a problem given that the number was One Hundred. Easy to remember, that.

Now, temporarily back in New Gorbals Police Station –and camped in the canteen, naturally - he was forced to twiddle his thumbs a bit as he waited for Lexy and Eleanor to decide whether or not to join him. He was hopeful, but he didn't want to tempt fate by putting any pressure on them. Still, this new Cambridge case was going to take plenty of thinking about, and he had plenty of time right now to do that. Two women with a deep personal connection pay a visit to that fine University city, eight years apart, and both disappear off the face of the earth. The first, the violinist Rhona Fraser, had now been officially presumed dead and a death certificate issued accordingly. But the second, Olivia Cranston, had only been missing for four months or so, her fate as yet unknown, but it was certainly too early to presume the worst. Like every policeman, he was familiar with the statistics. Eight out of ten adults who went missing were suffering with mental health issues, which was certainly the case with Olivia. The good news was that of the three hundred thousand or so reported incidents each year, the vast majority – ninety-seven percent - were found within just a few weeks. But that still left three percent who weren't, and that was nearly nine thousand individuals. For those missing more than a year, the statistics were even less favourable, but thankfully they were a long way from being at that stage yet with Olivia Cranston.

He was interrupted in his musings by the unexpected arrival of DC McDonald on the scene. She pulled out a chair opposite, the legs scraping across the tiled floor and emitting a nerve-jangling screech.

'Sorry about that sir,' she said, sitting down. 'So sir, I've been thinking about your offer. Is this a good time to discuss it?'

He smiled. 'Aye sure, go ahead.'

'I hope you don't mind sir, but I spoke to my Inspector here about it.' She hesitated for a moment. 'To cut a long story short, I floated the possibility of a secondment. A fairly short secondment, six months to a year. She was supportive.'

'A secondment?' Frank said, scratching his chin. 'Well, that would be a lot better than nothing, that's for sure.'

She nodded. 'I'm excited by the opportunity, but you know I'm quite ambitious. And to get to where I want to be, I need to have worked in as many different areas as possible. I've got an opportunity to join the organised crime team at the end of the year and I'd like to take that up.'

'Aye, I can understand why you'd want to do that.' He extended a hand towards her. 'Okay, let me welcome you on board for an exciting six-month ride. And when that's done, I'll try and persuade you to extend your stay,' he said, laughing.

Lexy shook his hand. 'I'd be rather cross if you didn't. But sir, you'll be pleased to know I come as a package deal. A two-for-one offer.'

He gave her an amused look. 'Pray explain young Lexy.'

She grinned. 'I've been talking to Eleanor. Or she's been talking to me if you want to be precise.'

'Oh aye, I forgot you were big mates,' he said. 'So what was she talking to you about? Mainly babies I expect.'

She laughed. 'Yes mainly babies, which kind of surprised me, because I'd never thought of Eleanor as a mum. But she did ask what I thought about your new department, and I said I thought it would be a dead interesting place to work. I think she was a bit fifty-fifty about it, so I said why not go for a secondment like I was doing?'

'And?'

'And that's what she's going to do. She had the name of some admin guy called Trevor and he said he could probably arrange it all and if she took your job, it would be on a higher grade and he could take care of all of that too.'

Frank laughed. 'Good old Trevor, he's rapidly becoming my best mate. So do you think she's going to say yes?'

'I think so sir. To be honest, she's a wee bit worried about working for you, but I told her you're a brilliant boss.'

'Thanks for lying on my behalf,' he said, laughing again. 'Anyway, since wee Eleanor doesn't take a blind bit notice of anything I say, it'll just be like business as usual. But that's great news Lexy. Woo-hoo! We're almost a team! Thank you so much.'

'Looking forward to it sir. Are we definitely debuting with that Cambridge missing persons case?'

He nodded. 'I've not cleared it with the Minister yet, but I'm confident she'll see the sense in starting with a fairly low-stakes investigation like this one. So yes, we will be.'

She paused for a moment. 'That's good, because I've been thinking about it quite a lot.'

'I wouldn't expect anything less. So what is it you've been thinking about?'

'That murder up in the Cairngorms sir, you know, the strangling of Naomi Neilson ten years ago. I really think we need to dig out these old files and take a deep dive. Four people who were on that expedition are dead for definite, and one's been missing for several months now, very possibly dead too. That's *seriously* weird, don't you think?'

He sighed. 'To be honest Lexy, my mind's been bouncing back and forward on that one. As I said in the pub the other day, it's almost too many deaths for it to be anything but a terrible if tragic coincidence. But then again, it wouldn't take much to persuade me to see it differently.'

'Let me look at it sir,' Lexy said earnestly. 'It wasn't that long ago, so I expect a few of the original investigation team will still be around to question. And I don't think there's any suggestion that there was a cock-up back then, so I expect we'll have no problem getting their cooperation.'

'Aye, you're right,' Frank agreed. 'All we're doing is looking to see how the events back then might have had an effect on what happened in the years afterwards.' He hesitated for a moment then said, 'Yes, go for it. Dive in and see what you can find out. And tie up with Ronnie. He's heading up to Cambridge in the next day or two to look at it from that angle.'

She smiled. 'Thank you sir, I will. It'll be interesting, I've no doubt about it.'

And although neither of them knew it just then, soon it was going to be getting a *whole* lot more interesting.

Chapter 10

It looked like the weather was going to be on his side for most of the next day's mission, although this being the Cairngorms, you were wise to treat any forecast with a healthy suspicion. Jimmy had decided to stay over at a nice bed-and-breakfast just outside Aviemore, mainly so that he could meet up with three of the guys from the mountain rescue team at a local pub for a meal and a couple of beers, but also so he could make an early start in the morning. Craig, Liz and Sandy had all been rostered on the night when Gina McQuarrie had failed to return from her early spring expedition to majestic Braeriach, and he was anxious to hear first-hand how and where they had discovered her body.

'It was a terrible night weather-wise and there wasn't any point in setting off until dawn,' Craig told him. 'I was particularly keen to be on the rescue myself because I'm a massive fan of Gina's. Not that it would have made any difference who it was,' he added hastily. 'But she was bloody gorgeous, wasn't she? I'll tell you man, what I would have given to have had just one night with her. We'd all have fancied that, eh?'

'Aye, well I suppose she was an attractive woman right enough,' Jimmy agreed noncommittally, thinking it was a strangely distasteful comment for the guy to make in the circumstances, particularly since they had only just met.

'He's got posters of her on his wall,' the man called Sandy said, raising an eyebrow. 'We always thought it was getting close to an obsession.'

'Away with you,' Craig laughed. 'A, that's not true and B, I wasn't obsessed with her. I just loved her music, that's all. But anyway, back to the rescue.' He paused for a moment then continued. 'So, we met up at six in the morning and took the Land Rover up the track that runs along Glen Einich, up to the wee loch at the top of the pass. It's the quickest route in, although it can be treacherous with snow and ice even at that time of year. It's not unusual for it still to be iced up in June even, never mind late April.'

'I know all about that, and I know the route too,' Jimmy said. 'An exciting drive I seem to remember. They dumped us up there once when I was in the army and left us for dead.'

Sandy laughed. 'That must have been fun. But aye, it's an exciting drive right enough, especially when Liz is driving. And she was that morning.'

'Bloody cheek,' the woman answered, then smiled at Jimmy. 'He only gets to say that because we're married.'

'I say it because it's bloody true,' Sandy replied affectionately. 'But no, it took us a good hour, but we got there just as it was getting light, at about five to eight or so.

There was five of us, and we had our tracker dog as well. He's another Sandy, a wee border collie. Smart as a tack and brave with it.'

'He's Robbie Cranston's dug,' Craig added. 'They're normally inseparable the pair of them, but Robbie was up to his ears with the annual cull, so his mate Mick was minding the dog for him.'

'The cull did you say? Jimmy asked. 'That's for the deer I suppose?'

'Aye, that's right,' Craig confirmed. 'Robbie's the ghillie at the Strathrothie estate. He's normally a stalwart on our rescues, but work comes first for all of us. Because we're all volunteers of course, every one of us.' He hesitated for a moment, as if unsure of whether he should say more. 'And anyway, Robbie's head wasn't in the best place with the business of his sister.'

'Hang on a minute,' Jimmy said, thinking. 'The woman who disappeared recently. In Cambridge.'

Craig nodded. 'That's right. Olivia. She's his sister. It's really done Robbie's head in. He spent weeks down there looking for her, but to no avail.'

'That's quite a coincidence,' Jimmy said, 'because that's a case that my brother is looking at, right at this very moment in fact.'

'They were very close, him and his sister,' Craig said. 'Cracking-looking girl too, but a bit flaky if you know what I mean,' he added, making a disparaging face. 'And gay as well. Shame that. But I hope they find her, obviously.'

Jimmy gave him a look but made no comment. 'You were telling me about the rescue.'

Craig smiled. 'Aye, I was. We parked up and got all the gear out, you know, the stretcher and all that, and set off as quick as we could, taking the route up by Einich Cairn.'

'That's a tough wee walk,' Jimmy said. 'Especially with all the kit. And that's another four thousand feet mountain, isn't it?'

Craig nodded. 'Yeah I think it is, or not far off anyway. And it was bloody icy on the way up, and there isn't really a track. So it took us two and half hours to get past Einich. We were bloody knackered, I can tell you. Anyway, it sort of widens out up there, I don't know if you know it, almost like a mini plateau, so the going gets a wee bit easier.'

'Not much easier,' Liz interjected, giving a wry smile. 'And there was six inches of lying snow that morning.'

'Yeah it was rough,' Sandy said. 'And there was no sign of Gina. So we decided to push on to Braeriach itself. She had been planning to come up over the top from the other direction, but we thought that maybe she hadn't made it that far and perhaps had bivouacked somewhere on the way up from Lairige.'

Liz was quiet for a moment. 'To be honest, we were worried that she might have fallen down Coire Bhrochain. Do you know it Jimmy?'

'Aye I do. It's that huge hollow which looks like someone's taken a big bite out of the mountain. I've seen it plenty of times from the Lairig Ghru pass and always thought it looked bloody dangerous.'

'It is very dangerous, but that doesn't stop some nutcases trying to ski down it,' Craig said, raising an eyebrow. 'So anyway, we had to go down and look, even although it would have added a couple of hours to our search. We were worried about daylight running out, so we decided to split up. Me and Sandy would go down into the corrie with Mick and the dog, and Liz and Allister would do a mile out-and-back towards the Lairige in case Gina was dug into a snow-hole somewhere along there. It's not best mountain-craft to split up, I know that, but we're all very experienced and the consensus was it was an acceptable risk to take.'

'And to cut a long story short, that's where we found her, right down in the corrie,' Sandy said. 'Lying face down with congealed blood all round her head.' He was silent for a moment. 'Must have slipped over the edge and banged her head on a rock on the way down. When they did the post-mortem they reckoned she would have died instantly. Probably four or five hundred feet further up the mountain we reckon.'

'Tragic,' Jimmy said, shaking his head in sympathy

Craig nodded. 'It's not exactly unknown either, much as I hate to say it. Every few years we get one up there. In fact there's a wee memorial plaque on the wall of the mountain rescue hut just a quarter a mile away from the spot. A guy lost his life there almost ten years ago to the day, and I remember it well, because it was one of the first rescues I was involved in when I joined the team. In fact this guy's body was found no more than twenty yards from where we found Gina.'

'Aye, that was the Gordon Baird guy, wasn't it?' Sandy said. 'The guy that was supposed to have murdered that girl. In the hotel at Nethy Bridge.'

Jimmy gave him a surprised look. 'Was that the Naomi Neilson case? My brother's a policeman, and he was talking about it just the other day.'

'That's right,' Sandy said. 'After Naomi's body was found, Baird took off into the mountains. They reckoned he killed himself by chucking himself over the edge of the corrie.'

'Heavy stuff,' Jimmy said.

'It was. And it was a bad day overall, because by a terrible coincidence another guy went missing the same day, a guy from Yorkshire, and *his* body's still not been found. Must have got deeply buried under a pile of snow or something and now it's probably encased in one of these blocks of ice that take forever to melt. It'll turn up one day, no doubt, completely out of the blue.'

'A tragic day right enough,' Jimmy said. 'But getting back to poor Gina, I guess you got her body onto the stretcher and battled your way back down to the track, to where you'd left your vehicle?'

Craig shook his head. 'Too difficult. It would have meant at least a two thousand feet climb to retrace our steps, and it's bloody steep in that gully. So we decided to head down to the Lairig Ghru and back along to Coylumbridge. A bit of a longer trek, but safer than the alternative.'

'And once we got down, they made me walk six miles or whatever it is back up the bloody track to fetch the Land Rover,' Sandy said ruefully.

'You drew the short straw then mate,' Jimmy said, laughing. 'But anyway, what do you guys think happened to Gina? Any theories?'

Craig shrugged. 'The visibility was poor, she was tired, she got too close to the edge of the ridge, she tripped or a sudden gust of wind caused her to lose her balance. Any or all of the above. And she was lovely,' he added wistfully. 'It was a great loss.'

Jimmy nodded. 'Aye, it was. But what you say makes sense.' He paused then smiled. 'You know what guys, you've all been an amazing help. The question now is, anyone for some more beers? And I'm buying, just so you know.'

***

He had managed to somehow drag himself out of bed with the six-thirty alarm and now, at eight-thirty on an early June morning, the sky was blue and the wind was blowing a moderate ten-mile-an-hour breeze from the west, which counted as a still day up in this neck of the woods. It was early summer now, so he wouldn't be facing exactly the same conditions as Gina McQuarrie had experienced during her walk, but nonetheless, he felt it important that he should retrace her steps precisely, mainly to be able to gauge her level of fatigue when she reached the ridge at Braeriach. Jimmy had parked his car in the same car-park as she had, on the road up to the ski centre, and was now about a mile into his walk, carrying a full pack just as she had on the day of her death. The woman had set herself a tough programme, posting on her social media that she intended to make the eight-mile slog up to the summit and then skirt down to Glen Einich for the eight mile trek back to the ski-road, following the rough track which had provided access to the mountain rescue guys' Land Rover. Apparently she had been super-fit, but factor in the unpredictable winter weather and it was a walk that would be challenging for even the most experienced mountain enthusiast. His own plan was a bit easier, but not by much. He would hike up from the car-park and put on as much of a sprint as he could, on the assumption that Gina wouldn't have been hanging about, given she had planned to cover not far off twenty miles of terrain in little more than eight hours of daylight. To do that, she would have to have been setting a pace of something like two to two-and-a-half miles per hour, no mean feat given the amount of climb on the route. But then again, he thought, that wouldn't be a factor if she had only intended for the trip to be one-way, as the Edinburgh & Glasgow Assurance Company seemed to be suggesting. For himself, he reckoned it would be around a two-and-a-half hour hike to reach the ridge, where he would conduct his survey and try and figure out what might have happened to Gina, after which he would retrace his steps back down to the ski road.

Under the crystal sky, you could see for miles, Cairn Gorm towering to the right of him as he started his ascent, majestic Ben Macdui standing not far behind. Both over four thousand feet in old money, they were number five and number two in the list of Britain's highest mountains, and today he hoped to conquer Braeriach, number three. The vista was unarguably breathtaking, but what he liked most about the mountain range was the absolute tranquillity, especially at this time of the year when the clattering ski-lifts were at rest, and on a day like today when the wind was trying to play ball. It was the place to come to if you wanted to think, and in the last month or so Jimmy had done a lot of thinking. It had all started that night at Maggie and Frank's wedding, where after one too many whiskies, and affected by the joyous sentimentality of the occasion, his finger had hovered over the phone number of his ex-wife Flora. But he hadn't called her, and he was glad that he hadn't, because somehow that day had been a watershed in his life, a realisation that there was no going back, and that he didn't need to anyway, because his life held so much promise if only he would grab it in both hands. Now, he was doing a job he loved, a job that took him into the mountains most weeks of the year, courtesy of the wee Outward-Bound business that he ran with his old army pal Stew Edwards. Better still, being his own boss meant he could devote a few dozen days every year helping out Bainbridge Associates when they needed him. And now, miraculously, there was a new woman in his life. Frida Larsen ran a bed and breakfast and tearoom in Braemar, where his business was based, and over the proceeding weeks he had found himself quadrupling his already-high caffeine input as he sought any excuse to pay another visit to her establishment in the hope she would serve him. She was just a year younger than him, slim and pretty with a shock of strawberry blonde hair that cascaded over her shoulders, its shade testimony to her obviously Nordic origins. They had immediately hit it off, discovering a shared love of the outdoors and folk-tinged rock music which complimented a mutually offbeat sense of humour. But it was Frida who had made the first move, telling him that she was bloody fed up serving him every day and that he should take her to a proper restaurant where *she* could be served for a change. So he did, and it had been a magical evening, and afterwards they had kissed, an outcome that was as natural as it was inevitable. Now he dared dream of a future together, making a home with the lovely Frida in a little white-washed cottage on the edge of a burbling stream, with a couple of kids chasing their dog through the adjacent wild-flower meadow. He hadn't dared tell Maggie and Frank about it yet, fearing the very act would curse the relationship before it had properly got started, but one day soon he planned to introduce her to them, and he was sure they would love her as much as he did.

Lost in such pleasant thoughts, he found five miles had passed without him noticing it. Now, checking his map, he saw that he would soon be swinging south-west off the Lairig Ghru path and starting the fierce ascent up to Braeriach. The going had been fairly easy up until then, but his map's tightly-packed contours heralded that things were about to get a whole lot tougher. Just one and a half miles or so to go, but these were the most challenging of the entire route, and it would have been twice as difficult for

Gina McQuarrie on that cold April day, with the path made indistinct by late-lying snow, making it treacherous underfoot too. All it would have taken was for the wind to whip up, adding a brutal wind-chill to the already sub-zero temperatures, to make the climb go from difficult to impossible. Had this been what had happened to the woman, he wondered, the battle to the summit leaving her so spent that she had lost her bearings and her judgement, making the fatal mistake that had plunged her down the Coire Brochain hollow? When he got there, he would once more take in the scene and try to figure out what could have happened. *If* he got there, he thought ruefully, realising he had been procrastinating at the foot of the ascent for a full five minutes, whilst his subconscious asked his conscious mind if this was really such a good idea. With a wry grin, he slung his backpack over his shoulders and set off. Three or four hundred feet into the climb, he could feel his thighs burning as the muscles complained, perfectly reasonably, about what they were being asked to do. But then quite suddenly the slope changed from ridiculous to almost benign, and he was able to catch his breath as the summit of Braeriach came into view for the first time, less than a mile distant by his reckoning. But then, to his annoyance and no little dismay, he saw that the route was about to descend several hundred feet into a gully before resuming the steep climb again. *Bugger*. Still, there was nothing for it but to push on if he wanted to get this mission completed. Half an hour later, he reached the corrie, allowing himself a brief smile of satisfaction as he planted an imaginary flag in the ground. Sweating, he threw down his backpack before grabbing his water-bottle from one of its external pockets and collapsing down onto the thin bracken, about fifty feet from the edge of the drop. He wasn't completely knackered, that was true, but it had been a worthy challenge nonetheless, and he was bloody certain that he wouldn't have fancied it one bit back when there was still snow around.

So, what could have happened to Gina on that fateful day? Her body had been found lying more than five hundred feet below, almost at the bottom of Bhrochain corrie, her death caused by a blow to the head, most likely from hitting a boulder on the way down. None of that was in dispute. What was in dispute was how and why she had gone over the edge in the first place. He supposed he better wander up and take a look. And as he stood up, something struck him, something he hadn't expected although it should have been obvious if he'd thought about it properly, or checked out the contours on his map. Because where he had been sitting, fifty feet or so from the edge, was also at least thirty feet or maybe more *below* the drop, and as a result, it was a quite a sharp wee climb to get up there. *Which got him thinking.* Parking the thought for a moment, he made his way up to the edge and looked over. It was dramatic, no doubt about that, and bloody steep too. But it wasn't a sheer drop, not like coastal cliffs, so if you just stepped over the edge by mistake, you wouldn't plummet through the air. No, you would slide, and the chances were your slide would fairly soon be arrested by perhaps a lone gorse bush, or less welcome, a boulder. And in any case, there was a perceptible ledge about sixty feet down, not wide but wide enough to knock most of the speed off any sliding climber. The fall *might* kill you of course, but it wasn't guaranteed by any means, making the corrie an unreliable accomplice should you be bent on suicide. No, if you wanted to be sure that the fall would kill you, you would have to somehow shoot yourself over the edge, like Wily Coyote chasing the Roadrunner in these old Looney-Tune cartoons. *But that was impossible, given how steep the slope up to that edge was.* It was hard enough to *walk* up to it, let alone run, so the likelihood of being able to create enough speed to propel yourself horizontally into fresh air, such that your fall would be vertical, was nil. His mind racing furiously, he sat down to think.

So almost certainly, this meant that Gina McQuarrie had not killed herself, which would be a great relief to her husband and family, if perhaps less so to Edinburgh & Glasgow Assurance, who would now be facing an unwelcome multi-million pound payout. He would take a few photographs of the scene to back up his logic, and he doubted if they would be able to dispute his conclusion. But as he sat under the bright sun, contemplating the scene again whilst enjoying the majestic scenery, something else struck him. If she hadn't jumped - couldn't have jumped in fact - and had simply tumbled over the edge because of poor visibility, why had her body been found so far down the corrie? It was possible of course that her slide had simply been unlucky enough to avoid any obstacles, or as the speed of her descent had picked up, any that had got in her way had been swept aside by her increasing momentum. Possible, but from what he had seen of the terrain first-hand, quite unlikely, especially since he had spotted that thin ledge sixty feet or so down. But now something else came to him, something that Craig has said last night in the pub - the fact that ten years ago there had been another death at the same spot, this one also suspected to be a suicide. *But that couldn't be true either, not if the man's body had been found in the same spot as Gina's.* Which, to his growing disbelief, left only one possibility - that in both cases, someone had pushed the victims with enough force for their initial fall to be near-vertical. It was a crazy thought, he knew that, but as Sherlock Holmes had once said, once you eliminate the impossible, whatever remains, no matter how improbable, must be the truth.

Now he would make the treacherous descent down the corrie so that he could see first-hand where Gina McQuarrie and Gordon Baird had met their deaths, seemingly identical events separated by almost ten years. And then tonight he would call Frank and Maggie to tell them that they had two new murder cases to get their teeth into.

Chapter 11

It was after nine o'clock when they received the unexpected call from Jimmy. Ollie was finally asleep, and Maggie and Frank had settled down in the living room with a glass of wine to enjoy the latest block-buster crime drama on the television. Or in Frank's case, to spend the entire hour loudly pointing out the implausibilities in both plot and police procedure, much to Maggie's annoyance.

'Hi Jimmy,' she said brightly. 'How are you? And by the way, I need to tell you we're already two glasses of wine into the evening. Anyway, I'll put you on speakerphone and hope that Frank doesn't slur too much.'

She heard her colleague laugh. *'Aye, I'm just having a wee dram myself after a tough day in the mountains. But listen, I found something out today which puts a massive new perspective on our case.'*

'What's that?' Frank asked.

'That Gina McQuarrie was probably murdered.'

'What?' Maggie blurted out. 'Are you *serious*?'

'Deadly serious. There's no way her body could have been found where it was if it had been an accident, nor was there any way she could have thrown herself over the edge of Coire Brochain. Nobody could do that. The slope up to the

edge is too steep to get enough momentum, even if you were as fit as Gina was.'

'Bloody hell,' Frank said. 'This is a turn up for the books, isn't it? And are you sure about this?'

'Ninety-five percent certain. And there's something else as well.' Jimmy paused for a moment before continuing. *'You remember that guy who supposedly murdered the girl in that Nethy Bridge hotel then committed suicide? Gordon Baird I think his name was? Well, I'll tell you what, he didn't kill himself either. No way. Impossible.'*

'I'm sorry to ask again Jimmy,' his brother said, speaking slowly, 'but are you definitely sure about this? Because if you are, this is something huge.'

'Same as I said about Gina. Ninety-five percent certain. For Baird's body to end up where it did, he had to have been pushed.'

'But this is crazy,' Maggie said, rifling a hand through her hair. 'It changes everything, doesn't it?'

Frank nodded. 'Yeah, on the face of it, it does.'

'So where do we go from here?' she said, thinking out loud. 'Does that mean we have to pass the Gina McQuarrie matter over to the police? I suppose we'll have to if it was murder.'

Frank gave her an uncertain look. 'Well, it'll be a Police Scotland matter obviously, and I'll have to talk to one of the brass up in the Grampian region to see what they want to do with it. But I can imagine we might have a wee bit of difficulty convincing them that Jimmy's analysis is right. No offence by the way bruv, but that's just the way they are. Particularly since the mountain rescue guys didn't put any suspicions in their report as far as I'm aware.'

'And what about the Gordon Baird one?' Jimmy asked. *'It's the same situation.'*

Frank shrugged. 'Same thing probably applies, and with it being a case that was quickly closed down all neat and tidy at the time, I doubt whether they will have much of an appetite for opening it up again. Although I suppose I might be able to persuade them that it might be worth my new unit taking a quick dekko at it,' he added. 'That would save them wasting their resources on it at any rate, which I expect they'll welcome.'

'But what do we tell the insurance company?' Maggie said, now worried. 'And does anybody know if a life policy still pays out if the insured person's been murdered?'

Frank raised an eyebrow. 'I came across a case like this a few years back. A City banker was murdered one dark evening as he was walking from his office to Liverpool Street station, a mugging that went terribly wrong. I remember he had a big life insurance policy, and it paid out to his widow with no problems. Which, when you think about it, is only right.'

'Yes, that makes sense,' she said, nodding. 'But what should we do now? Should we carry on with the investigation just as we were doing?'

Frank hesitated for a moment then said, 'I'm just talking off the top of my head here, but yes, I think you should carry on with what you were doing. At least until I get a response one way or the other from the Grampian lot.'

'Except, before my wee walk yesterday we were trying to work out whether or not she had killed herself,' Jimmy mused. *'Now, we think she's been murdered, and that's a whole different ballgame.'*

'It is,' Frank conceded. 'I would say you give it another week maximum, and then we'll regroup and see where we've got to.'

Maggie frowned. 'I'll have to speak to Charlie Wilson at Edinburgh & Glasgow first though. We can't be taking their money when we know now that Gina didn't commit suicide. I need to be honest with them, and if they decide to can the investigation, then so be it.'

'Aye, you're right about that Maggie,' Frank said. 'But actually, something else has just occurred to me, something which probably goes without saying.'

'What's that?' Jimmy asked.

'Well, with Sir Andrew McQuarrie being the beneficiary of the policy, it gives him the biggest motive to kill her, doesn't it? And if he does turn out to be the murderer, then Edinburgh & Glasgow won't exactly be jumping over themselves to pay him, even if the terms of the policy don't exclude murder.'

'So it's going to get very complicated,' Maggie said ruefully.

Frank nodded. 'Aye, it is. And something else goes without saying too, although I'm going to say it anyway.'

'What's that?' she asked.

'Just that if Gina McQuarrie was murdered, then that means there's a murderer still out there on the loose. And we all know that murderers will do anything to protect themselves if they think they're in danger of exposure.' He was silent for a moment. 'So it goes without saying that you two have to be bloody careful from this moment on.'

Chapter 12

What Sir Andrew hadn't told Maggie and Lori was that Gina's sister Laura McColl lived up in Aviemore. It wasn't the sort of interview you wanted to conduct over the phone, which was why the two bleary-eyed investigators had been at Queen Street Station to catch the 7.07am northbound service to Inverness. It was a nice morning and the journey afforded pleasant vistas once the city had been left behind, but Maggie hadn't noticed any of it, brooding as she had been on the difficult call she had to make to Charlie Wilson of Edinburgh & Glasgow Assurance. The dilemma was, what could she tell them? *We're thinking now that Gina might have been murdered.* Sometime soon the company would have to know, but not before the position became official, and they certainly couldn't be told before the difficult subject was broached with Gina's husband Sir Andrew. So in the end, she had decided there was no choice but to adopt a holding pattern, telling Wilson that suicide now looked unlikely but that there was further work to be done to establish exactly what had happened. Waiting until just past nine o'clock, then deciding she could put it off no longer, she made the call.

'That seemed a wee bit awkward,' Lori said after Maggie had hung up.

'Bloody awkward. But we can't tell them where we're going with this right now, can we? I feel really bad about it, and in fact, I've decided we won't charge any hours to the investigation until it's all out in the open. It wouldn't feel right.'

Lori nodded. 'Yeah, I can see that boss. Anyway, here comes the trolley. Let's grab a coffee and relax for a wee while.'

Maggie laughed. 'Actually, I'm going to have a little powernap if you don't mind. My alarm went off at half-five this morning.'

The train pulled into Aviemore on schedule and a few minutes later they were in a taxi en-route to Laura McColl's modest semi-detached home, located on a nineteen-seventies estate to the north of the village. The property had a small front garden with a weed-invested concreted driveway just long enough to accommodate a small car. A battered hatchback occupied the space, carelessly parked such that it encroached on the narrow path leading up to the front door.

'A bit different from Gina's Milngavie mansion, eh?' Lori whispered, raising an eyebrow.

Maggie smiled. 'Just a bit.' She reached out and pressed the doorbell. From somewhere in the house, a dog began to bark, and a few seconds later, the door opened.

'Laura?' Maggie said. 'I'm Maggie Bainbridge and this is my colleague, Lori Logan.'

'Yes, come in,' the woman said. Maggie guessed she was early-to-mid forties, quite pretty but overweight, with greying hair which looked as if it hadn't had a proper cut for months. She wore black jeans and a shapeless grey hoodie, adding to the impression that this was a woman who didn't care much about her personal appearance. They were led through to a small living room furnished with a well-worn sofa and an easy chair covered by a fleece throw. A faded Persian rug covered the wooden floor.

'Please, sit down,' the woman said. 'And can I get you a hot drink?' The dog barked again, and they could hear scratching against a hallway door. 'That's Paddy,' she said apologetically. 'He's a wee Jack Russell and he likes to make himself heard. But he likes to jump on laps and shed his hair everywhere too, so I'll spare you that.'

'He sounds nice,' Maggie said, laughing. 'But no, we had about five coffees on the train on the way up so we're good.' She paused for a moment. 'First of all Laura, can I say how sorry we are for your loss. Gina's husband Andrew told us that you and your sister were very close.'

'Yes, we were,' she said, her voice barely audible. 'Although we didn't see much of each other, we Facetimed a few times a week. I really miss my big sister.'

Maggie gave a sympathetic smile. 'It must be awful for you Laura.'

The woman sighed. 'What can you do? And my kids miss their auntie terribly too. They're only eight and five and they can't understand what has happened to her.'

'Poor wee things,' Lori said. 'They're at school now I suppose?'

Laura nodded. 'At the primary just round the corner. The school has been very good, but it's been hard for the wee ones.'

'So sad,' Maggie said. She paused again then said, 'Look Laura, I'm so sorry I have to do this, but as I told you on the phone, we're working for Gina's life insurer, and we're trying to get a picture of how your sister was feeling about life in the days and weeks before she died. I know it's a horrible thing, but it's something they have to do unfortunately.'

'They think she killed herself, don't they?' the woman said.

Maggie shook her head. 'No, they don't think that. But they need to eliminate the possibility. It's just their standard process when there's such a large sum of money involved.'

'Well, it's not as if Andrew needs the money, is it?' Laura said. Maggie detected something in the tone, bitterness certainly but perhaps a hint of envy too.

'They were well-off I think?' Lori said.

Laura nodded. 'Very. But I didn't mean to be horrible about money, because Gina was very good to me. My husband left me, you see. Two years ago.'

'I'm sorry to hear that,' Maggie said.

'No need to be. Johnny McColl was a pig and I'm glad to be rid of him. But it was tough financially at first, and Gina really helped me out.'

'You must have been very grateful.'

The woman nodded, then said quietly. 'Of course. I just wish I could have fixed her, but I couldn't.'

'What do you mean by that?' Maggie asked, surprised.

'You asked me how Gina was in the days and weeks before she died. You could have asked me how she was anytime in the last ten years, and I would have given you the same answer.' Laura paused then sighed. 'Poor Gina wasn't happy, and there was nothing I could do about it. I mean, I've been through some shit myself, but I've come out of it now, and although I don't have much, I've got my two boys and a wee job and I'm happy. But Gina could never recover from what happened to her, no matter how much material stuff she had.'

'What do you mean? Maggie asked again, narrowing her eyes.

'You know about the murder of Naomi Neilson I suppose?' Laura asked. 'Over in Nethy Bridge, ten years ago?'

Maggie nodded. 'Yes, but I only heard about it quite recently I must confess.'

'Did you know it was Gina who found her body?'

Maggie nodded sympathetically. 'Yes, I did. That must have been awful for her.'

The woman gave her a sad look. 'It was, and I don't think she ever recovered from it, if you want my opinion. Naomi and Gordon Baird were late down for breakfast, and Gina went to their bedroom assuming they must have overslept. The door was open and when she went in, she found Naomi lying on the bed, her face a gruesome purple and with that leather belt round her neck. It was such a horrible thing.'

'And the Baird guy had taken off into the mountains by then, hadn't he?' Lori said. 'They found him dead the next day and they said it was him who had killed Naomi.'

'Eventually, yes,' Laura said. 'But everyone was hauled off to the main police station in Inverness to be questioned. They were all held overnight, and it really spooked Gina. The police seemed to think at first that the whole group knew what had happened and were trying to cover it up, so they gave them a really hard time.'

'And this really affected Gina?' Maggie said. 'I can see why it might of course.'

'She had nightmares about it for years,' Laura said. 'About finding the body I mean. And then of course a couple of years later Rhona disappeared.' She was silent for a moment then said quietly, 'Gina might have eventually recovered from Naomi's horrible death, but then when Rhona disappeared, her world just came crashing round her.'

'Look, I need to ask you the difficult question,' Maggie said softly. 'Do you think all of this might have built up over the years such that suddenly Gina felt she couldn't go on? Because it would be understandable.'

'No, never,' Laura blurted out. 'Gina loved her kids, and she had her music and walking which she found a huge comfort. She wasn't happy, but she wouldn't have killed herself, no way.'

And we already know this, Maggie thought, although we can't share what we think *did* happen.

'And the marriage?' she continued. 'Would you say that was happy?'

Laura shrugged. 'I don't know, but how could it be, honestly, with Gina buried in her own unhappy little world? I think they were somehow bound together because of the Nethy Bridge tragedy. She didn't talk about it very much, but I always had this feeling, as if there was some terrible secret that could never be revealed.' She sighed again. 'But maybe I'm just imagining it. It was all so horrible.'

'So what do you think *did* happen to your sister?' Maggie asked.

'It was a tragic accident, that's all,' Laura said. 'People think it's only the inexperienced idiots who get into trouble up there, but it isn't. It only takes a moment's lapse in concentration and the mountain can bite you, no matter how experienced you are.'

'Did you know that your sister and her husband had taken out the insurance policy not long before she died?' Maggie asked. 'Did she ever discuss it with you, I wonder?'

Laura frowned. 'Not specifically, but I think there was some issue with money.'

'Really?' Maggie said, surprised. 'What makes you say that?'

The woman gave a sheepish look. 'Gina had been paying me an allowance. Six hundred pounds a month and I really needed it to get back on my feet. But then one day she called me, very apologetically, and said she and Andrew had some unexpected expenses to deal with and she would have to stop it for a few months. I mean, I couldn't say anything, but it did surprise me because they are very well off.'

'And Gina didn't give any hint as to why they needed the money?' Lori asked.

'No, and it wasn't any of my business, so I didn't ask,' Laura said sharply. 'And she had been very generous to me.'

'No, of course,' Maggie said. 'Look, I really appreciate how frank you've been with us Laura. I know it's been a very difficult period for you.' She hesitated for a moment. 'But there's one last thing I wondered if I could ask you, and it's this. Do you know if Gina had made a will?'

Laura shrugged. 'I really don't know. I assume so. But she did often joke that I would be very well off when she was dead, but that always upset me and I told her not to say it. But if there is any money, it'll go to my kids for when they're grown up.' Maggie watched as the woman raised a hand to wipe away a tear. 'I don't want her money, I just want Gina back. But I know that can't happen.'

Maggie got up and placed an arm around her shoulder. 'It's still so raw, but believe me, it will get better. You'll never forget her, but in time you'll remember mainly the good times you had with your sister, and that'll make you smile.'

The woman squeezed her hand. 'Thank you for that. And I'm sorry for crying.'

'Crying's good, really it is. But listen, we'll go now, and again, thank so much for helping us.'

***

'Poor woman,' Lori said as the made their way back to the station, this time on foot. 'She's really suffering, isn't she?'

'She is,' Maggie nodded. 'But what an interesting tale she had to tell.'

'Aye, you could very well imagine Gina being suicidal, with everything she'd gone through. Except we now know she couldn't have done herself in, from what Jimmy found out.'

'No, she couldn't have. But the big question is, where do we go from here? Because right now, I've got no idea.'

And it was true, Maggie thought. The sensational revelation, albeit still to be fully confirmed, that Gina McQuarrie had been murdered, had blown a huge hole in their Edinburgh & Glasgow assignment. Having said that, they had been asked to either confirm or rule out the possibility that Gina had killed herself, and the stark fact was, they had now done that. So there was no reason why she couldn't just phone Charlie Wilson again and tell him the truth and then let events take their course. But she had come to realise that finding out what had happened to Gina had now become utterly compelling for her, and there was no way she could simply just hand it over to the police. No, Bainbridge Associates would give the investigation a few more days, and next on the list would surely have to be a return visit to Sir Andrew McQuarrie.

At which the subject of money would almost certainly take centre stage.

Chapter 13

It had been a remarkable twenty-four hours or so, Frank thought, the outcome of his brother's Cairngorm expedition uncovering a brand-new murder and at the same time blowing a hole in a ten-year-old case that until then had looked rock-solid in its conclusions. He knew though that there were plenty of higher-ups in the force who would question Jimmy's evidence, and so it was far from a foregone conclusion that either case would turn into full-blown murder enquiries. After all, Jimmy's analysis, though thorough and credible, was at the end of the day just an expert opinion, and Frank had seen plenty of eminent expert witnesses being taken apart in court by smart-ass barristers. Tomorrow, he had a telephone call booked with the recently-appointed ACC who ran the Grampian division, one Alison White, whom he'd never met before, but he had some idea how it might pan out. *It was hard enough keeping on top of the current workload,* White would be thinking, *so why open up some ancient case that had been tidily put to bed all those years ago?* The Gina McQuarrie one was a different proposition though, it a recent incident that had been a headline-grabber over the last few months. White would be very much aware of the damage that could be caused if this new angle got into the papers and the police were seen to be doing nothing about it.

But the fact was, he really wasn't that bothered about getting the Naomi Neilson case officially opened up, because he could do everything he needed on that one under the umbrella of the Rhona Fraser/Olivia Cranston missing persons investigation. Both women had been at that hotel in Nethy Bridge on the morning Naomi's body had been found, and it was fair game to investigate whether that tragic event had a bearing on their subsequent disappearance. In fact, he'd already given DC Lexy McDonald the task of investigating the Neilson case, not that she needed any encouragement. He could tell already that the case had grabbed her, and he wouldn't have been surprised if she'd been up to midnight the previous night pouring all over the file. And in a couple of minutes he'd find out. Looking up from his desk, he saw Lexy approaching him, a broad smile on her face.

'Morning sir, are we doing the call here?' she said. 'And do you want me to log on for you?'

He gave her a sardonic smile. 'Actually, I think I'm up to speed with Zoom technology now.' He spun his laptop round to face her. 'Look, Ronnie's already on the line, live and kicking from Atlee House.'

'Morning Lexy,' French said brightly. *'Just waiting for Eleanor. She couldn't be arsed to come up the stairs to my manor so she's signing in at her desk.'*

As if on cue, another small window opened up on the screen and the stern features of the forensic officer appeared.

'Hi Eleanor,' Lexy said. 'Good to see you again.'

The greeting produced a half-smile at the other end of the line, which Frank acknowledged with a grin of his own. 'Aye, glad you could make it Eleanor.' He paused for a moment then continued. 'Well folks, this is the first team meeting of the National Independent Cold-Case Investigations Agency. It sounds pretty grand, doesn't it? And in further breaking news, we've now got a shiny headquarters building here in the fair city of Glasgow, and next month we'll have our team meeting in its spacious and salubrious conference suite. I know there's only the four of us right now, but the place has got enough for fifty, would you believe? You could play five-a-side football in there.'

'Will we get to meet our new guvnor too?' Ronnie asked. *'Dame what's-her-name?'*

'Dame Helen Dunbar,' Frank said, 'I've not met her myself, but that's what happens with these quango bosses, they only do a couple of days a month. But she seems a nice enough lady to be fair. And yes, I'll ask her to come to the meeting.'

'But you're the actual boss aren't you sir?' Lexy grinned. 'We take orders from you.'

He laughed. 'That's right, I'm in charge of this show and don't you bloody forget it.' He paused for a second. 'If that's alright with you Eleanor?'

Eleanor Campbell glowered but didn't say anything. 'Anyway,' he continued, 'isn't this a cracker of a case we've got on our hands? A real puzzler I would say. So maybe we start with Lexy and hear what she's got to say about the Naomi Neilson murder. Anything new to add from what we already know?'

Lexy nodded. 'Sure sir. The data guys got me my authorisation to look at the detailed files yesterday afternoon and I did a quick dive in last night. But nothing startling has leapt out at me as of yet, other than our colleagues seemed to have done a decent and thorough job at the time. After Naomi's body was found, someone dialled 999 and the call-handlers obviously realised right away the seriousness of the situation because they sent a DI and a DS down from Inverness. The pair locked the place down and got straight onto interviewing the group.'

'And what did everyone say?' Frank asked.

'That they hadn't seen or heard anything sir. Olivia Cranston and Rhona Fraser shared a room as did the McQuarries, and each said they'd gone to bed just past midnight and hadn't left their rooms until they came down to breakfast. And the hotel hasn't got CCTV in the corridors so there was no way of corroborating whether what they said was true or not. Also, neither of the couples admitted to knowing that Naomi and Baird had gone to bed together either.'

'See no evil, hear no evil, eh?' Frank said. 'In a wee cosy hotel like that, I find that a bit hard to believe.'

Lexy nodded. 'Yes, the SIO made a similar observation in one of the notes I saw. But obviously, it was impossible to prove one way or the other.'

'True,' Frank admitted. 'And it's probably neither here nor there anyway when I come to think of it. But sorry Lexy, I interrupted you. Carry on.'

'Okay sir. And you'll remember with the manner of her death, there was speculation that Baird and Naomi had been indulging in a sex game that went wrong.'

'*Asphyxiation,*' Eleanor said unexpectedly. '*You get a way better orgasm. It's like awesome.*'

Frank gave her a mildly horrified look. 'I won't ask how you know that.'

'Too much information I would say sir,' Lexy said, laughing. 'There was something else too. The post-mortem found evidence of a sedative in Naomi's blood stream. Rohypnol.'

'What, the date-rape drug?' Frank asked, furrow-browed. 'That doesn't fit the narrative of this being some sort of sex game gone wrong. This sounds a bit more disturbing than that.'

'Exactly sir,' Lexy agreed. 'But anyway, you'll remember all the others were whisked off to Inverness police station, where they were extensively questioned and held for the full twenty-four hours before being released. At the same time, they put out an all-points bulletin on Gordon Baird, and also broadcast an appeal on the local media. Pretty quickly his car was found at the Glen Einich car-park, and a few hours later a walker found a body at the bottom of the Bhrochain corrie.' She hesitated for a second. 'You can see why it seemed obvious at the time that Gordon Baird was the killer. He clearly had means and opportunity, although the motive wasn't quite so obvious. That's why they thought it might have been accidental.'

'Although not with Rohypnol involved,' Frank observed. 'But remind me, what verdict *did* the Fiscal come to in the end?'

'Murder sir. In the absence of firm evidence to the contrary.'

'With Gordon Baird as the perpetrator?'

She nodded. 'That's right. And I've been thinking sir. Just because we now think he didn't kill himself, that doesn't necessarily mean he wasn't the murderer.'

'True, but none of the others could have done him in either,' French cut in. *'Because they was all banged up in Inverness nick at the time.'*

'That's true Ronnie,' Frank said. 'It's a big puzzle right enough, but one we'll have some fun trying to unravel. Anything else Lexy?'

'Well, the interviewing team made quite a bit of the fact that Baird was a lecturer and Naomi was his student, as you might expect. Andrew McQuarrie was given a pretty hard time over that, because he was Baird's boss and he confessed to the team that Baird had a bit of history.'

Frank raised an eyebrow. 'What do you mean, history?'

Lexy shrugged. 'Apparently he'd been given a written warning in the past about inappropriate relations with undergraduates.'

'Sex, do you mean?'

She nodded. 'That would be my assumption sir. So obviously, McQuarrie knew about this particular relationship, and our team wanted to know why he hadn't put a stop to it.'

'And what was his answer?'

Lexy raised an eyebrow. 'He was pretty belligerent by all accounts. He said as far as he knew, they hadn't been in a relationship, and even if they had been, he wasn't going to do anything about it. He made it pretty clear that he didn't agree with the University's policy.'

'Charming guy,' Frank said.

'But there was something else that struck me sir,' Lexy said. 'Not something that I found in the file, just something I thought was odd, when I looked at their pictures.'

'What was that?'

'Naomi was beautiful sir, really beautiful. But Gordon Baird wasn't an attractive guy at all. And he was at least ten years older than her too. I showed his picture to Eleanor, and she thought the same.'

'Gross,' Eleanor said. *'Like seriously yuk.'*

'A bit of an odd relationship then?' Frank said. 'Although sometimes there's no accounting for taste. I still don't know what Maggie sees in me,' he added, laughing. 'Anyway, that is something to think about. So how about you Frenchie? How did you get on out in the Fens?'

'*Pretty good guv,*' French said. '*They allocated me a DC for the day, he showed me round the files. The Olivia Cranston girl is still a current case, although you wouldn't know it with the amount of time they're putting into it.*'

'But at least they're still working on it.'

French shrugged. '*Technically yes, but my DC says he's only able to give it a couple of hours a week, because of lots of other stuff going on. The thing is though, this Olivia bird has a history of mental health problems. They're reckoning she's just disappeared off her own bat, so I don't think their trying too hard in my opinion. But anyway, I think you know some of the background already, but I'll give you all a speedy update if you fancy it.*'

Frank nodded. 'Aye, we fancy it. Go ahead Frenchie.'

'*Right, so dealing with Rhona Fraser first, that's the eight year-old case. She'd come down to Cambridge with her band to do a concert. They were called the Skye-Larks if you're interested, but with 'sky' spelled like the Scottish island. Anyway, they travelled down from Glasgow in their van and arrived about four in the afternoon, that's according to the interviews with the other band-mates. Apparently Rhona was going to a gig that evening, just on her own, to see some rock band that she liked. This was a Thursday, by the way,'* French added.

'With you so far,' Lexy said.

'Okay. So next day, her band was due at the venue mid-morning for a rehearsal and sound check, but Rhona didn't turn up. And when she still hadn't appeared two hours later, they went back to their hotel to see if she was there, and when they couldn't find her, they got worried and called the police.'

'But wait a minute,' Frank said. 'I assume they were all staying at the same hotel? So why didn't they all travel to the rehearsal venue together that morning?'

French nodded. *'Yeah guv, that came up in the interviews. Her band-mates knew she had been at the gig the night before, so they assumed she had got back late and was having a bit of a lie-in. As well as that, apparently she never ate breakfast anyway. So they had expected her to make her own way there.'*

'Which she didn't,' Frank said.

'No, she didn't. Of course normally we wouldn't do anything much when someone's just been missing for a couple of hours, but the PC who took down the details was a smart lad

and he told them to call him back if Rhona hadn't turned up by the time of the band's concert.'

'And she didn't turn up.'

'No guv. So the gig was cancelled and the Cambridge boys kicked off a formal missing persons enquiry. A DC was allocated to the investigation for an initial three days, and did all the normal stuff, interviews with the band, looking at posts on social media, speaking to her family and associates in Glasgow on what her state of mind was etc etc. As I said, the standard stuff. But before you ask, no, there was nothing of concern to report on that score. She was happy, she had been looking forward very much to playing in Cambridge with her band, everything was good at home...'

'That would be her relationship with Olivia Cranston,' Frank interrupted.

French nodded. *'Yeah, that's right. The DC spoke to Cranston on the phone, who was obviously distraught but said everything was hunky-dory. After that, it was pretty quickly concluded that Rhona hadn't just decided to leg it somewhere.'*

'So then it either had to be an accident or something more sinister,' Lexy said.

'Yeah, as I said, they came to that conclusion pretty quickly, and then things started to move quite fast. The first thing of concern that emerged was that her bed hadn't been slept in, and the CCTV at the hotel didn't clock her coming back after the gig.'

'Worrying,' Lexy said.

'Yeah it is,' French agreed. *'Then they started trawling other CCTV sources for any other sight of her.'*

'And?' Frank asked.

'A couple of sightings. She was captured going into the concert venue at about quarter to eight, although they didn't get her leaving. And there was one more too, this one a bit weird.'

'What was that?'

'She got on a bus. A late one, about ten-past-eleven at night.'

'Why would she do that?' Lexy asked, puzzled.

French shrugged. 'Not worked that out yet. But listen, I've left the absolute best for last.' He paused for a moment. 'Because Olivia Cranston did the same. The exact same bus at more or less the exact same time. But eight years later.'

Frank gave a low whistle. 'Well that is damn interesting Ronnie,' he said. 'I assume you've got all the details, the route number and all that?'

'Sure guv. It was in the file. I was going to head back up there tomorrow and jump on it myself, just to see if anything obvious shouts out at me.'

'Sounds worthwhile. So what about Olivia Cranston. What's her story?'

French paused for a moment as if gathering his thoughts then said, *'Turns out Olivia had gone down to Cambridge for a job interview at King's College. A big job, as it happens, a professorship. She stayed the previous night at the Ely hotel, and the interview was at eleven the next morning and lasted nearly four hours. We don't know her exact movements afterwards, but one of the interview panel said she was intending to take a stroll along the river and get a drink. What we do know was she had booked a ticket for a gig that evening, some guy called Dan Jackson, who was playing at a venue called The Cambridge Musician. It's just a converted pub, but it's at the heart of the city's music scene, or so it says on their website.'*

'I know him,' Lexy said. 'They call him the future of folk.'

French gave her a wry look. *'I've heard his stuff. It's a bloody dirge.'*

'But isn't it an interesting coincidence that both women decided to go to a gig on their visits to Cambridge?' Frank mused. 'And remember, this is nearly eight years apart.'

'Yeah, I thought that too guv. But anyway, the venue's foyer CCTV clocks her going in at about a quarter to eight.' He paused again. *'But here's another weird thing. You see, the CCTV catches her leaving again just before eight.'*

'What, before the concert had started?' Lexy said, surprised.

'Seems like it,' French said, shrugging. *'And then she's off the radar until she gets caught getting on that bus.'*

'And what about the bus's own CCTV?' Frank asked. 'Nothing on that?'

'They didn't have it eight years ago. And it wasn't working on Olivia's unfortunately.'

Frank sighed. 'Bloody typical. But did the Cambridge team not interview the bus driver?'

'Actually, that's quite interesting guv,' French said. *'The guy driving Olivia's bus was interviewed, but he didn't remember her getting on or off. Which is obviously useless. But I don't think they pushed him too hard, so I'm going to nip back up there and have a strong go at him myself.'*

'That's a good shout,' Frank said. 'But please, no actual violence.'

French laughed. *'I'll do my best. But listen guv, here's a thing. I've only had a quick skim of the file, but I didn't see anything that suggests the driver of Rhona's bus was ever spoken to.'*

'That's a bit sloppy, isn't it?' Lexy said.

French nodded. *'Yeah, it is. But I'm going to have a go at tracking down the geezer myself. He or she might not still work there and even if they do, they probably won't remember anything, but it's worth a shout.'*

Until now Eleanor Campbell had been silent, but out of the blue she said, *'I can like set up a mapping sweep against the electoral roll database, and cross-reference it against the bus route.'*

Frank gave her a puzzled look. 'I know it's me, but I don't quite follow. Can you spell it out in words of less than one syllable, none of which are technical?'

French guffawed, getting a scolding look from the forensic officer in return.

'So like, Olivia and Rhona must have been going to see someone, right?' she continued.

'Or following someone,' Lexy said, looking thoughtful.

'Aye, that's a good point,' Frank said. 'But sorry Eleanor, we interrupt you. Carry on.'

'So if we start to build up a database of people connected to the two cases, for example starting with the dudes who interviewed Olivia and maybe whoever booked Rhona's band, we can upload their addresses and see if the bus route goes anywhere near. That might help us work out who Rhona and Olivia were going to see.'

Frank was silent for a moment as he assimilated what she meant, then, finally understanding, said. 'Aye, that's very clever. Go ahead and do that Eleanor please.' Then he paused for a moment. 'But just to get this straight, the last time either woman was seen was when they stepped on to that bus. And after that, nothing?'

'Nothing guv,' French said. *'Although as I think I said, the local guys are still treating Olivia's case as a live investigation.*

Frank gave a sardonic smile. 'A live investigation they're devoting a whole half-hour a month to. But not to worry, it seems as if you've got a wee plan of action Frenchie.'

French gave him a thumbs-up. *'Yeah, all set guv.'*

'And what about you Lexy?' Frank continued. 'What's your plans?'

She frowned. 'I think we need to look very carefully at Gordon Baird's accident, don't we? Because if he didn't kill himself, that throws everything up in the air.'

***

And Lexy was right, Frank thought, because if Baird's death was murder, not suicide, did that mean that Naomi Neilson's death had to be revisited too? If Baird had accidentally caused the young undergraduate's death as part of some bizarre sex game, then you could understand the guy feeling unbearable remorse such that he felt compelled to take his own life. But according to Jimmy, he *hadn't* killed himself.

Yes, there was no doubt about it. This thing was turning into a whole new can of worms.

Chapter 14

A bit of smooth talking with her PA had secured Frank an eleven-thirty appointment with Assistant Chief Constable Alison White, and he had decided to bring Jimmy along too in the role of expert witness. It was a bit of a pain that the meeting was at Division headquarters in Aberdeen, meaning a three-hour train trip up from Glasgow that morning, but it was the kind of thing you really had to do face-to-face. Now here they were in the reception area, his brother having made the much shorter journey over from his Braemar office by car.

'All set then mate?' Frank asked after they had announced themselves to the desk sergeant. 'By the way, I've not actually met the ACC, but I've heard she's a bit of a tough cookie. Mind you, they all are,' he added. 'It's standard issue with the job. And she's new to the position. Came up from the Norfolk force a few months ago.'

Jimmy grinned. 'A bit of culture-shock then I would imagine. Anyway, I've drawn a wee diagram that shows the topography at the top of the ridge. I don't think it should be that hard to explain what I think happened, even to someone who's not seen a mountain before.'

'Big word, topography, ' Frank said, grinning. 'I hope she can understand what you're talking about.'

His brother shrugged. 'I don't know how else to describe it. But I think my sketch will make it clear what the lie of the land is up there.'

They heard the click as the remote door lock opened, the sergeant simultaneously gesturing for them to come through.

'Right, follow me boys.' He led them down a wide corridor which ended at a door bearing the name of the ACC. After a discreet knock, he cautiously pushed it open. 'Your visitors ma'am. A pair of Stewarts.'

Seated at her large desk, she glanced up over her reading glasses and pointed towards two chairs opposite.

'Thank you ma'am,' Frank said, pulling out the first chair. 'I'm DCI Frank Stewart and this is my brother Jimmy. He's a civilian, just so you know.'

The ACC raised an eyebrow. 'I know who you are Stewart. They tell me you're the guy who lost Brian Pollock his job a couple of years back. I hope you're not coming after me now.'

'No ma'am, your job's quite safe with me,' he said, 'and to be fair, I think it was Chief Constable Pollock who lost himself his job. I was just doing mine.'

'And now I hear you're being set up as judge and jury in some new shiny government quango?' The obvious cynicism in her tone confirmed what he already knew, that the brass didn't like the idea of his new unit one bit.

'Not much different from what my department does now ma'am,' he said diplomatically. 'Same objectives, just different paymasters. And again, personally, I'll just be doing my job.' He gave her an emollient smile. 'But it's not a cold case we're here to talk about today. Not the first one at least.'

'Yes, it's Gina McQuarrie, isn't it? The woman who died up on Braeriach.'

'That's her ma'am. But you speak as if you know the mountain.'

She smiled. 'I don't know it yet. But between you and me, that's one of the reasons why I took this job. I want to spend as much time up there as I possibly can. It's beautiful.'

Frank nodded towards his brother. 'Well here's a man that can show you around if you need a guide. But anyway, just to give you some super-quick background, my wife Maggie runs a private investigations agency and Jimmy here works for her part-time. Maggie was commissioned by Edinburgh & Glasgow Assurance to confirm that Gina hadn't killed herself. A bit unsavoury I know, but the McQuarries had quite recently taken out a life insurance policy worth a cool three million quid.'

'Your wife did you say?' White said, raising an eyebrow. 'Sounds like you're running a family business. Or a corner shop.'

'Not really,' he said, laughing. 'It's just a coincidence that the Gina McQuarrie thing overlaps with another case we're looking at. But to cut a long story short, Maggie's firm was picked mainly because Jimmy here runs an outward-bound school and knows the Cairngorms like the back of his hand.'

His brother nodded. 'My mission was to work out whether her death had been an accident or whether she had killed herself. And what I discovered was it was neither.' He placed his sketch on her desk, facing her. 'Look, this is the precipice where she fell, and this is the slope that leads up to it. And here, about sixty feet down or so below the drop, is a narrow ledge. But not so narrow that it couldn't stop a body falling any further.'

The ACC examined the sketch with evident interest. 'Okay, I think I can picture that,' she said. 'So what's it telling us?'

'Gina was found right at the bottom of the corrie, hundreds of feet down and the only way that could have happened was if she had been propelled over the edge with enough force to clear that wee ledge. You wouldn't clear it if you just stumbled and fell, and you couldn't run up that steep slope fast enough to launch yourself over it either. I mean if you were intent on killing yourself.'

'So you're saying she was pushed?' White said.

Jimmy nodded. 'Must have been. Which makes it murder in my book.'

'Which is why I'm here ma'am,' Frank said. 'It's your decision, but it seems to me like we need to re-look at Gina's death.'

The ACC hesitated for a moment before speaking.

'You've rather thrown this at me Frank,' she said. 'Obviously, with Gina McQuarrie being in the public eye, there'll have to be a press conference if we're going to open a murder enquiry. And not to be disrespectful, but your brother is a civilian with no official position.' She smiled at Jimmy. 'And I'm not dismissing your expertise for one minute, but there would be questions if we launched an investigation based entirely on a single uncorroborated opinion.'

He laughed. 'Yeah, from a part-time detective who runs a wee outward-bound school. I can see how that would look.'

'It's not just that,' she continued, 'because unless you're going to tell me differently Frank, there doesn't seem to be anything else that firmly points to it being murder.'

He gave her a rueful look. 'You're right ma'am. Apart from the results of Jimmy's investigation, we don't have anything right now. We've no idea what the motive might be, or who might have had the means or opportunity to carry out the crime. But to be fair, we haven't actually started looking very hard yet.' He paused for a moment. 'Although something *has* come up that's quite interesting.'

She gave him a searching look. 'And what's that?'

'An article in the *Chronicle* suggested Gina's husband Sir Andrew McQuarrie is planning to pack up his family and move to America. It's only speculation at this stage, but it's a factor to be considered.'

'Well I suppose it's often the husband who turns out to have done it,' she said wryly, 'but I don't think we've got *quite* enough yet to detain him at the airport.'

Frank laughed. 'No, not exactly ma'am.'

'Okay,' she said, evidently thinking out loud. 'We must have a good few officers in this division who know the mountains as well as you do Jimmy. I'll ask around, and then maybe you could take one of them to the scene and let us see it for ourselves.'

He gave an enthusiastic nod. 'I'd very much welcome a second opinion. And what about we take one of the mountain rescue team with us as well? Three heads are better than one and all that.'

'Yes, that's a good idea, I'll try and get that sorted as soon as we're done here.' She gave Frank a questioning look. 'And in the meantime, are you going to continue with your enquiries?'.

'We're not actually doing anything right now ma'am,' he said, his tone apologetic. 'This has been a Bainbridge Associates show up until this point.'

'And we're kind of in limbo,' Jimmy interjected. 'In some ways we've done our job for the insurance company, in that we've ruled out suicide. Although I don't think they'll be expecting it to be murder,' he added ruefully.

'Have you told them your suspicions? White asked, sounding concerned.

Jimmy shook his head. 'No no, we were very conscious we couldn't give them even a whiff of that until the investigation becomes official. As I said, we're in a bit of a limbo.'

She looked at Frank. 'Well given what you told me about the husband, you should probably carry on for a few days until we've done our official assessment.' She paused for a moment then frowned. 'But I don't suppose it's in your remit, either your old department or your new one.'

He laughed. 'We're basically guns for hire ma'am. We'll take on any type of investigation if we're asked.'

'And what about budget? Because I can't really release any spend until it's official.'

'I've got a guy by the name of Park who can help me with that. But I think it'll be okay.'

'Alright,' she said firmly, 'so just one week maximum, and it needs to be kept totally low-key, understand? Because we don't want anything getting into the media until we know how things stand.'

He gave a thumbs-up. 'Understood ma'am. Now remember I mentioned there was a second wee matter...?'

***

It hadn't surprised him of course that ACC White was less than keen to resurrect a ten-year old murder investigation, especially one where back in the day the *who-done-it* had seemed so utterly clear. She'd listened politely enough, but it hadn't taken her long to reach her verdict. *It was the logical conclusion that Gordon Baird had killed himself in remorse for killing his girlfriend. There was no way of knowing at the time whether that killing was murder or an accident as a result of a sex game, and there's no way of knowing today. There's nothing the police would have done differently, meaning no lessons to be learned. So nothing to be gained from re-opening the matter and not a good use of scarce investigative resources.*

That was it as far as she was concerned, and Frank wasn't entirely unsympathetic to either her reasoning or her conclusion. But the thing was, if Gordon Baird *had* been murdered in the mountains, and by the same MO that had taken Gina McQuarrie's life, then it had to be at least fifty-fifty that he hadn't killed Naomi Neilson. Which meant that her real killer might still be out there, and that was never a satisfactory state of affairs. Now it was becoming more apparent that the disappearances of Olivia Cranston and Rhona Fraser and the murder of Gina McQuarrie and the identical death of Gordon Baird were in fact strands of the same matter and had to be approached as such. He'd mull on it overnight, and if he felt the same way in the morning - which he was pretty sure he would -he'd put in a wee call to his political master Katherine Collins. Because *this* was looking very much like a worthy matter with which to launch a new cold-case unit. And a matter that definitely needed the help of Bainbridge Associates.

Chapter 15

Ever since Jimmy's investigations had suggested, sensationally, that Gina McQuarrie might have been murdered up on remote Braeriarch, Maggie had been facing the follow-up meeting with Sir Andrew with some trepidation. And now, as a result of the startling story which had been emerging in that morning's media, her meeting was looking about ten times more awkward. She and Lori had met first thing for a fortifying coffee at the Bikini Barista cafe, and were now hurrying up University Avenue on route to their appointment at McQuarrie's office, discussing this intriguing breaking news as they went.

'So he's *resigned*,' Lori was saying. 'That's a turn up for the books, isn't it? With him being so famous and everything.'

Maggie shrugged. 'Well perhaps. But remember Yash's article suggesting he would be very welcome in the US? Well now the TV news guys are speculating that he might be discussing a tenure post at Stanford in California. That's one of the leading Universities in the world, and it just shows how his theory has become hugely-respected globally. He's in great demand in the world of economics.'

'Aye, and he'll probably be earning a packet over there as well,' her associate said. 'Maybe that's why he's going, do you think? For a great big pile of dosh?'

'Perhaps you can ask him,' Maggie said. 'But tactfully,' she added, with a wry smile.

A few minutes later, they were sat in the reception area of the Adam Smith building, awaiting his arrival.

'You know, I was surprised that he agreed to see us again,' Lori mused. 'He didn't have to.'

'Yeah, I was thinking about that too,' Maggie said. And she *had* thought about it, long and hard, and there had only been one logical conclusion. McQuarrie, despite his outward material prosperity, either needed or wanted very badly the money from his dead wife's life insurance policy. And without a positive tick in the box from Bainbridge Associates, the Edinburgh & Glasgow Assurance Company wasn't going to give it to him.

'Here he is,' Maggie said, nudging her associate then getting to her feet. She held out a hand as he approached. 'Andrew. Thank you for seeing us again.'

'That's okay,' he said. 'But look, we need to do this here, because I don't have much time this morning.'

'No problem,' Maggie said, sitting down again. 'I hope you don't mind me raising this, but I heard the news of your Stanford appointment on the TV. That must be exciting for you.'

He gave a terse smile. 'Yes, it is. But nothing's confirmed yet. We're just in discussions.'

'But you've already resigned your position here?' Lori said. 'Is that right?'

He nodded. 'I badly need a change of scenery after all that's happened. And I think it would be good for my kids too. But we're not here to talk about that,' he added impatiently. 'We need to get the insurance business concluded. I assume that's why you're here, and that you've got some news for me?'

Maggie nodded. 'Yes, we're nearly done with it. You know that my colleague Jimmy Stewart has completed his survey of the scene of your wife's accident. He's just weighing up his final conclusions, and then...'

'What is there to weigh up?' McQuarrie interrupted. 'My wife didn't kill herself, that should be obvious to anyone with half a brain.'

Pleased to be able to answer truthfully, Maggie said, 'That does seem to be the conclusion. Although since there weren't any actual witnesses to your wife's tragic death, Jimmy's report will have to have a caveat to the effect that he's unable to be one hundred percent certain.' She paused for a moment. 'But I guess that's just a technicality,' she added, less truthfully. Then with an apologetic look she continued, 'Anyway, there's just one final thing we need to clear up with you. And Andrew, I'm afraid you might find it rather intrusive, but unfortunately, it's something we need to get out of the way.'

For a moment, he looked as if he was going to give a sharp reply, then with visible effort, he managed to compose himself.

'Yes, of course,' he said, thin-lipped. 'Please, ask away.'

'We talked to Emma King,' she said. 'And to her credit, she was scrupulously confidential in everything she shared with us. But she did tell us a little about the recent reorganisation of your finances, something you yourself mentioned when we last met. She helped with an exercise to improve your liquidity, that was how she put it.'

'So?' he said. This time there was no disguising his displeasure about the direction of the conversation. 'What of it?'

'The thing is,' Lori said, 'we wondered why you needed to get your hands on that cash.'

He gave them both a look of annoyance. 'You know, you're right, this is bloody intrusive. And quite frankly, it's none of your business either.'

Maggie smiled sympathetically. 'Ordinarily of course you would be right. But the thing is Andrew, because of the situation with the life insurance, it becomes more difficult. You and your wife's finances have to come under some scrutiny I'm afraid.' She paused for a moment. 'And that means unfortunately, we need to have some explanation why you needed to do what you did.'

He hesitated, as if debating with himself how to answer. Then with an audible sigh he said, 'Okay, if you *must* know, Gina was planning to leave me.'

'Leave you?' Maggie said, astonished.

He gave her a wry look. 'You sound surprised. Well I was too, let me tell you. She didn't want us to sell the Milngavie house because of the effect it would have on our kids, but she needed money to buy her own place, it was as simple as that. So there, now you know. Satisfied?'

'That must have been hard for you Andrew,' she said, 'but thank you for sharing it with us.' Then immediately she thought, do I actually believe this? Because if Gina really was going to leave her husband, surely she would have wanted to separate all their financial affairs. So why take out a big joint life insurance policy? Somewhat perplexed, she continued, 'Andrew, this is quite a material piece of information you've shared with us. I'm assuming it will be okay if we put a paragraph about this in our report?

Obviously the company will keep the matter completely confidential, and it'll only be seen by a small handful of their most senior staff. But I hope it will be enough to put the matter to bed.' She hesitated before continuing again. 'What I mean is, it would seem unlikely your wife would have killed herself if she was making plans to leave the marriage and purchase a property for herself.'

'Exactly,' he said, sounding bitter. 'Gina had decided to swan off into her wonderful new life leaving me to pick up the pieces, that was the truth of the matter. So why don't you put that in your bloody report.'

Maggie gave him a sympathetic smile. 'We'll report the situation, of course, but as diplomatically as we can.'

He answered quickly. 'Sure, fine, just make sure you do. The whole bloody thing has already dragged on far too long.' With that, he got up and then made what looked like a forced smile. 'Thank you. But now if you don't mind, I need to get on with my day.'

***

Back at the Bikini Barista cafe, there was plenty to talk about and it was Lorilynn Logan who was doing most of the talking.

'Do you believe him Maggie?' she asked, her words tumbling out in a gushing torrent. 'Because I changed my mind about a million times when we were walking back from the meeting. See, first I remember her sister saying she wasn't sure about the state of the marriage, so maybe Gina *was* going to leave him, and yeah, it would definitely explain why they were trying to free up the cash. But then I thought, it doesn't explain why they took out the insurance policy, does it? And then I remembered that Emma King had said it was Gina who had wanted them to take it out in the first place, so how does that fit? And then I thought, they did the same cash thing eight years ago, and if that was because she was going to leave him, then she would surely have done it by now.' She grinned. 'Actually boss, I've no idea what I think.'

Maggie laughed. 'Yes, it is hard to fathom. But in answer to your question Lori, well no, I'm not sure I do believe him.'

'Why not?'

'Forgive me, because I'm thinking out loud here, but as far as this US move is concerned, well I should have thought the last thing you would want to do when your kids have lost their mum is to inject even more disruption into their lives. Why would you want to rip them away from their home and their school and their friends and of course their grandparents too?' She paused for a moment. 'So here's my crazy theory for what it's worth. Four months ago, something big occurred in their lives, something totally unexpected and dramatic enough to set off this chain of events. Something that caused a panic for cash, and caused Gina to believe that her life or her husband's life or perhaps both their lives were in danger, so causing her to review their life insurance provisions. And then a few short weeks afterwards, she's found dead at the bottom of that corrie, a tragedy we now believe was no accident.'

'Phew,' Lori said. 'That's some theory. But I can see where you're coming from.'

Maggie nodded. 'And that's all it is right now, a theory. But I don't believe Sir Andrew McQuarrie is heading to the US to pursue his great career dream. No, I think he's running away from something.'

Chapter 16

Over breakfast, and much to her amusement, Maggie had listened in to a long video call Frank was having with his new colleague Trevor Park, who seemed to occupy a role in the organisation which was half-way between accountant and concierge. It was apparently the first time her husband - and gosh, it still seemed a great novelty to be using that word- had actually clocked sight of Park, who turned out to be ridiculously young, or at least ridiculously young-looking, his unremarkable face thin and pock-marked, and with a grey pallor which suggested he didn't spend much time in the great outdoors. It was apparent too that he came equipped with a humour bypass, something Frank had already noted in two or three previous phone conversations. But he was efficient and helpful, if rather prone to over-elaborate explanation, currently being demonstrated as he strove to answer Frank's question as to whether the unit had any budget to expend on a short investigation into the circumstances of Gina McQuarrie's death.

'The unit's been set up with a first-year operation budget of two-point-four million pounds, which covers headcount for seven full-time ex-police investigators and nine investigators with legal qualifications, plus three forensic officers and four administrative assistants. There's a travel budget, to include the provision of motor vehicles, of ninety-six thousand

pounds, and further provision for the procurement of sub-contract services up to four hundred and eighty-six thousand per accounting year.'

'Good to know,' Frank said, raising an eyebrow. 'But how does that answer my question?'

Park disappeared out of sight for a moment, re-appearing with a printed page of spreadsheet, which he held up and scrutinised. '*Presently, there's committed spend for three investigators - DCI Frank Stewart, - that's you of course - DCs Ronald French and Alexa McDonald and one Senior Forensic Officer, Eleanor Campbell. So we're currently projecting a considerable underspend for this current fiscal year.*'

'That's good to know as well,' Frank said, shooting Maggie a sideways look of amusement. 'So is that a *yes*, then?'

Park managed a half-smile. '*Yes, it's a yes. We need to set up a case-number of course to track expenditure, but I can do that.*'

Frank gave him a thumbs-up, then paused for a moment. 'And Trevor, let's say I wanted to procure some of these sub-contract services of which you speak, how do I go about that?'

'*That falls under sections forty-seven and forty-nine of the public-sector standard procurement framework*,' Park said.

'*It's a straightforward process*,' he added, apparently without irony.

Frank laughed. 'I look forward to finding out. Anyway, e-mail me an outline of what I need to do and we can look at that one a wee bit later. And thanks for your help.'

'Interesting guy,' Maggie said after the call had ended.

'You think so? I wouldn't like to be stuck with him in the kitchen at a party.'

She laughed. 'You don't like parties.'

'Aye true. But you know what I mean.'

'But is it going to be alright to use Bainbridge Associates on our new and exciting combined investigation?' she asked. 'We obviously don't want you rubbing up against a conflict of interest.'

He shook his head. 'No no, I'll be playing it strictly by the book, once our Trev tells us exactly what that means. But I suspect I'll need to write a project specification and you'll have to submit a proposal with prices and terms of references and CVs of your team, and then we'll both have to sign a contract.'

Maggie laughed again. 'You haven't the faintest clue what any of that means, have you?

'Not a clue. But Trevor will put us right, I'm sure. Just as long as he puts in a clause that obliges the subcontractor to kiss the Senior Investigating Officer on demand. That's me, by the way.'

'Kiss you on *demand*, you cheeky sod?' she said, giving a mock grimace. She leant over and pecked him on the cheek. 'Okay, there's one on account. But just don't get used to it, okay? Because I don't do *anything* on demand.'

'What about making babies?' he said, raising a tentative eyebrow.

She laughed. 'For that, I'll make an exception.'

***

The case launch meeting was by necessity a virtual affair, scheduled to start at 10.30. Given the confidential nature of the upcoming discussions, Maggie and Lori were in their Byres Road office rather than the more convivial atmosphere of the Bikini Barista cafe two doors down. Jimmy had joined from Braemar, but not, as far as Maggie could tell, from his little office, but from the small cafe he had casually mentioned from time to time and evidently loved. Frank and Lexy McDonald were in an interview room somewhere in the depths of New Gorbals police station, and Ronnie French and Eleanor Campbell had dialled in from Atlee House, sitting at the forensic officer's desk on the deserted first floor of the building. Unusually, and mainly on account of DC McDonald having been in charge of organising the get-together, the technology had cooperated, and everyone was signed in on schedule and ready to go.

'Okay guys, we'll get started, shall we?' Frank shouted at his laptop. 'So, first of all I should say that due to a virtuosic display of administrative brilliance on my part, or rather, of a bloke called Trevor, we've been able to secure the services of Bainbridge Associates as official investigative sub-contractors on this case. So Maggie, Jimmy and Lori, welcome to the National Independent Cold-Case Investigations Agency. That's Niccia for short, although it doesn't exactly trip off the tongue.'

She grinned. 'It's brilliant. We're all looking forward to being proper detectives."

'You're lawyers,' Frank said. 'You'll never be proper detectives. But moving on...,' he added, returning her grin.

'Now in theory, I'm SIO on the case, but I know in practice I've got zero chance of getting any of you lot to pay a blind bit of notice to anything I say. And the fact is, this is going to be a damn complicated investigation, and we'll need everyone to be chipping in with ideas if we're going to have any chance of solving this thing.' He gave Maggie a wry look. 'Not that I would have any chance of stopping that happening even if I wanted to.' He paused for a moment before continuing. 'I've had some ideas on how we might divvi this thing up, which I'll share in a second. But as I said, we need everyone to chip in, so I'm looking forward to hearing your ideas.'

'Is this all one big case now guv?' French asked. 'The Cambridge business and Gina McQuarrie's death and that ten-year old murder case up north?'

Frank nodded. 'Aye Ronnie, I believe now they're all wrapped up together. Lots of different strands mind, but all deeply connected. So as a result, we've quite a few lines of inquiry to pursue.' He paused again, giving his head a scratch before continuing.

'So Frenchie, you're looking after the Cambridge bit. We need to find out what happened to Rhona Fraser and Olivia Cranston, and specifically why the hell they both got on that late-night bus.'

'On it guv,' French said, nodding. 'I've spoken to the bus company, and they've given me the name of the driver who was on the number three when Olivia got on it that night. I'll be following that up sharpish to see if he remembers anything.'

'And I did that analysis,' Eleanor interrupted. 'Of the households or business premises along the route of the bus that are within ten minutes' walk of a bus-stop.' She paused for a moment, looking pleased with herself. 'And the answer is eighteen hundred and six.'

Maggie, detecting that Frank was about to say something humorous but unhelpful, cut in.

'That's very illuminating Eleanor,' she said. 'My hunch is that both women might have been following someone. So that's eighteen hundred and six potential addresses where this person might live.'

'Or work,' French supplemented. 'Could be a shop or a pub or something I suppose.'

'Yes, that's true,' Maggie conceded.

'I can hack a list of names from the electoral database,' Eleanor said. 'In fact, that's what I was planning to do next. Then we'll have names to go with the addresses.'

Frank gave her a sharp look. 'I know you're only using the bloody hack word to wind me up, you wee devil. But yeah, go ahead, because it sounds like a good idea.'

'It'll be a lot of bloody names to trawl through though,' French complained. 'It'll take me weeks to go through them all.'

Frank laughed. 'Frenchie, one day soon we'll replace you with AI and then you'll be begging for a long list of names to trawl through.'

'No I won't guv, he said, grinning. 'I'll be retired, remember?'

'How could I forget?' Frank said. 'Anyway, we'll worry about that list when we get to it. So, anything else you need Ronnie?'

The DC pondered for a moment. 'Actually guv, we could do with more background on the Olivia woman. I was thinking maybe Lexy could do a bit of digging?'

'Aye, that's a good idea,' Frank said. 'What do you think Lexy? Up for that?'

She nodded. 'Yes sir. In fact, I was just thinking myself that we need a bit more background.'

'Good stuff. And I was also hoping that you would keep hammering through the old Nethy Bridge files, add some lateral thinking, and see if you can come up with an alternative theory that fits the facts. Now that we know Gordon Baird was murdered.'

'Will do sir,' she answered enthusiastically.

'Right, where are we?' he said, pausing for a moment.

'You were talking about Gordon Baird,' Jimmy interjected. 'I think I need to take a look at the circumstances around his death. I'd start with the mountain rescue guys and see if they've kept any records of who was up there that day.'

'Do they keep these records?' Maggie said, thinking out loud. 'And will they be complete? Because I know you're supposed to tell someone where you're planning to go, but there's a lot of idiots who just set off in t-shirts and flip-flops and tell nobody.'

Jimmy sighed. 'Aye, that's true enough. But the mountain rescue guys have maintained a self-reporting online database for a good few years now, so they'll still have that I expect. And if not, they'll have the duty rosters. Worst case, I can talk to whoever was on duty that day and see if they remember anything.'

'Sounds like a plan,' Maggie said. 'So, what about me and Lori, Mr SIO?' she continued, giving Frank a fond look. 'Got any plans for us?'

He nodded. 'Aye I do, and I'm afraid you're going to be getting the toughest job of all.'

'We're up for it,' Lori gushed. 'We love tough jobs, me and Maggie. So what is it?'

'If we're going to re-open Naomi Neilson's murder case, someone needs to talk to her mum and dad,' he said quietly. 'And I think it would be better if that person was a mother herself. It'll be a difficult conversation I know,' he added apologetically, 'but it's something we have to do I'm afraid.'

'I'm fine with that,' Maggie said. 'And we'll do it as soon as we can.'

'Good good,' he said, then gave a satisfied smile. 'It feels as if it's gradually coming together.'

'And what about you?' she said, raising an eyebrow. 'Are you going to be doing anything? Or are you going to be just sitting on your backside drinking coffee and dishing out orders?'

He laughed. 'Every army needs a general, any history book will tell you that.' He paused for a moment and scratched his head again. 'So team, how does that all sound? Anybody got anything to add?'

There was an outbreak of silence as the team members individually pondered on his question. But then suddenly the silence was broken by a female voice with a sweet highland accent, one that none of them had heard before. Jimmy darling, would you like another coffee?

'Shh, I'm still on my call.' His rebuke was firm but gentle, but it was also too late.

'Aye aye, what's this then?' Frank said, grinning.

Up in Braemar, there was an embarrassed silence, and then the face of a beautiful young woman appeared alongside Jimmy's. 'This is Frida,' he said awkwardly. 'I've been meaning to introduce her to you all for a wee while now.'

Chapter 17

Jimmy had been forced to park his investigation of Gordon Baird's death for a few days, with him and his business partner Stew Edwards committed to taking a party of Edinburgh civil servants on their outward-bound company's signature three-day Cairngorm endurance trek. However, somewhat disingenuously he had to admit, he had planned the adventure so that it followed the route taken by the mountain rescue guys when they had set out to search for Gina McQuarrie, and taking the party right by the exact same spot where she had met her death. The group had stopped for a half-hour hydration and nourishment break in the saddle that led up to Braeriach, allowing Jimmy the opportunity to re-examine the crime scene. Given that he would soon have the job of convincing an experienced local police officer that his analysis of the situation was correct, he approached this second visit with an open mind and some trepidation. But no, there was nothing he saw that made him change his opinion - unquestionably, Gordon Baird and Gina McQuarrie had been forcibly propelled over the edge, clearing the potentially arresting ledge before falling to their deaths.

Now Jimmy was over in Aviemore, where he had arranged to meet with Sandy McDade from the mountain rescue team, together with his new colleague DC Lexy McDonald, who had driven up from Glasgow that morning. The venue was the *Infamous Grouse* pub, which had evidently become the unofficial headquarters of the team and had inexplicably been allowed to keep using its cheeky name by the international beverage giant that owned the trademark to the *Famous* whisky brand. At ten-thirty in the morning however, a wee dram wasn't on the menu, famous or otherwise. Swinging through the door, he saw that Lexy and Sandy had already arrived and had grabbed a table over in the corner. He raised an arm in greeting and strode over to join them.

'Hi Jimmy,' Lexy said brightly. 'Me and Sandy have already introduced ourselves and we've ordered some coffees.'

Jimmy gave the man a warm smile. 'Good to see you again Sandy,' he said, shaking hands.

'So what's this all about?' McDade said. 'You said on the phone you wanted to talk about a couple of deaths from ten years ago, and now it seems it's a police matter.'

'Aye, sorry about the subterfuge Sandy,' Lexy said apologetically. 'It's a situation that's moving really fast and we can't tell you the full story right now, because we don't actually know it ourselves. But we really need your assistance.'

McDade smiled. 'Well of course, I'll do whatever I can to help.'

'I see you've brought your laptop,' Jimmy said, nodding at the device. 'Does that get us on to your database?'

'Yep, it's all here,' he confirmed. 'Or at least everything *we* have. Remember, lots of eejits head into the hills without telling a soul.'

'Aye, I know that,' Jimmy said ruefully. 'So for Lexy's benefit, would you mind explaining how this thing works?'

'Yeah, I suppose you and your mate Stew use it all the time,' McDade said. 'So you'll be familiar with it.'

Jimmy gave a wry smile. 'Me yes, Stew not so much. But I think I'm managing to persuade him of the sense in it.'

'I hope you do,' McDade said, opening up his computer as he spoke. 'So Lexy, the system's quite simple really. If you're a responsible walker, you log on and give an outline of your intentions. Start place and time, size of your party, your route and how long you expect it to take you, that sort of thing. Two or three of the outdoor equipment shops in the village have got touchscreens too, where you can record your plans.'

'And do you hold on to these records?' she asked.

McDade nodded. 'Sure. They're not of much use, but they don't take up much space either so there's never been any need to get rid of them.'

'Which is going to be very handy for us,' Jimmy said.

'Anyway Jimmy,' McDade said, 'I looked up the records on the day you were interested in. 17th March 2014, I think that was it?' Not waiting for an answer, he continued. 'Turns out there were two parties who had signified their intention to take on Braeriach that day.' He paused then punched a few characters into the laptop. 'Firstly, there was the other guy who sadly died. Robert Harrison was his name, from Sheffield. He'd posted his route the previous day and said that he was getting up at four in the morning to drive up and hoped to be setting off from the carpark at about ten. Mad keen obviously,' he added, 'but then there's a lot of folks like that.'

'When you say *died*,' Jimmy said, 'I suppose technically we mean *disappeared*. Because they've still not found his body, have they?'

'No, they haven't,' McDade conceded. 'But the situation's not totally without precedent you know. I looked at the records going way back, and they show we get one incident like that every nine or ten years or so. And there was still plenty of snow and ice around that day, but it was warming, and there had been two or three pretty significant avalanches in the previous days. Of course we'll probably never know for sure, but the Fiscal's conclusion at the enquiry was that Mr Harrison was caught in an avalanche and his body deeply buried as a result. It's the only explanation really.'

'I guess so,' Jimmy said, although not totally convinced. 'And the route he took was pretty much the same route we think Baird took. That's based on the fact Baird's car was found at the Glen Einich carpark too.'

'That's my assumption,' McDade said.

'So, anyone else who was planning a Braeriach expedition that day?' Jimmy asked.

McDade nodded. 'There was a big group from an Aberdeen University hiking club. Twenty-odd walkers in their party, and according to what they posted on the database, they were setting off from the ski carpark and going up via Cairn Gorm and Ben McDhui.'

'That's the same route I did, and the same as Gina McQuarrie's,' Jimmy said, then pondered for a moment. 'So the chances are this group would have passed both Baird and Harrison at some point in their day.'

'Aye, assuming everyone kept to their plans, they would have,' McDade agreed.

'Do you have a contact name from the Uni group?' Lexy asked him. 'Although whoever it was would have graduated and been long gone by now, I expect,' she added, evidently thinking out loud.

McDade peered at the screen of his laptop. 'Yep, a girl called Liz Thompson. We've got a contact mobile phone number too for what it's worth. Although I'd be surprised if she's still using it now.'

Jimmy laughed. 'That's the benefit of having an ace detective on our team. DC McDonald here will have Miss Thompson tracked down in no time.'

'Thanks for the compliment, undeserved though it is,' she said. 'So Sandy, is it you that will be coming up with us tomorrow as the mountain rescue representative?'

He shook his head. 'No, I'm working I'm afraid. But we've got someone who's perfect for you.' He hesitated for a moment. 'It's Robbie Cranston.'

'Cranston?' Jimmy said, surprised. 'That's the missing woman's brother, isn't it?'

'That's right,' McDade said. 'He knows the mountain very well and was keen to help. I think he needs something to take his mind off what's happened.'

***

'So are you still up for tomorrow's wee walk?' Jimmy asked after McDade had left them to return to work. 'Because it's not an easy one, even for a fit young woman like you.'

Lexy laughed. 'It sounds better when you describe it as a wee walk, and even better when you fib about my fitness. But I used to often take myself into the mountains when I lived at home, so I'm not a total rookie. And besides, Frank kind of persuaded me that I should tag along on the trip because of its importance to the case.'

He gave her a wry smile. 'Aye, but I notice he didn't volunteer to go himself.'

'He doesn't do hills he told me. Besides that, I really want to see the crime scene for myself, and remember, it's Olivia's brother Robbie who's going to be the mountain rescue representative. So I'll get the chance to speak to him on the way down. Ronnie French wants some more background on his sister.'

'Makes sense,' he said. 'By the way, do you know the guy from the police who's coming up with us?'

She shook her head. 'No, I've never met him before. Callum Reid's his name. He's a uniform sergeant from Inverness.'

'Well, it'll be an interesting day out, that's for sure.' As he said it, he felt again a wave of self-doubt sweep over him. Tomorrow, he would be back up at the corrie with two independent experts who would have to be persuaded that his murder theory held water. The more he thought about it, the less sure he felt. But there was nothing he could do other than lay out his logic and see if they were prepared to corroborate it.

Forcing the matter to the back of his mind he said, 'And we've got the missing girl's brother with us too, which will be interesting. He's a ghillie, isn't he?'

She nodded. 'That's right. At Strathrothie estate, over at Tomintoul. He lives in a lodge house which I guess comes with the job. But I'll tell you what Jimmy, it's not a job I'd like to do. It must be horrible having to shoot all these magnificent beasts, even although I know it needs doing. They say it's a quick death, but it's still not nice.'

Jimmy gave her an understanding look. 'Problem is, deer don't have any predators ever since the wolves died out, and if they're not culled, they cause massive destruction to the natural environment. It's sad but it's true unfortunately. And hunting and stalking them is a very important income source for these big estates.' He paused for a second then said, 'Anyway, we've got plenty of time, so why don't we see if we can figure out how we might track down this Liz Thompson? Any ideas where to start?'

She gave him a knowing look. 'With Google of course. Search for *Liz Thompson, Aberdeen University.*'

'You're serious, aren't you?' he said, suppressing a laugh.

'Deadly serious. Go on, punch it into your phone. And maybe add a year. 2014. To narrow it down a bit.'

'All right, I will.' He took out his phone, tapped on the app then typed in the search phrase.

'And go for *images*,' Lexy instructed. 'It would be good to see what this woman looks like.'

'Affirmative.' He tapped the link and watched as the search results filled his screen. And then let out a *wow* when he saw what had appeared at the top.

'That's *got* to be her,' he said incredulously, spinning his phone round so she could see it.

'Her Facebook profile. Wow,' Lexy echoed, wearing a huge grin. The photograph was of a type that Jimmy had seen a thousand times before, he in fact having been behind the camera for dozens of them, that of the inexperienced climber beaming a proud smile after conquering their first Highland summit. This climber was the opposite of inexperienced of course, but nonetheless Liz Thompson's picture was a classic of the genre, her pretty face weather-beaten and triumphant, a mass of auburn hair held in check by a gaudy headband, sunglasses perched on top of her head. A glistening crystal-blue sky framed the scene, forming a perfect background to what she would have known *had* to be her new profile picture.

'It's her all right,' Lexy said. 'See here, Aberdeen Uni Hikers is listed as one of her Groups and it says too that she graduated in 2015. She's from Glasgow, went to school in Hillhead, and now works as a chartered accountant in Edinburgh.'

'Bloody hell,' Jimmy said admiringly. 'Is proper police work always this easy?'

She laughed. 'No, not always, unfortunately. But the fact is, just about everyone is on some sort of social media these days. I mean, even my lovely grandma up in the Isles is on Facebook. And so unless you set out to deliberately cover your digital tracks, just about anyone can be found with a few clicks.'

He nodded. 'Aye, that's true I suppose. So how do we get in touch with this Liz? Shall I send her a private message?'

She grinned. 'Well actually, Police Scotland has an official Facebook page itself. Don't you think a request for help would be much better coming from that source?'

***

Within an hour of DC McDonald's request, the woman had replied by email, confirming she would be more than happy to help and provided a mobile phone number. Lexy responded instantly, explaining it would be an investigator from the newly-formed Independent Cold-Cases Agency who would be in touch, that investigator having been chosen because of his deep knowledge of the mountains. And one hour after that, Jimmy was on a call with Liz Thompson.

'Is this a good time Liz?' he began. 'Because I guess you're at work right now?'

He heard her laugh. *'Well yes I am, but I've been working like crazy these last few weeks, so I think they owe me a half-hour break.'*

'I'm sure they do,' he said. 'But just one thing if you don't mind. Are you somewhere you can't be overheard? Because what I'd like to ask you is connected to a historic crime that is being re-examined. So it's very sensitive.'

'I have my own office,' she said, with just the hint of edge to her voice. He wondered if this had become an automatic response from a successful woman sick and tired of putting up with condescending male arseholes. Present company excepted, he hoped.

'Ah right, that's great,' he replied. 'So as DC McDonald mentioned to you, we're re-examining the death of Gordon Baird up on Braeriach ten years ago. You'll remember it yourself of course because you were up on the mountain that day with the university hiking club.'

'Yes, I remember it,' she said. *'It was a terrible terrible day.'* She was silent for a moment. *'But why are you only looking at Baird? Because another climber went missing that day too.'*

He'd expected the point to be raised, and he'd known too it was going to be awkward.

'Yes, there was another climber,' he said, speaking carefully. 'A Sheffield man called Robert Harrison. But right now, for reasons I can't yet disclose, our focus is on Gordon Baird. But that doesn't mean we aren't concerned about finding out what happened to Mr Harrison. Because we are. Very much so.'

Out of the blue she said, '*We saw them you know. Both of them.*'

'That was the first question I was going to ask,' Jimmy said, feeling his excitement rise. 'Where on your route were these sightings?'

'*It was just as our group was dropping into the saddle beyond the Brochain corrie,*' she said. '*At the start of the south-west descent, if you know it?*'

'Aye, I know where you are,' he interjected. 'Carry on, please.'

'*Okay. So ten minutes earlier we'd had our wee celebration on the summit and were putting on a bit of pace on the descent.*' She laughed. '*We were always desperate to get to the pub back in those days.*'

'And who was it you saw there?' he asked. 'Which one?'

'No no, you misunderstand me. We saw them both. At almost the same time.'

'What?' he shot out, not able to hide his astonishment. 'You mean they were together? Baird and Harrison?' he added, as if they could be talking about anyone else.

'No, I don't think they were actually together,' Thompson clarified. 'We bumped into Gordon Baird first, and you don't just walk straight past someone up there in the middle of nowhere without stopping for a chat. Our lot were in high spirits after their climb, and I remember one of the lads pulling out a hipflask and more or less forcing Baird to take a swig. And it was whilst all this was going on that Robert Harrison appeared. He was probably seven or eight minutes behind Baird, but I doubt one would have been aware of the other.'

'Okay,' Jimmy said, forming a picture in his mind. 'And so I guess Harrison turns up and is more or less obliged to join in with these revelries.'

'He was in great spirits,' she said. 'I chatted to him myself. He'd set off from Sheffield at some crazy time that morning and was absolutely buzzing to be up in the mountain.'

'And what about Baird? How was his mood?'

She sighed. '*Well obviously, we know now what had happened. He was agitated and distracted, and anxious to get on his way.*'

Jimmy nodded. 'So did the two of them eventually leave together?'

'*Not exactly together. Harrison was having a laugh with a couple of the girls in our group when Baird set off. So he was probably two to three minutes behind Baird, something like that.*'

'And that was the last you saw of them I suppose? The only reason I ask is that according to what he posted with the mountain rescue guys, Robert Harrison intended to ascend Braeriach then come straight back down again, back to where he'd left his car. That made me wonder if he might have caught your party up, but obviously not.' He paused again as he framed his next question. 'And back then Liz, I assume the police spoke to you guys?'

'*Yeah, they followed up with a few of us. And we told them exactly what I've just told you. Because that's what happened.*'

'Yes, of course,' he said. He hesitated then asked. 'Liz, you know these mountains as well as anyone on the planet. Can I ask you, what do you think happened to Robert Harrison?

Could he have been lost in an avalanche? Because that's what the enquiry concluded.'

He heard her sigh. *'It's a horrible thing to say, but although he was nice, I thought he was a little bit too full of himself. As a for instance, about the first thing he said to me was that he'd done eighty-two Munroes the previous year. He was cocky, super-cocky even.'* She hesitated. *'You know yourself how easy it is for walkers to underestimate the danger of the Cairngorms. And I wouldn't be surprised if he was one of them.'*

***

It had been a *very* useful call, of that there was no doubt, particularly the revelation that Baird and Harrison - one now dead and one missing, presumed dead - had met on that fateful day. He was ruling out the possibility that anyone in Liz Thompson's ebullient student party had killed Baird, firstly on the grounds that the suggestion was wildly improbable, and secondly the fact that the group's encounter with the man had occurred almost a mile from where he died. Which seemed to leave only Robert Harrison as the possible perpetrator, a suggestion that seemed equally crazy to Jimmy. As far as he knew, Harrison and Baird were complete strangers, so if Harrison *was* the murderer, what could the motive possibly have been? Did Harrison catch up on Baird, and then did they have an argument about something, an argument that spiralled into violence? It wasn't impossible, but it was surely extremely unlikely. So, was there a third person involved, someone who had been tackling Braeriach from the north-eastern direction, following the route taken by the student party but an hour or more behind them? Jimmy gave a deep sigh as he contemplated this new possibility. Because if this is what *had* happened, then his investigation would come crashing to a stop before it had even started.

Chapter 18

It wasn't an assignment that Maggie was looking forward to, but it was one she'd decided was best tackled on her own. Her new associate Lori Logan was a young woman with many admirable qualities, but her get-up-and-go demeanour could sometimes jar in a situation where tact and empathy was required. Naomi Neilson's parents Bill and Patricia lived in Glasgow, in the neat suburb of Bearsden, and conveniently just two miles from Maggie and Frank's rented Milngavie bungalow. The meeting had been arranged for eight-thirty in the evening, allowing Maggie to see Ollie safely in bed before taking the short drive to the Neilson's home. The phone call arranging the meeting had been difficult enough, with Maggie only able to say that some new information had emerged related to the death of Gordon Baird, and that a specialist government cold-case unit had been engaged to look at their daughter's case again. Now she was standing in the Neilson's neat covered porch, breathing deeply before summoning the courage to push their doorbell.

The door was opened by a bespectacled grey-haired man in his fifties, who looked her up and down then said, 'Maggie I assume. I'm Bill. Please come in.'

'Thank you Bill,' she answered, grateful that they were to be on first-name terms. She followed him through a wide hallway and into a comfortably-furnished living room. A woman sat on a sofa where she had evidently been tackling a crossword in a puzzle-book. She set the book aside and smiled wanly. 'Hello,' she said. 'I'm Patricia. Patricia Neilson. Naomi's mum.'

'I'm Maggie,' she said. 'And I'm so terribly sorry that we're meeting in these circumstances.'

The woman gave her a sad look, then said. 'Would you like a cup of tea? I was just about to put the kettle on. And please, sit down,' she added, gesturing to the spare place beside her.

'No tea for me thank you Patricia,' she answered as she settled on the sofa. She would have quite liked a cup, but that would have meant five minutes or more of agonising small-talk with the couple whilst it was being prepared, and she was anxious to avoid that by getting straight onto the subject in hand. 'Let me just start by explaining who I am,' she said, smiling warmly. 'I'm Maggie Bainbridge, and I'm a lawyer who works mainly as a private investigator. So I'm not a police officer, just to make that clear. But as I said on the phone, the government has recently set up a specialist cold-case unit, and they decided in their wisdom that it should have a wider staffing mix, to include legal professionals as well as serving police officers. And as such, I've been engaged to work on the reopening of Naomi's case.'

'I don't see the point of this,' Bill Neilson said sharply. 'We'll never get over Naomi's death, but we've come to terms with it. What good will come of raking it all up again? Because nothing you or anyone else can do can bring our daughter back.'

Maggie nodded. 'Yes, I can understand that Bill, and we will obviously handle the matter as sensitively as we can.' She paused for a moment. 'But we now have reason to believe that Gordon Baird didn't kill himself, but in fact was murdered. And that unfortunately means that the case must be re-examined.'

'They said she did dirty things,' his wife spat out. *'Sex* games they called it in the papers. But my Naomi would never have done anything like that. She was a good girl, a very good girl. And a very clever girl.'

It must have been agony for Bill and Patricia, Maggie thought, all that salacious speculation about their daughter splashed all over the media, but that didn't mean it wasn't true. However, the truth or otherwise of that speculation was not top of her current list of concerns.

'Had you ever met Gordon Baird, either of you?' she asked. 'Were they a couple, boyfriend and girlfriend I mean?'

'He was her lecturer and tutor,' Bill Neilson said coldly. 'I assume they knew one another, but they weren't going *out*.

He was ten or fifteen years older than her. And she always had plenty of boyfriends her own age.'

'If there was sex, then he must have *raped* her,' Patricia said, raising her voice. 'We said that to the police, but they wouldn't listen.'

Maggie nodded sympathetically but made no immediate comment. The fact was, had there been evidence of assault, sexual or otherwise, then that would have been centre-stage in the police investigation. But she hadn't heard Lexy mention anything like that following her review of the file.

'She was very pretty and very clever too,' she said. 'You must have been so proud of her.'

'She was going to Oxford you know,' Naomi's mother said, evidently in response to Maggie's eulogy. 'To do post-graduate research. And not *everybody* gets that opportunity,' she added with a distinct air of self-regard. 'They said it was one of the most interesting research proposals they had ever seen,' she continued boastfully. 'Of course, she needed a first-class honours to do it. And not everybody gets a first, do they? But Naomi did.'

Maggie gave the woman a wry look. 'Well, I certainly didn't,' she said. 'But I guess Naomi always was a high achiever. Straight As in her Highers I expect.'

She saw the husband give his wife a sharp look, as if chastening her against taking the subject any further. Patricia shrugged, and then with a definite hint of disappointment said quietly, 'Yes, she did well enough.'

Her husband smiled as he evidently reminisced about his daughter. 'She always liked the boys more than she liked studying, did our Naomi,' he said fondly. 'Just as well she was clever enough to make up for it eh?' The question appeared to be aimed at no-one in particular but succeeded in riling his wife.

'You shouldn't *say* that,' she said angrily. 'It was *you*, always indulging her, daddy's special little girl. It was *me* who was pushing her to be everything she could be. Even when she was at university, it was still the same. You were making stupid excuses for all the failed exams, I was forcing her to face reality.'

He shook his head but said nothing, Maggie regretting that she seemed to have opened up an old wound between the couple.

'I'm sorry this is so difficult for you both,' she said. 'Perhaps I should let you know what will happen next.'

'Please, that would be good,' Bill Neilson said, his face crumpled with sadness.

'A detective will be carefully reviewing all the case files to see if she can shed new light on what happened that night. In parallel, the team will be investigating the murder of Gordon Baird to see if we can identify who killed him. We may re-interview some of the people who were spoken with back then, in the light of this new information.' She paused for a moment before continuing. 'Bill, I know you have questioned why we should be doing this, and of course it won't bring poor Naomi back. But it is possible that it wasn't Graham Baird who was responsible for your daughter's death. And that may mean that her real killer has still to face justice.'

Maggie paused then stretched out and placed her hand on Patricia Neilson's forearm. 'And we may be able to disprove those very distressing allegations too,' she said softly. 'It would be good if your lovely daughter's reputation wasn't sullied by these distasteful rumours. You would want that, wouldn't you?'

The woman nodded sadly. 'Yes of course. Of course. Please, do that for me.'

***

Lori had been disappointed not to have been invited to the meeting with the Neilsons but had been part-mollified by the promise of an early and comprehensive report of the proceedings. Accordingly, the two of them had rendezvoused at the Bikini Barista cafe first thing the next morning.'

'So how did it go?' the girl asked eagerly, as they settled in a table in the corner.

'They're broken people,' Maggie said. 'It was awful. So terribly sad.'

'And did you learn anything interesting that will help us with the case?'

She looked at her uncertainly. 'I learned some interesting things, yes. Whether they help with the case is a different matter. I need to do some serious thinking about them before I can answer that question.'

Lori laughed. 'You're dead good at serious thinking. But give me a for instance.'

'Okay,' Maggie said. 'Well, it seems that Naomi was one for the boys, not that there's anything the least bit special about that in a girl of her age. But it didn't please her mother. I got the impression that Naomi had been a disappointment to her. There was also a hint that she had had trouble with her exams at uni. But then she seemed to have pulled her socks up, because she ended up getting a first.'

'Aye, after she was dead,' Lori added.

'Yes, that's right. She had done her exams but didn't get to celebrate the results. It was very sad. And to add to the sadness, it seems she'd had an offer to do a post-graduate research degree at Oxford University. That was contingent on her getting her first,' she added.

Her associate gave her a blank look. 'What does contingent mean?'

'Sorry, it means that she had to get her first-class honours, otherwise she wouldn't get to take up her research place.'

'Aye okay, got that now,' Lori said. 'And what about her shagging her lecturer? Did you learn anything about that?'

Maggie laughed. 'I do like the way you put things Lori. But I didn't get the impression they were in a relationship. I'm thinking out loud here, but maybe they had a few too many on that night, and it just *happened*. And then it all went horribly wrong.'

But there had to be more to it than that, she thought, because Gordon Baird, whether he had been feeling remorseful or not, *hadn't committed suicide*. He had been murdered, and until they found out who was responsible for that, she knew they would not have the key to unlocking the mystery of Naomi Neilson's death.

Chapter 19

As fate would have it, it was a ghastly day for the mission, the rain falling in sheets and a mist limiting visibility to no more than five or six metres. He and Lexy had driven up to the ski-centre from Aviemore for the eight o'clock rendezvous with their two expedition colleagues, and as he pressed his nose against the window in a forlorn hope that things might be improving, Jimmy wondered again about the sense of letting DC McDonald join the trip.

'If I was you, I'd just stay here and track us on the GPS,' he said to her, half-joking, half-serious. 'The weather's crap here and it'll be even crapper up in the pass.'

She gave him a smug smile. 'Nah, you don't get rid of me that easily. Besides, Callum texted me this morning to say we're going up on the quad.'

For a brief second, he struggled to remember who Callum was but then it came to him. Sergeant Callum Reid, Police Scotland's mountain man from Inverness.

He gave her a doubtful look. 'What? I don't think so. The national park authority would have a fit about it.'

'Police business trumps everything, especially since this is a potential murder enquiry. Anyway, I expect he got a warrant or a special permit or something. '

He shrugged. 'I suppose you're right. But I didn't know the police had a fleet of quad bikes at their disposal. Are they white with a wee blue light on top?'

She laughed. 'I don't know, I've never seen one. Sergeant Reid's bringing it down on a trailer from Inverness. In fact, he should be here any minute now,' she added, glancing at the time on her phone. Simultaneously, a text alert popped on to her screen. *Just walking in now. Wearing a police Hi-Viz.*

'Guess that's him,' Jimmy said, pointing to a man who had appeared in the doorway and was now conspicuously scanning the room. Lexy stood up and waved vigorously. Reid raised a hand in response and came over to greet them. He was a huge guy, dressed in black salopettes and a red walking jacket beneath his police tabard, with a blue woolly hat pulled down so that it almost touched his eyebrows.

'Bloody awful out there,' he said, sighing. 'I'm Callum Reid from Inverness nick, by the way. You must be DC McDonald,' he added, smiling at Lexy, 'and you're Jimmy .'

'That's right. Jimmy Stewart. We're just waiting on Robbie to arrive.'

'Good job we're not walking today Callum,' Lexy said. 'I'm sure glad you could bring your wee mini jeep thing with you.'

'Aye, well we're only taking it up as far as the Ptarmigan restaurant,' he said. 'The rest we have to do on foot I'm afraid.'

Jimmy caught Lexy's disappointed look and jumped in. 'That breaks the back of it though. Knocks nearly two miles of the distance and gives us a couple of thousand feet head start too on the climb.' And what he'd said was more or less true, although they'd still have three or four miles of tough walking to do, and a few thousand feet of climb too. But it was definitely better than nothing.

'Yeah, sounds great,' she said brightly, although her expression suggested she might be feeling something different. A few minutes later, Robbie Cranston arrived, directing a warm smile of recognition towards the Inverness policeman, whom he had evidently met before.

'Good to see you again Callum,' he said. 'And you two... Jimmy Stewart and DC McDonald I presume?'

Jimmy nodded and stretched out a hand in greeting. 'Got it in one. Good to meet you.' He hesitated before giving the man a sympathetic smile. 'And we're both very sorry about what's happened to your sister. It must be awful for you and your family.'

He gave them a sad look. 'Aye, it's awful but we haven't given up hope. Olivia always suffered with her mental health and we're praying that she just had a wee breakdown and has taken off somewhere.'

'I hope that's what's happened Robbie,' Jimmy said. 'I know the police are still trying hard to find her. They'll be doing everything they can. And DC McDonald here has joined that team, so I know you'll be in good hands.'

Lexy nodded. 'On that subject Robbie, would it be okay if you and I had a ten-minute chat once we get down to terra firma again? I've a colleague working in Cambridge right now and he wants to find out as much about Olivia as possible.'

'Aye sure,' Cranston said distractedly. He was silent for a moment then said, 'Well, it's a bloody awful day out there, couldn't have picked a worse one.'

'You're right there,' Callum Reid said. 'I'll just go and get the quad off the trailer, it'll only take five minutes. See you out the front.'

Twenty minutes later, after a cold and wet ride in the uncomfortable vehicle, they'd reached the restaurant, located just a couple of hundred feet or so below the summit of Cairn Gorm.

'We'll need to park up the buggy here,' the sergeant said. 'But it'll be waiting for us for the scoot back down. And I'm sure we'll be pleased to see it on a day like this.'

Yes alright, Jimmy thought, half-annoyed, half-amused. *No need to keep reminding us how bloody awful the weather is.*

'Next stop Coire Brochain then?' Reid said, swinging a heavy rucksack onto his back. 'Seventy minutes or so by my reckoning, something like that?'

'What, have you got another quad bike tucked away in that bag?' Jimmy said, giving him a look. 'We'll just take it at a nice steady pace I think.' *For Lexy's sake*, he was going to add, then thought better of it, knowing she wouldn't thank him for giving her any special treatment. Not long after they set off, the rain eased a little and the mist began to lift, affording a view of Ben McDhui rising impressively to the left of their route. Soon they would be making a sharp right and starting the steepest part of the walk, a test in any conditions and certainly today. But looking at his colleague, he saw she was coping admirably, her breathing steady and her stride moderately paced but confident.

'Enjoying it?' he said.

'Immensely,' she instantly shot back, making him laugh. She nodded to Reid and Cranston, who were ahead of them and making effortless progress. 'But you should have told me we were walking with a pair of mountain goats.'

'They're men of the hills, what do you expect? Anyway, I bet your sergeant's got a wee gas stove in that backpack of his, so he'll make us a nice cuppa when we get to the corrie.'

It was nearly two hours after they'd left the Ptarmigan that Jimmy and Lexy reached the edge of the Coire Brochain corrie, some fifteen minutes behind Reid and Cranston. To their mutual amusement, they saw that Sergeant Callum Reid had indeed brought a stove, together with an aluminium camping pot and four small plastic beakers.

'Tea up guys,' he said. 'Water from that nice wee highland burn over there, but no Hob-Nobs I'm afraid. I ate the whole packet on the way down from Inverness.'

'I'll remember that,' Jimmy said, accepting a cup. 'So what do you think then guys? Have you had a look at the scene?'

'Dangerous place,' Reid said, taking a sip from his tea. 'You could easily slip off the edge in this mist, never mind when it's twice as dense.'

'I'll second that,' Robbie Cranston said. 'Especially when it's treacherous underfoot with the snow and ice.'

Jimmy nodded. 'But come and have a good look over the edge,' he said, beckoning to them. 'About fifty or sixty feet down, maybe more. There's a ledge. Do you see it?'

'Aye, that would probably stop anyone falling further,' Reid said, pursing his lips. 'At least I think so. But if you did hit it, the impact would most likely kill you stone dead. I mean, there's a pile of rocks down there for a start, which wouldn't exactly cushion your fall. And as you said Jimmy, it's at least fifty feet below us. Quite a drop.'

'You're probably right about it killing you Callum,' Jimmy conceded. 'But do you see what I'm saying? To *clear* that ledge, you would have to be propelled outwards, very forcibly. And that would take a hefty shove.'

'I can see that, aye,' Reid said. 'And that's what you believe happened to Gina?'

'That's what I think *must* have happened,' Jimmy said. 'If it was an accident, she would have been found on that ledge. Same if she'd tried to kill herself.'

'So you're saying it would be the same if someone jumped?' Cranston said, a sceptical edge to his voice. 'You know, if they were trying to do themselves in? They wouldn't have cleared the ledge?'

'Aye, I am,' Jimmy answered, nodding. 'Because you see the slope up to the edge here?' he continued, pointing behind them. 'It's a bloody steep ramp. You'd need to be an Olympic sprinter to get enough speed to launch yourself from that.'

'I'm not sure about that,' Cranston said, still sceptical. 'I think you could jump out from just standing here on the edge, without any run up.'

'You could,' Jimmy agreed, 'but you wouldn't get out far enough to clear the ledge, I'm pretty sure of that.'

Reid put his hands on his hips, then leant over and looked down. 'Yeah, you're right I think. It's probably sticking out ten or twelve feet horizontally after you've taken the slope into account.' He paused and grinned. 'But I tell you what guys, I bet none of us fancy doing a practical experiment.'

'I'll wear a parachute and have a go at it if you want,' Lexy said, grinning. 'But seriously, I couldn't run up this hill, never mind jumping off at the end of it. I agree with Jimmy, no-one could do it.'

'Aye, well the thing is,' Reid said, evidently keen to focus back on the job in hand. 'I've got to decide if Gina McQuarrie's sad death could only have been murder and then report back to my ACC. And that's what you're saying Jimmy, isn't it, that it had to be murder? And what about you Robbie? Do you agree with Jimmy's analysis?'

Cranston was quiet for a moment, then said. 'Well, sort of. There is a lot of sense in what you're saying Jimmy, no doubt about that.' Jimmy looked at him, narrow-eyed, waiting for the *but* he thought was sure to come. And he was not to be disappointed.

'But there's just one thing,' Cranston continued. 'What if she had tried to kill herself, and she comes crashing down on the ledge, but she somehow *survives* the fall? She's still determined to go through with it, so she manages to get up and jump from the ledge. Then falls to her death and ends up where she was found, at the bottom of the corrie.'

With a sinking heart, Jimmy recognised the fatal flaw in his previous logic. Sure, it was hugely unlikely that anyone could survive the fall onto the ledge, but he had to concede that it was perhaps just possible. Maybe, for instance, the ledge had been covered with a thick bank of snow that served to cushion Gina's initial fall? And then, as Cranston was suggesting, she managed to somehow stagger to her feet and complete her act of self-destruction. And what if the self-same thing had happened in the Gordon Baird case? However improbable, it was a possibility he should have thought about, and he could kick himself for not seeing it before. And now it seemed Reid was having the same doubts.

'There's something in what you say Robbie,' he said, speaking slowly as if picturing the possibility in his mind. 'It's very unlikely, but I suppose it's just possible.'

'More than possible,' Cranston said, 'My view is that most people would survive that fall. They wouldn't be in great shape, but they would be alive.'

'No, no way,' Jimmy said, shaking his head. 'As Callum said, those rocks down there would be lethal if you landed on one. You'd bust your head or break your back. One or the other, definitely.'

'Tough one, this,' Reid mused. 'As I said a second ago, I think surviving that fall would be unlikely. But not impossible.'

The way he said it failed to disguise what the sergeant evidently was now feeling. *Unlikely sure, but a whole lot more likely than some dubious murder theory.* 'I think we've probably seen enough,' he continued, taking a few steps back from the edge. 'Let's get ourselves moving and see if we can get back to the Ptarmigan before the bloody rain starts again.'

***

Jimmy made the descent in a daze, his mind endlessly churning over his seemingly flawed analysis of the scene of Gina McQuarrie's demise. What an *idiot* he'd been. He *should* have seen the possibility that someone could have survived the fall onto the ledge, even if that possibility was only one in a thousand. The trouble was, those odds, long though they were, were enough to raise a question mark over his postulation that Gina had been murdered and would surely be enough to persuade Sergeant Callum Reid to play it safe with his recommendation to his Assistant Chief Constable. More than that, it would mean he and Maggie would have to look again at what they were going to say to Edinburgh & Glasgow Assurance. *Did she or did she not kill herself?* Who could now say with any certainty? It was a bloody mess, and it was going to get a whole lot worse after he called Frank to give him the bad news.

Chapter 20

ACC Alison White hadn't even bothered to call Frank with her verdict. Instead, he'd received a WhatsApp which was a masterclass in both brevity and bluntness. *Insufficient evidence to open up a McQuarrie murder enquiry. Naomi Neilson ditto. Thx.* He'd predicted the outcome in advance of course, after the conversation with his brother, and now, with there to be no official re-opening of either matter, there was an urgent need for a Plan B. Accordingly, a video call had been scheduled and was about to kick off, to be attended by himself, DC Lexy McDonald, Maggie and Jimmy. He was in New Gorbals police station's canteen with Lexy, Maggie was in her Byres Road office and Jimmy was up in Braemar. And it was the latter who spoke first.

'Look guys, I'm really sorry to have ballsed this up,' he said. 'I have to hold my hands up, I should have spotted the possibility at the time. That was a big oversight on my part.'

'Nonsense bruv,' Frank said. 'Because whilst you've been fretting up there in the wild north, there's been conversations going on down here. Oh aye, there has been. Deep conversations.'

Jimmy laughed. 'That sounds ominous.'

'Frank and I talked,' Maggie continued, 'and we're more certain than ever that Gina didn't kill herself. She was a loving mum, and a woman with enormous talents, and no matter how bad things got in her life, she would always have had the wherewithal to overcome any obstacle. She would never have killed herself.'

'Exactly,' Lexy continued. 'And I've been up there, and I saw that wee ledge with my own eyes. If it had been an accident, Gina's body would have been found on the ledge. And it wasn't.'

Maggie nodded. 'So that means Gina McQuarrie was murdered. And *that* means our case has to proceed on that basis, whatever ACC Alison White thinks or says. We've all discussed it Jimmy, and we all came to the same conclusion.'

'But can you do that Frank?' he asked. 'Not if your big boss the ACC has ruled against it, surely?'

His brother laughed. 'Luckily Jimmy-boy, I'm a man with many bosses. And the one that trumps them all – not including you Maggie, of course,' he added hastily, 'is my *newest* big boss, one Katherine Collins, who is our minister of state for crime and policing, according to the wee business card she gave me. I've talked to her and been given the go-ahead for the Cambridge disappearances of Olivia Cranston and Rhona Fraser to be the pilot case for my new cold-case unit.'

'And we know Olivia and Rhona were both present on that fateful night up in Nethy Bridge when Naomi Neilson died,' Maggie added. 'As was Gina. It's all mixed up together. If we want to find out what happened to these poor women, we have to look back in history. We wouldn't be doing our jobs properly otherwise. Irrespective of what ACC White might think.'

Frank grinned. 'Yes, to put it in a nutshell, and forgive my crudeness, we're giving the proverbial two fingers to the good ACC. We carry on with our investigations exactly as we'd planned, the only difference being is we can't say to anyone that we think Gina and Gordon Baird were murdered. That's something we keep to ourselves until we work out who killed them. Understand?'

Everyone nodded, then Maggie said, 'It's going to be tricky dealing with Sir Andrew, isn't it? Because he's obviously a suspect for his wife's murder. *The* prime suspect probably,' she added.

'It makes it difficult for us police to get involved,' Frank admitted. 'But you and Jimmy and Lori are still working on the Edinburgh & Glasgow matter, so you've plenty of legitimate reasons to talk to him. It'll be fine.' He paused for a moment. 'There is one thing though. Everything that Lexy and I do from now on has to be a ratifiable spin-off from anything we discover down in Cambridge. That's what we need to do if we want to keep this thing legit with my police brass.' He paused again and sighed deeply.

'Which means for the time being we're in the hands of the dream-team of French and Campbell.'

***

The direction of the case now satisfactorily agreed, Frank grabbed himself another coffee at the counter – supplemented by an iced-gingerbread square, a Scottish delicacy that he had sorely missed during his years in London – and dialled French's number. Twenty rings were about his average as far as answering was concerned, but this time the laconic DC surprised him by answering on the third or fourth.

'Ronnie me old son,' he said in a terrible approximation of a Cockney accent, 'how are you getting along? Any progress to report to your guvnor?'

'Not bad guv,' French said pleasantly. *'I'm just holed up in a nice caff at the moment having a bit of a think-through and a bit of breakfast to go with it.'*

'It's half-past eleven by my watch but it's good to see you're putting the graft in,' Frank said, shamelessly taking a bite from his own cake. 'Anyway, wee Lexy's spoken to Olivia Cranston's brother like you asked. We can either cover that now or wait until you've given me your stop-press news from Cambridge.'

'Whatever guv. You go first if you like, and I'll get stuck into me sausage and bacon whilst you're talking.'

'I'll assume that you're trying to be funny Frenchie,' Frank said, laughing. 'But as far as the brother is concerned, there's not too much to report on that front. The bottom line is Robbie Cranston fears his sister has killed herself. Sure, he's clinging to the hope that she's just disappeared off somewhere, but I don't think he believes that one bit. The thing is, Olivia has a long history of mental illness, and he thinks going back to the city where her lover disappeared must have tipped her over the edge. And just so you know, Lexy says he's angry too that the local police aren't making more effort to find her body. Which, I'm guessing, is probably at the bottom of the river somewhere.'

'It ain't very deep, that river,' French said. *'It hardly comes up to your knees. It won't be in there.'*

'Fair point,' Frank conceded. 'And I suppose we're making the assumption that if she *has* killed herself, she did it in Cambridge. Whereas there's no reason why she couldn't have taken off somewhere else to do it. The fact is Frenchie, she could be anywhere.'

'Yeah, you're right guv. But I've thought about her mental illness situation. You see the thing is, Olivia was in Cambridge for a big job interview, and she obviously knew if she got offered the job she'd be living there. If you want to know my opinion, it's likely she deliberately wanted to move there to be close to the spirit of her Rhona. All that spiritual stuff's bollocks I know,' he added, sounding apologetic, *'but loads of people believe in it, don't they? And somehow that doesn't stack up with her killing herself.'*

'No, I suppose it doesn't,' Frank admitted. 'Anyway, what have you got to tell me?'

'This and that, this and that. First of all guv, I checked with the college where she had her interview, and a professor geezer there told me they were all very impressed with her and had phoned her the very next day to offer her the job, but they got no response. Nothing back from their messages either. Nothing. He sounded a bit peeved until I told him she'd gone missing that day.'

'And he didn't know?' Frank said, surprised. 'When it must have been all over the local papers?'

'These geezers only read academic journals,' French said. *'He was a bit of an airy-fairy head-in the-clouds sort of guy.'*

'But does that mean then that Olivia had already come to some harm by then? Within twenty-four hours of the interview?'

'That's what I feared guv,' French said. *'But the prof said that she was really enthusiastic and excited at the interview. As I said, it don't stack up with her topping herself, even if she was a total nut-job.'*

Frank struggled to suppress a laugh. 'Good old Ronnie, the king of political correctness. But now that means we must be considering murder.' He paused for a moment. 'What's the local plod's thinking on this?'

'There's no body, is there? It's still a missing person as far as they're concerned, and none of us try too hard on them cases, do we guv? And as luck would have it, a guy was murdered last night and they're moving nearly everybody on to the investigation. That guy was found in the Cam by the way, but someone had stabbed him four times in the stomach before they dumped his body.'

Frank sighed. 'Aye well, I can understand why they're switching all their resources onto the new murder case, we'd all do the same. But at some stage we're going to have to persuade them to try a bit harder on ours. Anyway, how have you got on with chasing up the bus drivers?'

'Stroke of luck on that one guv,' French said laconically. *'I didn't adam-and-eve it myself, but it turns out the same guy's been driving on that route for over fifteen years now. Harry Potter's the guy's name.'*

'Really?' Frank interrupted, laughing.

'Yeah, really guv. Anyway, he was the driver the night Rhona disappeared and the same for Olivia.'

'Bloody hell, you wouldn't expect that, would you?' Frank said. 'And did our wizard guy remember anything about either night? I suppose it's a big ask in Rhona's case, given it was eight years ago now,' he added, answering his own question.

'Well actually he did guv. There was nothing in Rhona's file to say that he was questioned back then by the way, but he says he was.'

'Brilliant,' Frank said sarcastically. 'Just shows how seriously the Cambridge plod were taking her disappearance if they couldn't be arsed to keep the records up to date.'

'Agree guv,' French said. *'Anyway, he said then that he vaguely remembered a girl matching Rhona's description getting on, but he didn't remember her getting off.'*

'That's no great help, is it?' Frank complained. 'We've already got CCTV of her getting on the bloody bus. Same with Olivia.'

'Yeah but hold your horses guv. See, what he did remember in both cases was that nobody got on or off the bus for the first couple of miles. He said that was normal because the first part of the route is around the city centre and although there's a lot of shoppers and students getting on and off during the day, that doesn't happen so much at night .'

'So?' Frank asked, not immediately seeing where French was going with this.

'It means that we've got a lot less bus stops to worry about, which means we've got a lot less addresses where the geezer the women was following might live. If you get my drift.'

'Aye, you're *right* Frenchie,' Frank said. He felt his excitement level rise as suddenly something came to him. In fact, *two* things came to him.

'Ronnie, do you know how to get Eleanor on this call? I don't know how to do one of these three-way connection thingies myself.'

'No problem guv. Bear with, bear with.'

A few seconds later, Frank heard a ring, and a few seconds after that, the call was answered.

'*Hi Ronnie,*' Eleanor said in a pleasant tone. '*How can I help?*'

'*The guvnor's on the line*,' he said. '*He's got something to ask you.*'

'*Hello Frank,*' she said, the tone distinctly less cheery. '*What do you want? Because I'm busy at the moment.*'

'Of course. You always are,' he answered, grinning. 'Look, I'm assuming you can get access to the older electoral records as well as the current ones, am I right?'

'*Like yeah. They keep them online for every electoral cycle. Going back to when they were first computerised.*'

'Brilliant. So does that mean we – sorry, I mean you – does that mean *you* could compare addresses between two electoral registers and see if the same person or people are living there?'

'*Yeah, easy,*' she said. '*Like three lines of code.*'

'Fantastic. You see, some good work from DC French here has narrowed down the number of addresses the guy who was been followed could be going to. What do you think Ronnie? How many bus-stops are still in play?'

'About eight or nine now guv. Them ones are the last on the route.'

'And the thing is,' Frank continued, thinking out loud, 'there'll have been a fair amount of moving in and out of the area over an eight-year period. There's always a lot of churn in a university town like Cambridge. It seems that our guy, assuming it is a guy, has been at the same address all that time, but there'll be a lot of addresses where that's not the case. Eliminating the movers is going to narrow down our list of names quite a bit I'd imagine. So we end up with a list of people who lived in the area when Rhona Fraser went missing and are still there. Incidentally, what's this place called? The place where the bus goes?'

'A place called Cherry Hinton,' French said. *'I took a trip there the other day. Pleasant enough suburb.'*

'And you can get us this list with just three lines of code Eleanor?' Frank asked. 'Sounds like a couple of minutes work maybe?' As soon as he said it, he knew he shouldn't have, because there was nothing the feisty forensic geek hated more than an amateur pronouncing on the timeframe of one of her projects. He tried to retrieve the situation with a hasty *but I'll let you work that out of course*, but it was already too late. In a few seconds time, he and Ronnie were going to be on the end of a long and convoluted technical exposition, and there was nothing to do but grit your teeth and try and keep your mouth shut until you were sure she was done.

'It's not that easy,' she began with, this an introductory passage he had heard many times before. *'I've got to get login credentials from Central IT Security Governance, and that takes like five signatures to get permission. Then I have to build a production environment and a test environment and migrate the data into them from the central repository. Then I have to write the code, obviously, then desk-review it, then test it, before I do a production run.'* There was a silence, but both Frank and French were experienced enough to know not to fill it, on the expectation she was simply pausing for breath. But it seemed in fact she was done, adding a simple *that's it* to finish.

'That's great Eleanor,' he said. 'And I know it sounds very involved, but I'd be very grateful if you can get on to that as soon as you can. Now Frenchie,' he continued, 'I've had another thought.'

'So have I guv,' his DC said. *'It struck me that this geezer must have been taking that same bus for years, and I assumed he was going home after working in town. I thought if we randomly pull some of the CCTV the bus company has got from that service going back over a few years, there's a good chance we'll get a mugshot of the guy.'*

Frank laughed. 'You've stolen my thunder Ronnie, but I suppose they say great minds think alike.'

'*Or fools seldom differ,*' Eleanor said sourly, but then awkwardly added, '*but I'm not saying you two are fools or anything. It's like just a saying.*'

'We like to play the fool though sometimes,' Frank said, laughing. 'It's very important for maintaining team morale. Anyway, so you're going off to dig out some CCTV, are you Ronnie?'

'*That's the plan guv,*' French agreed. '*They're very helpful at the bus company so I should be able to get this sorted tomorrow with a bit of luck.*'

'Okay then you two,' Frank said ebulliently. 'Go to it and we'll speak again in a couple of days.'

***

Contemplating it afterwards, Frank thought this might well be the moment that seemed to arrive in every case, that sweet moment when a couple of pieces of the jigsaw fell into place and for the first time you began to get sight of the complete picture. A few days ago, Eleanor had estimated that there might be, what was it, a couple of thousand households within ten minutes' walk of a bus stop on that route? Now with Ronnie having eliminated around half of them from the search, that might come down to as few as one thousand. Once Eleanor had performed her IT wizardry and got them a list of people who lived in the catchment area eight years ago and were still there, that might half again. A list of just five hundred names fell firmly into the territory of a door-to-door exercise, with a wee team of three or four uniforms being easily able to complete the door-knocking within a week. Add to that the fact that they might have a mugshot for reference, courtesy of the bus company's on-board CCTV cameras, and the chances of them tracking down the guy that Olivia and Rhona had been following had multiplied immeasurably.

Because the more he thought about it, the more he was convinced *that* was what must have happened. Two women from Scotland, two women whose lives were closely intertwined, had chanced to visit Cambridge, and, presumably to their shock and surprise, had bumped into someone they had not expected to see. What had been in their minds, he wondered, as they set out to follow this figure from their past? Had there been a confrontation that ended in violence, with both women murdered and their bodies coldly disposed of? Right now, it was all just supposition, but in Frank's opinion, it was a supposition based on a highly credible premise.

A premise that might turn into something more once they'd tracked down the mystery man.

Chapter 21

Ronnie French's news from Cambridge was both exciting and encouraging, which in Maggie's mind went some way to offsetting the disappointing outcome of Jimmy's Braeriach expedition with Sergeant Callum Reid and Olivia Cranston's brother Robbie. Okay, ACC White had been unwilling to officially designate Gina McQuarrie's death as murder, but that didn't mean the woman *hadn't* been unlawfully killed, a point she was making forcibly as she and Frank powered into one of Stevie's excellent breakfasts at the Bikini Barista cafe. Lori was with them too, and Jimmy had joined on a video call, Maggie amused at his wistful longing for the full Scottish that they were enjoying.

'I'll tell you what,' she said through a mouthful of toast, 'this wee setback should just make us doubly determined to crack on with the case, and I mean every aspect of the case. Not just Gina, Naomi Neilson too, and Gordon Baird. Everything.'

'*Did you just say 'wee' there?*' Jimmy asked on the line from Braemar, evidently amused.

'Did I?' she said, giving a questioning look. 'I didn't notice. But you just hear it so often up here that I wouldn't be surprised if I did. At least I'm not saying *aye* yet, but I'm sure that'll come too.'

'Aye, it will Maggie, in a wee while you'll be talking just like a wee Glasgow lassie,' Lori said, chuckling. 'But does this mean we're going all-out on the case then? Because that'll be dead amazing if we are.'

'I've made a list,' Maggie said. 'I hope you don't mind Frank. I'm not trying to put you out of a job, honest.'

He gave her a wry look. 'So that's what you were scribbling in your wee notebook when I was playing that football video game with Ollie last night? I *thought* you were looking serious.'

'There was no point in me playing, because I'm so rubbish I can't give him a game anymore. Besides, there were so much stuff spinning round my head that I had to write it down otherwise I would have gone nuts.'

'Alright,' he said. 'We'd better hear it then. Fire away, please.'

'Okay,' she said, her excitement obvious, 'and this is in no particular order I should say.' She paused for a moment before continuing. 'So, question one. Why was a beautiful girl like Naomi Neilson sleeping with Gordon Baird? He was much older than her for a start, and from his pictures he was no Brad Pitt either.'

'But *was* she sleeping with him?' Lori interjected. 'What I mean is, were they a sort of regular item, or did they just end up going to bed that night as a one-off? It happens you know,' she added, a sheepish note creeping in to her voice, 'when you have one too many double vodkas. Not that I'm speaking from experience or anything of course.'

'Heaven forbid,' Maggie said, raising an eyebrow. 'But whatever the case, we need to come up with a theory as to why and see if it stacks up.'

Frank gave an appreciative nod. 'Yep, I like that. What's next?'

'The next one's Gordon Baird's death up on Braeriach. I want Jimmy to carry on with his investigation until we get to the bottom of what happened. We ignore Callum Reid and Robbie Cranston's doubts and proceed on the basis that he was murdered. Because he was. We all know that,' she added.

Jimmy sighed. *'I'll do that Maggie of course, but I must admit I'm completely flummoxed at the moment.'*

'He *was* murdered, and you know he was,' she repeated. 'So please keep trying. That big brain of yours will crack it, I have every confidence in you.'

He laughed. *'I'm not sure about my big brain. But yeah, I'll crack on with it.'*

'Good,' she said. 'And whilst you're at it, I want you to do the same thing for Gina McQuarrie. She was murdered too, we know she was. You know *how* it was done, which has got to lead you to the *who*. Frank and I will try to work out the *why*.'

He gave a thumbs up. *'Of course, I'll do that, no problem.'*

'Great. Next,' Frank barked.

'The next one is one I'm going to take on myself,' she continued, 'and apologies, because it's all massively vague in my head right now. It's just that there's something about the subject of academic qualifications that's nagging me.'

'Not with you I'm afraid,' her husband said, furrowing his brow.

She gave a half-smile. 'Yes, I'm not *quite* sure where I'm going with this myself to be honest. But we heard about Naomi needing a first to get that post-graduate research post in Oxford, didn't we? And we heard from her parents that she'd had trouble with her exams, and when she was at school, that she preferred boys to studying. And then there's Sir Andrew McQuarrie, who you remember, was no high-flyer and then suddenly he's an economic genius and the darling of the media and gets a knighthood to boot. I know, it doesn't make much sense, any of it,' she added apologetically, 'but as I said, it's just something that's been nagging away at me.'

'It is interesting, now that I think about it,' Frank said. 'Because funnily enough, Lexy mentioned something similar after her chat with Robbie Cranston the other day, not something she really gave much weight to. His sister had always been a bit flaky mentally, that was the general gist of the conversation, right back to when she was at school. But apparently, she always particularly fretted about her exam results, and always got herself so worked up that she didn't do as well as she should. Maybe you should add that to your considerations, do you think? Maybe look and see what sort of degree she ended up with?'

'I'll do that Frank, thanks.' She paused again, gathering her thoughts. 'Okay,' she said, speaking slowly and shooting Frank a sweet smile. 'This next one is the item I think might cause you a little bit of difficulty my darling, but I'm going to raise it anyway.'

'We're all one team now, aren't we?' Lori said supportively. 'All for one and one for all.'

He gave the girl a sardonic look. 'I'll hear what it is first, thank you, before I commit to that philosophy.'

'It's the money,' Maggie said. 'We know that on two occasions, the McQuarries had to make an urgent call for cash, and huge amounts of it too. One occasion was eight years ago, the other a few weeks ago, just shortly before Gina's death.'

'He told us she was planning to leave him and needed the money to buy a place of her own,' Lori reminded them.

'And we all know that's complete bollocks,' Maggie said firmly. 'Gina wouldn't have sloped off to live in some dismal flat leaving her kids with their dad in that beautiful big house. So where was this money coming from and where was it going, that's what we need to find out. And for that, we need the services of one Miss Eleanor Campbell.' She gave Frank a smiley questioning look. 'What do you say my darling? Can you put her at our disposal? *Please*?'

He sighed. 'You're asking her to access their bank accounts I suppose?' he said, then answered his own question. 'Aye you are.'

'*If this was an official murder enquiry you'd do it, no bother,*' Jimmy interjected.

'Aye, but it's *not*,' Frank shot back. 'There are laws in this country about that sort of stuff, as I'm sure you know. We need warrants for a start. We don't just let geeky hackers loose on the internet. Especially if these geeky hackers work for us.'

Lori gave him a thoughtful look. 'But I think you said last time that we can do stuff if we can show a connection back to the official Rhona and Olivia case, didn't you?'

'I did,' he admitted, giving her a suspicious look back.

'Rhona Fraser disappears eight years ago and there's a sudden panic for money,' Lori continued. 'Olivia Cranston disappears a few weeks ago, there's a sudden panic for money. I might be a mile off here, but that looks very much like a connection to the Cambridge case to me.'

'She's right you know,' Maggie said excitedly, not giving him a chance to respond, and then stopped suddenly as a thought came to her. 'And I'll tell you what,' she continued, 'this could be more than just a tenuous connection.'

'What are you getting at?' Jimmy said.

'Actually, I don't know what I'm getting at, not right now,' she said, sounding slightly deflated. 'But it *must* be more than just a coincidence, and perhaps when we see where the money was going to, it will all click into place.'

Frank gave a resigned sigh. 'Aye well, I suppose I *can* make a case for getting our wee troublemaker involved. And right now, I'm technically still working for 12B, so I can ask Jill Smart to kick off the paperwork, and Jill usually trusts me on this sort of stuff. Leave it with me.'

'Excellent. So, back to my list.'

'Bloody hell, there's *more*?' Frank said.

Maggie nodded. 'I'm afraid so, although it gets a bit more tentative now. Anyway, I've been thinking about Sir Andrew McQuarrie again. And bluntly, I don't think we've properly considered the possibility that he killed his wife.'

'He looked and sounded properly devastated about her death that first time we talked to him,' Lori said doubtfully. 'There was even a couple of tears, and I don't think he was faking them.'

'Well, you're hardly going to be dancing up and down and saying *I'm really glad my wife's dead,* are you?' Maggie said. 'And sorry Lori, that sounded horribly critical, I didn't mean it to, I was just thinking out loud. But what if it was all just a skilful act, him playing the grieving husband when all along he's just waiting to collect his three million quid insurance money then head off to a shiny new life in the States?'

'*Do you think he might have another woman over there?*' Jimmy asked thoughtfully. '*Because these academic types are always jetting off to fancy international conferences, aren't they? Maybe he met someone when he was on one of them.*'

'It's a possibility, a good possibility,' She paused for a moment then said, 'But you see the big thing is, he's not been asked that question that suspects are always asked on TV detective dramas.'

Lori jumped in, nodding. 'Sir Andrew, would you mind telling me where you were on the day your wife died?'

'Got it in one.' Maggie said. 'He's the husband, the prime suspect and a guy who benefits hugely from his wife's death. We've let him off lightly, we really have. We need to put some pressure on him in my opinion.'

Frank gave her a sharp look. 'It might be news to you, but you're not allowed to beat a confession out of a suspect anymore. And obviously, I can't ask that question, not with the case still being unofficial. I'd be on a bloody harassment charge before you know what's what.'

'Can I do it?' Lori said, her eyes shining. 'I've always wanted to say that to somebody, just like on the telly.'

Maggie laughed. 'The job's yours Lori, as long as you don't mind me covering my eyes with embarrassment when you say it.'

'I'd like to be there to see that too,' Jimmy said. *'Can you take a wee video Maggie?'*

'Absolutely. It needs to be recorded for posterity.'

'By the way, I've noticed there's not much on your list for the actual police to do,' Frank interrupted. 'Apart from Ronnie of course. Are you trying to tell us something, and me in particular?'

She laughed again. 'No, of course not. And don't forget, our super-smart DC McDonald is scouring the old Neilson files to try and figure out what really happened that night up in Nethy Bridge. That's going to be absolutely huge in terms of making sense of this whole thing, and if anyone can figure it out, it'll be Lexy.' She paused and gave him a cheeky grin. 'Besides darling, I've always thought your forte was using your great age and experience to steer the ship. The elder statesman. The wise old owl.'

'Bollocks to all of that,' he said, giving a mock grimace. 'I want to slap the wee blue light on top of my car and scream down the road with sirens blazing, in pursuit of the baddies. I'm a man of action, me,' he added. 'Just so you know.'

'If you say so, although thousands might disagree,' she grinned. 'But what do you think everyone? Plenty to get our teeth into?'

'Too much,' Frank said. 'But, no, you've done a brilliant job Maggie, really fantastic.' He raised his hands above his head in an extravagant stretch, then yawned. 'So, I'll just sit back and relax until it's all done. Give me a wee buzz when you need me to make some arrests and I'll sort out some handcuffs.'

Chapter 22

It was simply the intensity of their schedules that had prevented Jimmy arranging an event where his gang could meet Frida for the first time, and with every meeting or video call so tightly focussed on the case, he hadn't *quite* had the chance to tell them that he'd moved in with her either. At least, that's what he had convinced himself was the reason. Or was it that he was worried how they might react, given he had only known the lovely girl for ten or twelve weeks, if that? *Marry in haste, repent in leisure* was the old saying, one that had rather fallen out of fashion given that not so many people were tying the knot these days, but the warning still held relevance. He thought that might be the gist of what Maggie and Frank would say, but he didn't care. Frida Larsen was wonderful, it was as simple as that, although he couldn't forget the last time he had fallen for a Scandinavian woman, it had ended in disaster. But Frida was nothing like Astrid Sorenson, the country music star who had once stolen his heart and ruined his life at the same time. He realised now that Sorenson had been little more than a comfort blanket when he had been struggling to stay sane during his time in the Helmand Province hellhole. Their crazy relationship had resulted in too many people getting hurt, himself included, not that he felt sorry for himself. What he had felt afterwards was pure shame, and he had found it was an emotion that was virtually impossible to shake off. But with Frida Larsen, everything was different. Frida Larsen was wonderful. In fact, the more he thought about it – and he had been thinking about it a lot lately - the more he considered he might already be in love with her.

She stretched over and kissed him full on the lips, taking him by surprise since he thought she was still asleep.

'Good *morning* darling,' she said lasciviously. 'You look thoughtful.'

He smiled. 'I was thinking about you,' he said truthfully.

She snuggled up to him. 'About last night?'

'Aye, that too. You seemed to show very little respect for my date with a four-thousand-foot mountain this morning. I didn't get to sleep until past two o'clock.'

'I didn't hear you complaining. And anyway, you're a very fit man. With *fantastic* stamina,' she giggled.

'Aye, all right,' he said, now faintly embarrassed by the direction of the conversation. 'I'll just dive up and make us some coffee and a wee bit of toast. Then I'm going to drive over to the ski centre rather than do the walk from here. It knocks a good few miles off it each way.'

She sighed. 'I've got a vanload of supplies due in this morning, so I need to be up and about myself.'

They sat at her kitchen table in contented silence, she engrossed in her laptop as she reviewed her tearoom's expected deliveries, he sipping coffee and thinking about the day's mission and how he could best piece together what had happened to Gina McQuarrie and Gordon Baird. Of course, he reflected, cold logic suggested that he could probably make just as good progress if he stayed here in Frida's cosy kitchen and applied the old grey cells. But no, that wouldn't do at all, he knew that. He *had* to be at the scene once more, where he could close his eyes and breathe in the sharp mountain air and imagine he had been a witness at both murders.

'I'll get off now Frida,' he said, getting up then kissing her gently on the forehead. 'And see if you're planning on a repeat performance tonight, can we have steak for tea?'

***

The ninety-minute drive over to the Cairngorm ski centre had been productive, in so much that it gave him time to recognise the key difference between the two murders, a difference he realised was acute despite their shared MO, and one that hadn't struck him before. The thing was, Gordon Baird's murder *had* to be totally unpremeditated. Nobody had known that he was going to take off into the mountains after the death of Naomi Neilson, save perhaps for some of the walking party who were staying at the Nethy Bridge hotel the previous night, and they'd all been accounted for by the local police, who had interviewed each of them not long after Naomi's body had been discovered. Whereas in Gina's case, there was every likelihood that the murder *was* premeditated. She had posted her route not only on the mountain rescue team's website, he had discovered, but also on her own Facebook page too. And with her being one of Scotland's biggest music stars, literally thousands of her followers would have found out in advance about her intention to tackle Braeriach single-handedly. Which meant that anyone who had wanted to kill her would have had plenty of opportunity to prepare and plan for it. But who was it, that was the question? Opportunity and means were crystal-clear, but that left motive, and that was anything *but* clear. Her husband would have to be on that list because husbands always were, but other than Sir Andrew, who might have wanted to kill the national treasure that was Gina McQuarrie?

The carpark was quiet, just a dozen or so vehicles parked near to the buildings that housed the lower station of the moribund funicular railway, a crumbling edifice that had been added to a national register of ineptitude which included a couple of massively late and over-budget ferries, an NHS waiting list that seem to have nearly every citizen on it, and an education system that turned out kids with third-world levels of achievement. But politics wasn't his thing, so all he could do was gently curse the fact that he could have been whisked up to the top of Cairngorm in ten minutes had the railway been in operation. But no matter, today he was travelling light, with a small backpack containing essential emergency supplies, including a torch and compass, a pair of old-school items so often omitted by walkers who foolishly relied on their phones' battery holding out. Fine if everything went to plan, but up here, with a change in the weather liable to bite you in the arse at any moment, the plan could quickly go out the window. With a bit of army-level pace, he was reckoning on just seventy minutes to get to the corrie, where he would spend an hour or so stress-testing his theory again, before making an equally quick descent. In the event, he clocked it at just over eighty-five minutes, which he wasn't too disappointed with, although he'd found himself struggling for breath at some of the steeper points on the route. Still, at thirty-five, he was not far off the fitness level he'd had in his army prime, and up here no-one was shooting at you, which made it a whole lot more relaxing.

So here he was back at the scene, for the third time in not many more weeks. Facing into a brisk easterly, he stood as close to the edge as he dared and stared down at the ledge below. It had been mainly Robbie Cranston who'd raised the doubts about his theory, and looking back, he realised the guy had been pretty insistent too, which had gone a long way to persuading Sergeant Callum Reid that declaring Gina McQuarrie's death as murder would be unsafe. Cranston's contention had been that someone could survive the fall onto the ledge, and if they were intent on killing themselves, could continue the undertaking by jumping or rolling off it. So how far down was it? He'd studied the map before he'd left Frida's, but the contours were packed together such that it was impossible to see exactly where the ledge started and finished. Before, he'd thought fifty feet or so, but the map suggested it was more. But now it was a question that would be answered by empirical experiment. The slope down to the ledge was steep, in fact almost vertical, but he'd spent three horrible weeks during his army training learning how to climb up and down a cliff-face without the benefit of ropes or carabineers, the sadistic sergeant major in charge insisting all you needed were strong fingers and a lot of bottle. Strong fingers he still had; bottle, that was a bit less certain. With a sigh, he spun round one hundred and eighty degrees, then took the first tentative step down, eyes fixed on his boots in order to find a stable foothold. Much of the slope was bare rock, but there were occasional clumps of vegetation sprouting from cracks in the surface which might be capable of supporting his weight or forming a handle he could grab hold of. Trouble was, these weren't laid out like the convenient ladder pattern you might find on an indoor climbing wall, nor could you be sure they wouldn't come away in your hand or disintegrate under your foot. You had two feet and two hands, and you needed to make sure three out of the four of them were firmly anchored before you made your next move, and it was many times more difficult going down than climbing up, since it was hard to see where to put your feet. He sighed again, wondering if this was such a great idea, but he badly wanted to get down on that ledge, and he wanted to have a reasonably accurate estimate of how far down it actually was, which he would be able to calculate from counting the number of individual moves he made during his descent. So, there was nothing for it but to take a deep breath and get on with it. At least going down he would have gravity on his side, although you wouldn't want too much of it, he thought wryly.

It took more than half-an-hour for him to finally reach the ledge, with more than a few heart-stopping moments on the way. Relieved, he threw his backpack on the ground and collapsed on his back alongside it, closing his eyes and waiting for his elevated heart rate to fall to something approaching normal. He rested a couple of minutes and then did the calculation. It had taken about forty or so individual moves to get down to the ledge, and he estimated each would have taken him down two to three feet, depending on how much he'd had to stretch on any particular one. So, the distance down from where he started was actually more like eighty or ninety feet, further than his visual assessment had reckoned. No way could anyone survive that fall, especially now that he could see close-up the array of jagged granite rocks that almost covered the surface of the ledge. Last night for good measure he'd looked it up on Google, and learned that above forty feet, the chances of surviving that fall were almost zero, and he also read an interesting if obvious maxim; *it's not the fall that kills you, it's the landing.* Yes, anyone landing here would be killed instantly, irrespective of what Robbie Cranston might think. He recognised it might have been a wasted effort climbing down here, but no matter, he'd enjoyed the challenge of the descent, and at least he'd eradicated the doubt that had crept in to his mind since his last visit to the scene with Cranston and Callum Reid. Unclipping a pocket of his backpack, he removed his water bottle, took a swig and then closed his eyes. Ten minutes later he awoke with a start, taking several seconds to remember where he was, then smiled wryly to himself as he recognised what might have happened if he'd rolled over in his sleep. He got to his feet and stretched, then slung the backpack over his shoulders in preparation for the return ascent. But as he did so, something caught his eye, a couple of feet ahead of him where the ledge was starting to narrow. *Footprints.* Surprised, he knelt down to get a closer look. The prints had been made by a walking boot, not much doubt about that given the pattern they had left. He hovered his own foot over one of them to judge the size. A little bit smaller perhaps, maybe a size nine or ten in comparison with his own size twelve, but probably a man's print. He looked around again to see if there were any others, but there didn't seem to be. So, whoever had climbed down – or had climbed up from the foot of the corrie, he recognised that could be a possibility also– had been on their own, which struck him as a little odd. He could imagine climbing clubs taking on the challenge of the ascent or descent, but they would normally make the attempt with at least one buddy, for sensible safety reasons. He took out his phone and snapped a couple of them, although doubting if they had any relevance to Gina's death. But then, something else attracted his attention, a little flash of colour just on the edge of his peripheral vision. Spinning round to get a closer look, he saw it was a small patch of cloth that had snagged on a particularly jagged rock, the patch a vivid shade of red. Carefully he picked it up and scrutinised it. The material had the look and feel of the water-and-wind-proof fabric used on high-performance outdoor clothing, of the sort he himself was wearing that day. Someone had been here and torn their jacket on a rock, probably much to their annoyance, given the eyewatering cost of these upmarket garments. He tucked the patch into a pocket and then turned his mind to the ascent.

***

The climb back up the corrie was completed without drama, and with the return hike to the carpark start-point essentially downhill and therefore able to be accomplished just about on automatic pilot, he was able to do some serious thinking about the two baffling murders. As far as Gordon Baird was concerned, there might have been a ton of folks in the world with a ton of motives to kill him, but he was only on that mountain because he'd panicked after Naomi Neilson's body was discovered in his hotel room. No-one could have predicted he would have done that, and so there was no way that his murder could have been premeditated. Worse still, the list of possible suspects wasn't a list at all since it had only one name on it, that of Robert Harrison, who tragically had died himself on that day, and whose body had never been found. *Could* he have killed Baird, perhaps because of some argument that had sprung up when they unexpectedly met at the edge of Coire Bhrochain? Then, his mind in turmoil after what he had done, had he made some fatal mistake leading to his own death? Jimmy had gone over this scenario in his head a hundred times in the preceding days but no matter how hard he tried, he just couldn't come up with any other explanation. *Harrison and Baird had a fall-out. Harrison shoved Baird over the edge with great force, killing him. Later, Harrison died in an accident. End of story.* That must have been what happened, and it had bugger-all to do with Naomi Neilson's death. *Fact*.

Discouraged, Jimmy parked that matter and turned his attention to Gina McQuarrie. *Her* death was premeditated, there was no doubt about that, because she had broadcast to half the world her intention of making a solo expedition to Braeriach. Pre-armed with this knowledge, her killer could easily have lain in wait for her before pushing her to her death. That was one of the perils of fame of course, that you might attract the attention of some inadequate nutter who wanted to make his mark on the world by doing you harm. There was nothing he could do to investigate that himself, but maybe Eleanor Campbell could work some of her cyber-magic, to see if some saddo had been looking at Gina's Facebook page a hundred times a day or sending her disturbing messages. When he got back to civilisation, he would ring Frank and see if the IT wizard could look into that.

It took about fifty minutes to reach Cairn Gorm, and suddenly fancying a quick coffee, he decided to detour via the Ptarmigan restaurant. As it came into view, he noticed a team of workmen who appeared to be carrying out some unspecified operations on the elevated concrete track of the funicular railway just where it entered the adjacent top station. In true British fashion, only one of the hi-viz-jacketed workers seemed to be doing anything, the other three standing with hands on hips, no doubt offering sage advice to their colleague. But if this was an indication that the system was to be brought back to life, then it was a development to be applauded, although he noted the name of a prominent English civil engineering firm on the back of the men's jackets. Smiling to himself, he pushed open the sturdy door and joined a short queue at the counter. On a whim, he ordered a hot chocolate and accompanied it with a chocolate bar, a twin choice he knew would have met the approval of his brother. The restaurant was near empty, and he found a window table that afforded a fine view down the mountain, where beautiful Loch Morlich could be seen glistening in the distance under the weak sun. Just as he sat down, his phone rang. It was Frida.

'Hi darling,' she said brightly. *'I thought I'd just give you a quick call to see how you've got on.'*

His heart gave a skip at the sound of her voice. 'Aye, not bad thanks. Cleared a few things in my head I suppose, although I'm not sure I've really made any progress. Looking forward to getting back though. Should be no more than two hours I hope, traffic permitting. And thanks for calling, it's lovely to hear your voice. Even although it's only six hours since I last heard it,' he added, laughing.

'Actually, I didn't really call to ask you how you'd got on,' she said, with a discernible note of mischief.

'No? So why did you call?' he asked.

She giggled. *'Just to say it's steak for tea. Hurry back.'*

After they'd hung up, it was as if someone had taken a jet-wash to his head, blasting away the fog that had stopped him thinking clearly. Because suddenly, he started to see things in a different light. With Gina, whilst it was true that she had broadcast her plans to her legion of social media followers, he realised that what she had posted was bereft of the details that any would-be stalker would require to be able to ambush her on the mountain. *Expedition to Braeriach next Monday, Excited! Can't wait!* That was all she had posted. No timetable, and more importantly, no details of the route she intended to take, so no one would have known if she was intending to start from Glen Einich or tackle it from the Cairn Gorm direction. Whereas on the mountain rescue service's database, she had, as was recommended, posted full details. And now Jimmy's mind was cast back to his first meeting with the rescue team in the pub in Aviemore. Craig, that was the guy's name, the guy that had made him slightly uncomfortable with his effusive eulogies about the dead woman. It was a crazy thought of course, but any of these mountain rescue guys would have had access to the database, and so would have known her route and timetable in advance. *Including Craig.* He smiled wryly to himself as he reflected that he, Jimmy Stewart, a supposed crack member of Maggie Bainbridge's team of super-sleuths, didn't even know the guy's surname.

But it was on the Gordon Baird case where the epiphany hit him like a train powering out of a tunnel, and already he was kicking himself about how *stupid* he had been up until now. *The thing was, he had been looking at it completely the wrong way round.* Ever since he'd spoken to Liz Thompson of the Aberdeen University hiking club, it had seemed so so obvious that Robert Harrison was the only person who could possibly have murdered Gordon Baird.

Except, he now realised, that premise was complete and utter horlicks. Now, he urgently needed to speak with Maggie and Frank and Lexy, whom, he hoped, could provide answers to the tsunami of questions now rushing round his head.

Answers, he was sure, that would be the key to unlocking the whole case.

Chapter 23

McQuarrie financial cyber-hack complete. Have news. Don't call right now. Busy.

The WhatsApp from Eleanor was both typically short-and-not-sweet and deliberately phrased to wind him up, but it contained sufficient portent of a positive outcome such that Frank felt compelled to call her right away, despite her rejoinder to the contrary. He didn't expect her to answer, but to his surprise, she did, responding with a terse and entirely characteristic *what?*

'Got your message Eleanor, I'm excited,' he said. 'So, what's the big news you've got for me? Come on, don't keep me in suspense.'

'I would have called you if I'd time to talk, like obviously. But I haven't.'

'But yet here we are, talking,' he said, struggling to suppress a laugh. 'Come on, *please.* You can speak at lightning speed, and I promise not to interrupt, not even once.'

'You always promise that and you always interrupt,' she said sourly.

'But I *really* promise this time, honest. Look, go ahead. I won't say another word from this second unless you ask me to. Other than the occasional point of clarification,' he added, to clarify, 'which I think is allowed under the rules.'

There was a silence at the end of the phone before she finally said, '*It was like an amazingly complicated trail to follow.*' Again, she was silent, as if tempting him to speak, but he wasn't falling for that, not this early in proceedings. He let her continue. '*The McQuarries have six different bank accounts,*' she said, '*because Sir Andrew and Gina both have limited company accounts and Gina has another LLP with Rhona Fraser and that's got a separate account too. And one's in Jersey.*'

It was a little disconcerting hearing her speak of the deceased Gina and Rhona in the present tense, but he certainly wasn't going to pull her up on that one. Biting his lip, he waited for her to continue.

'*The total banking assets of the pair prior to a transaction that occurred eleven weeks ago was nine-hundred and thirty-five thousand, two hundred and forty-six pounds,*' she said, sounding as if she was reading from notes. Startled by the huge amount, he felt a *bloody hell* coming on but just about managed to keep it to himself.

'*After that transaction, the balance on all accounts was three hundred and thirty-six thousand exactly. That transaction was made first by transferring from the Jersey-*

based LLP into an account in the name of Sir Andrew, and then out to the recipient entity.'

Mentally, he did the calculation. Near enough six hundred thousand had been paid out of their accounts, which was a bloody giant sum by anyone's standards. He assumed if he was able to maintain his patience, Eleanor would tell him who the beneficiary was. But he couldn't.

'Bloody hell,' he exclaimed. 'That's a shedload of money Eleanor. So where did it go? I presume you know?'

'It wasn't easy,' she said, *'but yeah, I know. It went to a company,'* she continued. *'A company called Gregory & Clarke Trading Ltd, which is owned by another company called Gregory & Clarke Group Holdings Ltd. Which is owned by a company called Gregory & Clarke Partners, which is registered offshore. In the Cayman Islands.'*

He felt his heart sinking a little at this news. They'd been through this sort of stuff many times before, he and Eleanor, and he knew exactly how difficult it could be to track down the individual or individuals behind this kind of financial pyramid. Which of course was the whole reason it had been set up that way in the first place.

'And no idea of who's behind these organisations I guess?' he said.

'That's like interesting,' she said, which was as unexpected as it was enigmatic. *'There were no directors listed in the Cayman parent company of course. That's like standard practice.'*

And she was right of course, it was standard practice, if financial obfuscation was your objective. Two UK registered companies, one an operating unit, one a holding company, the latter recorded as the sole shareholder of the former, the latter in turn by an anonymous Cayman-registered corporate entity. Interested law-enforcement agencies might be able to see how the money flowed, but it was a lot more difficult if not impossible to see who it was flowing *to*. Except, Eleanor had used the word *interesting*. In the next few seconds, he hoped to find out why. Except, she evidently had more to bring to the discussion before that revelation.

'I looked at all their bank accounts from eight years ago too, like you asked,' she continued, *'and two things were like mega-interesting. First, they had a lot more money then, like nearly five million. And second, it was all in the Gina and Rhona LLP company. A lot of it invested in US securities, not cash.'*

That was certainly interesting, he thought, in so much that it showed just how much the two young violinists must have made from Skye Lament and all its spin-offs. Back then, Sir Andrew's groundbreaking economic theory had been in the public domain for less than a year, so had presumably not yet turned into the money-maker it was subsequently to become.

'But they needed cash I thought?' he asked quickly. 'And by the way, that was a clarification, not an interruption.'

'Yeah, they did,' Eleanor agreed, evidently having already forgotten about her no-interruptions directive. *'I traced the transactions they made on their stock-trading platform. They held a lot of tech stocks which had done quite well, but the Dow Jones was in a downturn. No-one was selling shares at that point in time, but I guess they had like no choice. They sold three hundred thousand pounds of stock in one day. Two years later they would have been worth a million, maybe more.'*

'But something was forcing them to sell,' he said, thinking out loud. 'Something both urgent and bloody compelling too.'

'I don't know anything about that,' Eleanor said. *'But the money was transferred the same day to Gregory & Clarke Trading.'*

'Okay,' he said. 'And were you able to find out anything about this Gregory & Clarke outfit? Like what their business is or anything like that?'

'I checked first with Companies House,' she answered. *'Both the operating company and the holding company are late with filing their accounts and their annual report. Three years late in both cases. In fact, they've only twice filed accounts, once ten years ago and once six years ago. It's a thing,'* she added.

'What do you mean, a thing?'

'It's what you do if you want to avoid financial scrutiny. It's breaking the law, technically, but they give you like a gazillion warnings before they take any real action.'

'Sounds well dodgy,' Frank mused. 'And as to their business, any clue to what that is?'

'I looked up their Articles of Association,' she replied. *'No clue there. Both set up as off-the-shelf companies that could be in any business.'*

Frank nodded ruefully. 'Aye, that's standard practice as well. Particularly popular amongst our organised crime fraternity.'

'But they did make one schoolboy error,' she said, then immediately fell silent.

He laughed. 'You're a wee devil Eleanor Campbell, so you are, and I know you're doing this deliberately to raise my heart rate. So come on, tell me. What was this schoolboy error of which you have just spoken?'

'It's like quite complicated.'

'I wouldn't expect anything else,' he said, still laughing. 'Now come on, bloody well get on with it.'

'The firms that offer these company registration services set up like hundreds and hundreds of companies in advance and invent cool names that make them sound more important or longer-established than they are.'

'Like Gregory & Clarke.'

'Exactly. And they advertise. On the internet. So I searched. And I found an advert from ten years ago. Placed by a firm called Capital Corporate Services. And they have an office and they're like still in business. In Peckham.' It had taken her about two seconds flat to spit out the torrent of words, and he furrowed his brow, struggling to process exactly what she had just told him.

'Eleanor, this is bloody fantastic work,' he managed as he cottoned on. 'This means we can go and knock on the door of this Peckham outfit and see if they have any records of who bought the shell companies. Bloody fantastic work,' he repeated.

'*Ronnie already has,*' she said, her tone throwaway, as if the information was of no consequence.

'Sorry, did you say that Frenchie's already been to see these guys?' he said, open-mouthed.

'*Like yeah. And it's guy, not guys. And the guy's a girl. Or more like a woman actually. That's what Ronnie told me.*'

'What, you two have already been *discussing* all this?' he said, shaking his head. 'Without *me*?' He laughed again. 'Great use of the old initiative, the pair of you. So how did the boy Ronnie get on? Did he find out anything, do you know?'

'*You can ask him yourself,*' she said. '*He's here. I'll put us on speakerphone.*'

'*Morning guv,*' French boomed. '*Yeah, like Eleanor told you, I called in on these Capital Corporate Service geezers yesterday, over in Peckham. They've got one of them shopfront offices on the High Street.*'

'Not one of Del-Boy's ventures, was it?' Frank said, knowing Eleanor would be oblivious to the cultural reference.

'*Nah guv, don't think so,*' he laughed. '*But they do all sorts. Photocopying, passport photos, overseas money transfers, that kind of malarkey. Run by a nice woman called Chandra Singh. Been in the business nearly twenty years she told me.*'

'Dodgy would you say?'

'Nah, I'd say she was legit. A nice old bird trying to make an honest living. There's dozens of these registered office plaques plastered all over the front of her place by the way. She does that too, as part of her company services thing. Acts as the registered office for all sorts of businesses.'

Frank nodded. 'By law, companies need to a have a sign on the wall of their registered office, don't they, even if they don't conduct any business there? And the practice isn't iffy, because I happen to know that some of the biggest companies in the country have their registered office at their lawyers' or accountants' offices. It just makes their statutory admin load a lot easier. Although I doubt that's why our boys Gregory & Clarke are doing it.'

'No, I doubt it too guv,' French agreed. *'I'd say it was all about hiding the paper trail in their case. But they didn't hide it well enough,'* he added, his tone betraying the slightest hint of self-satisfaction, which was not like the unassuming DC at all. Which meant that whatever he'd discovered, it must have been something big, and Frank was now desperate to find out what it was.

'So come on Frenchie, don't do that Campbell thing and stretch it out for ever,' he said. 'You need to tell me what you found out, and you need to tell me right now.'

'*I will guv,*' French said, '*but I can tell you right away, you won't bloody adam-and-eve it. No way. It's mental, it really is.*'

Frank laughed. 'Well, if I ever get to hear it, I can tell you if I agree with you or not. So bloody get on with it.'

'*Sure guv. It turns out that Mrs Singh keeps excellent records and was able to tell me that the two UK Gregory & Clarke companies were purchased for four hundred and fifty quid on the 15th of July 2013, paid for by a credit card in the name of P D Berrycloth. Peter David Berrycloth.*'

Before Frank could say anything, Eleanor cut in. '*Then Ronnie asked me if I could find any records of the Berrycloth dude.*'

'That's nice,' Frank said sardonically. 'And did you? Find any records of this dude, as you call him?'

'*Yeah, I did, and it was like mega-interesting. Because I didn't actually have to do a database search at all. Which saved me like a ton of coding.*'

'Sorry, I don't think I'm following you,' Frank said, trying hard to keep his growing exasperation in check. But he knew from bitter experience that it didn't pay to try and chivvy along the tetchy Forensic Officer. Eleanor divulged information at her own pace or not at all, and you just had to put up with that, if you didn't want to start the third world war.

'I also completed that other exercise you asked me to, to compare these two Cambridge Electoral databases, you remember? The one from now and the one from eight years ago? Where we were looking for dudes who hadn't moved house in that period? And who lived within ten minutes' walk of the last seven bus-stops on the number three route?'

'Aye, I remember.'

'*He was on the list*,' she said. '*Peter David Berrycloth. 125 Aldeburgh Crescent.*'

'Bloody hell,' Frank exclaimed. 'This guy lives in *Cambridge*? And are we sure it's the same guy? Although there can't be too many Peter Berrycloths in the country I would imagine.'

'*It's the same guy, defo*,' Eleanor confirmed. '*I checked the address that was registered against the credit card. I also checked the Cambridge Council Tax database too, and he moved to that address ten years ago. And I checked the Land Registry database to find out how much he paid for the property...*'

'Bloomin' heck.' Frank said, 'you've been busy. And by the way, this isn't an interruption. This is a wee pat on the back, which I think you'll find is allowed under the rules of engagement.'

'... *which was three hundred and ninety-two thousand pounds,*' she continued, with a perceptible softening in her tone. '*Which is quite a lot.*'

'So what the hell are you waiting for then Ronnie?' Frank said excitedly. 'Clamp the wee blue light on top of your motor and get up there pronto.'

'*Too late guv,*' French said laconically.

'What do you mean, too late?'

'*Didn't I tell you guv that you wouldn't believe my story?*' French replied, a discernible note of triumph in his voice. '*And when I tell you this, I'll have slam-dunk proved it.*' He paused for a second then continued, '*You see, Peter Berrycloth's the geezer who got murdered last week. Stabbed four times in the chest then chucked into the Cam.*'

***

It was the most unbelievable development, causing Frank to recall with amusement a throwaway comment he had made earlier in the case, that they were now in the hands of Eleanor Campbell and Ronnie French as far as making any progress with the investigation was concerned. Well, the dynamic duo had come good, with the sensational revelation that a random Cambridge murder victim wasn't random at all but was seemingly intimately connected to their investigation. Furthermore, with the guy's connection to the McQuarries unveiled, there had to be a greater than even chance that Berrycloth was the man that Rhona Fraser and Olivia Cranston had followed onto that same late-night bus, eight years apart. The man would have friends and workmates in Cambridge and perhaps a wife or partner too, and in no time at all Ronnie and Lexy would be asking them the questions that would unravel all the details of his life. There was a bleaker consequence to the discovery though, because Frank had a feeling in his gut that this man's murder made it more likely that Rhona Fraser and Olivia Cranston had been murdered too. But by whom, that was the question? Right at this moment he hadn't the faintest idea, but he wasn't worried about that. The key thing was that the investigation was finally going to pick up pace, and soon all the pieces would nicely fall into place, like they always did. And there was something else too, a thought that suddenly brought a smile to his face. It had emerged that Sir Andrew and Gina McQuarrie had had a very close financial connection to a series of companies seemingly set up by Peter Berrycloth, and now the man had been killed. That meant that it was now perfectly legitimate for the police to question Sir Andrew, and goodness, didn't he have some difficult ones to answer? For an enjoyable half an hour Frank let the ins and outs of the investigation circle round his head, as he slowly started to knock the disparate strands into some sort of coherent shape. So engrossed was he in this absorbing task that it was another thirty minutes before something startling - and a fact that had slipped his mind completely - suddenly leapt up and metaphorically slapped him in the face.

Gina McQuarrie's maiden name was Berrycloth.

Chapter 24

It didn't take Maggie long to recognise that the further sensational developments in Cambridge meant there would have to be some significant changes to the plan she'd agreed with Frank only a few days earlier. Specifically, with Andrew McQuarrie now connected to the murder of the mysterious Peter Berrycloth, he was now a person of interest for that crime and any interviews that took place from now on would be one hundred percent the responsibility of the police. Nor would it be Frank's new cold-case team who would be leading these interviews either. That would fall within the bailiwick of the Cambridge murder squad, and in fact she had already learned from her husband that they were sending a detective up the next day to question the economist. She smiled again as she thought about the craziness of Frank Stewart being her husband, a reality she still sometimes found hard to believe, despite that unarguable fact that she had definitely been the bride at the wedding, and it had been the happiest day of her life too. But was that amazing day soon to be relegated to an honourable second place, she wondered, should their quest for a baby come to fruition? That would be too wonderful for words, and immediately she banished the thought from her mind, worried that the very act of thinking about it would somehow jinx the likelihood of it coming true. Not that she and Frank weren't making a concerted effort to *make* it come true, her somewhat bleary-eyed appearance this morning a pleasant testament to that fact.

To add to her excitement, Jimmy had evidently made discoveries up on bleak Braeriach of almost equal significance, and later that day there would be a call with Frank's team to work out how to proceed with them. But before then, there was work to be done, and important work at that. *They were getting close to the solution.* She could feel it in her bones, and even although she didn't have a clue right now what that solution was, she was certain that two important meetings that were happening later that day would cause much of it to cascade into place. Conveniently, and remarkably too, these encounters were to happen simultaneously, because for the first time ever, Maggie was entrusting a major assignment to her new assistant Lori Logan, who was to have a phone conversation with Gina McQuarrie's sister Laura McColl. Lori's mission, putting it bluntly, was to find out who the *hell* Peter Berrycloth was. Because with an unusual surname like that, it was surely odds-on that he and Gina were related in some way, particularly since information had just come in from Ronnie French that 'the dead geezer was another Jock', to quote the DC verbatim. He wasn't her brother, they knew that, Laura being her only sibling. A cousin perhaps, or maybe even an uncle? Hopefully, Lori would find out, which would see another piece of the jigsaw clicking into place. Now Maggie was heading back over to Bearsden, for a second meeting with Bill and Patricia Neilson. She wasn't at all sure how she would be received, given on her last visit she had raised their hopes that their daughter's case would be re-opened, only for these hopes to be dashed by Assistant Chief Constable White. Still, she would just have to deal with that, and at least she could bring some news that White's decision might yet be reversed, given what Jimmy had worked out following his third visit up Braeriach.

It was Patricia Neilson who answered the ring on the doorbell. The woman was probably in her mid to late fifties, Maggie had calculated, based on her daughter's age, but today she looked a good decade older. Silver-haired, her lined and haggard face showed every inch of the suffering she must have endured this past decade. Her daughter had been beautiful, and it was likely the mother had been the same, but that beauty would have vanished on the day she and her husband received the terrible news that every parent dreaded.

'Come in Maggie,' Patricia said. 'It's just me today. Bill's gone to the golf. He's there a lot,' she added, her voice betraying no reproach. Even if she resented her husband's frequent absences, Maggie doubted that this defeated woman would have any stomach left for a fight.

'Thank you Patricia, it's good of you to see me,' Maggie said, following her host down the hall to the living-room. 'And I'm sorry we had that setback about reopening Naomi's case. But since we last spoke, there have been further developments. I don't want to raise your hopes again, but it's a promising line of enquiry I think.'

'That's good,' the woman said, her tone listless, then gestured to the sofa. 'Please, sit down.'

This time it seemed there was to be no offer of tea or coffee, not that Maggie wanted either. But it was perhaps an indication of Patricia Neilson's state of mind, engulfed in a suffocating melancholy that made even the simplest everyday tasks impossibly difficult to face.

'I won't take up too much of your time Patricia,' Maggie said quietly, 'because I know how painful it must be to talk about Naomi.'

The woman's eyes seemed to brighten a little. 'It is painful, but it's nice too. It helps me remember her. I often close my eyes and picture her sitting over there as a little girl, in her pyjamas, eating her toast and drinking her milk. It was our routine, every night before bedtime.' She gave a short laugh. 'We were still doing it when she was eight or nine. Daft I know, but it was so lovely.'

'That must have been *so* nice,' Maggie said, feeling a lump in her throat. She wanted to tell this sad woman that she too had a child and that at the age of eight, her darling Ollie still had *his* toast before bed, and that her husband Frank often tried to sneak him a caramel wafer to go with it. But she held back, suspecting that rather than creating a bonding moment, it might cause Patricia Neilson to return to her terrible loss. 'And Patricia, I want to talk, if I may, about something I know you must be incredibly proud of. I'm meaning Naomi's academic achievements and particularly her final year at university.'

Patricia smiled. 'She was a very clever girl you know. And she was very diligent about her studies, never mind what her father says or thinks.'

Maggie remembered that on her last visit there had been some conflict between the couple on the subject and resolved to choose her words carefully. 'Naomi got a first-class honours, and that's an exceptional achievement from a university like Glasgow. Especially in a complex subject like Economics. She must have been a very hard worker.'

The woman nodded slowly. 'Bill's right, although I would never let him hear me say it. She loved dancing and she loved drinking and yes, she loved boys...'

'Pardon me for interrupting,' Maggie said, giving the woman a warm smile. 'You're describing a young woman who loved life. And bringing her up to feel that way is an achievement you should be very proud of Patricia.'

She nodded. 'You're right of course Maggie. But Naomi wasn't really a hard worker I'm afraid. She was gifted at everything she did and relied on that to scrape through her exams, right from when she was at school. That was why she had her panic attacks in her final year.'

Maggie gave her a surprised look. 'I didn't know Naomi of course, but that doesn't seem like her, not from what you and your husband have told me about her.'

'No, it wasn't like her at all,' Naomi's mother agreed. 'But she was so set on winning that higher degree research place at Oxford, but she needed a first to get in. She shared a flat in Hillhead, but she always came back to stay with us for a few days at Christmas, and that year she was in a terrible state. She'd made a bit of a mess of the mid-year exams and was predicted to just scrape an upper second.'

'It happens to lots of students in their final year,' Maggie said sympathetically. 'The sudden realisation that there's a mountain of work to get through and not much time in which to do it.'

'That was exactly where Naomi was. She was in despair, and I'd never seen her like that before. It was heartbreaking for Bill and me.'

'And yet she got her first in the end.'

Patricia laughed. 'Yes, she did. And that was Naomi all over. She was always skating on thin ice but somehow the ice never cracked.' She stopped abruptly. 'Until it did of course,' she added, her voice fading to a sad whisper.

'I presume that Oxford University did award Naomi her place, since she had achieved the entry qualifications?' Maggie asked.

'They did. They wrote us a very nice letter after they found out about her death, saying how much they'd been excited by her dissertation and how much they had been looking forward to her joining the faculty. It was a great comfort to both Bill and me.'

'It would be nice to see that,' Maggie said, 'and the dissertation too, that would be really interesting. Although I won't understand a word of it of course.'

The woman shrugged. 'It's in her old room somewhere, in that great pile of boxes.' She nodded in the direction of the hallway. 'I don't go in there. Bill got me a cleaning lady and she goes in from time to time to dust.'

Maggie took a breath then said quietly, 'Patricia, would you mind if I went and looked for it? I'll try not to disturb anything.'

'Do what you like,' she answered. 'I won't ever be going in there again. Two of her flatmates packed all her things in boxes and brought them round. They've been lying there ever since.' She raised her arm and pointed down the hall. 'It's the second door on the left. It's still got her name plaque on the door from when she was little. It's a *My Little Pony* one,' she added sadly. 'She used to love them. These and Sylvanian Families. She had them all.'

'That's really nice Patricia,' Maggie said, giving a half-smile as she stood up. 'And thank you for letting me look in Naomi's room. I won't be long.'

The door to the room was slightly ajar, allowing Maggie to open it with a gentle push, which somehow felt appropriately respectful. The Neilsons had lived in this house over thirty years she had learned, and so this would have been their daughter's room since birth. The decor reflected the girl's journey from baby to teenager, the wallpaper a vivid pink, dotted with wispy white clouds and floating teddy-bears holding bunches of balloons. But now much of it was obscured by posters of already-forgotten boy bands, interspersed with images of Taylor Swift in her early teenage country-singer phase, wearing a Stetson and clutching a National guitar. The quilt cover on the single bed matched the wallpaper but was faded after years of service, hinting that it had been a favourite of the dead girl. A trio of smiling soft toys sat side-by-side in front of the pillow, probably unmoved since the day Naomi left for university. In the corner were the objects that Maggie was most interested in. Five plastic storage boxes, stacked in two piles, and evidently untouched since being packed up and delivered by Naomi's flatmates, a task that must have been traumatic for the youngsters who would still have been grieving their murdered friend. She took the lid off the box at the top of the first pile and peered inside. Just clothes, bundled and crushed down to fit into the confined space available. Maggie replaced the lid then lifted the box onto the floor. The second box contained more of the same and was quickly dismissed. The third, at the bottom of the pile, contained only textbooks. There was more than a dozen of them, she estimated, and probably quite valuable too, and she wondered if she ought to offer to help Mrs Neilson to sell them, since the woman had made it clear she would never again set foot in the room. That would be something she would ponder, but now there were just two boxes left to examine. Maggie removed the lid from the first of the two and scrutinised the contents. This looked more promising; a neatly stacked pile of yellow A4 booklets, which on closer inspection turned out to be examination papers, marked and returned to Naomi Neilson, the grade which had been awarded by the markers hand-written in red ink on the front. She picked up a few at random and looked at the grades - some 'Bs', a couple of 'Cs' and one 'Pass', which presumably was just enough to scrape through but unworthy of a specific grade. This for the girl who had been conferred a first-class honours degree, which would have enabled her to take up a prestigious post-graduate research place at Oxford had she lived. She lifted the rest of the papers from the box and set them down at the foot of the bed.

Now only one item remained in the container, a navy-blue ring binder stamped with the crest of the university. Maggie picked it up and read the title, which had been typed on a slip of paper and slid into a transparent pocket on the front of the binder. Her heart began to beat a little faster as she realised she had found what she was looking for. *This was it, the thesis that Naomi had submitted in support of her application to Oxford University.* It was a thick document, five hundred pages or more she estimated, but she had no interest in opening it, let alone reading it.

Because the title told her everything she needed to know.

***

Lori had called just as Maggie left the Neilsons' home, and they quickly decided to rendezvous at the Bikini Barista cafe for a full update of the girl's conversation with Gina McQuarrie's sister. Fifteen minutes later they were camped up at a window table. As fortification, coffee and iced gingerbread squares had been ordered, the latter a delicacy that Frank had recommended to her a while back and to which she was now seriously addicted.

'How did you get on at the Neilsons?' Lori asked. 'Find what you were looking for?'

Maggie gave a huge smile of satisfaction. 'I did, yes, hidden away at the bottom of a box where it had been lying for ten years.'

'Does that mean...?' her associate asked, wide-eyed with astonishment.

'Yeah, it bloody does,' Maggie said. 'And what about you? Have you found out who our Peter Berrycloth guy is?'

'Aye well, yes and no,' Lori said. 'It's a bit complicated and I don't think I've been able to figure it all out yet. But Laura was really helpful. She's staying at the McQuarries' house for a couple of weeks by the way, with her kids. She said the McQuarrie twins are really struggling with the death of their mum and Sir Andrew was desperate for some help.'

'Yes, I can understand that,' Maggie said. 'When my first husband was killed it was so traumatic for Ollie. I wouldn't have survived without my mum by my side.'

'It's the twins' birthday in a couple of days, and they're having a party in a wee hall in Milngavie,' Lori explained. 'Laura's got the job of organising it. It's a kind of leaving party too, since they'll be heading off to America soon.'

Maggie nodded. 'They're teenagers, aren't they? It'll be good to give them something big to focus on I guess. Poor kids,' she added. 'Anyway, tell me what you found out, and if it's complicated, maybe we can figure it out together.'

Lori nodded. 'Right. Well, there *are* other Berrycloths in their family, Laura told me. Remember, her and her sister's parents moved up to Newtonmore from Kent, and that was nearly fifty years ago. Her dad Simon is eighty-three now incidentally and still going strong, although they lost their mum three years ago. But the thing is, their dad had an older brother. His name was Paul, although he's dead now.'

'And he was a Berrycloth, obviously,' Maggie interjected. 'Paul Berrycloth.'

'Right. He and his wife stayed in Kent, and they had a son. Just the one.'

Maggie gave her a look. 'Surely it can't be as simple as that. Is *he* Peter Berrycloth? The son?'

Lori shook her head and sighed. 'He's *a* Peter Berrycloth. But he's not our guy.' She paused for a moment. 'Remember DC French found out the guy murdered in Cambridge was Scottish? Or a Jock as he put it?'

'And this son of Paul obviously isn't Scottish,' Maggie said, disappointed. She frowned. 'He's Gina and Laura's cousin of course, isn't he? I must admit, I always find these relationship things are always so hard to get straight in your head. Does Laura still see her cousin, did she say? And did Gina keep up with him too?'

'It's quite a sad story,' Lori said. 'Peter was disabled from birth, both mentally and physically unfortunately. The two girls did visit him during their childhood, and they kept it up when they were adults too. Peter's in a care home now in Kent and has been for more than ten years. Laura told me that Gina and her husband had to organise it after his father and mother died. They actually died within months of one another and so there was no-one to look after their son.'

'What a sad story. And there's no other strands of the family that Laura knows of? Even distant relatives?'

'No, she didn't think so. Berrycloth's a very unusual name and I Googled it. But not much comes up. Nothing you could connect to the family.'

Maggie sighed. 'Well at least we've eliminated that link, and I suppose the Cambridge murder squad will be tracing the dead man's nearest and dearest as part of their extensive enquiries. I'm sure they'll find out who this man was.' She looked up and smiled. 'Anyway, here's the excellent Stevie on his way with our order. Maybe some caffeine and calories are what we need to turbo-charge our brain cells.'

The proprietor greeted them in his customary ebullient manner as he laid their order on the table. 'Here you go, youse guys. Two double-strength americanos and two double-size gingerbread squares with the super-thick icing on top.'

'Thanks Stevie, you're a lifesaver,' Maggie said, amused, 'but did we order the double-size? I don't think we did.'

'That's your wee loyalty upgrade,' he said, grinning. 'But you can pretend they're still the normal-size ones in disguise if you like. Then they'll only have half the calories.'

She laughed. 'I wish. But maybe I'll take half home for Frank. Or maybe I won't. What do you think Lori?'

Glancing up, she saw her young associate was deep in thought.

'No, it *cannae* just be a coincidence,' she said emphatically, her stare out the window evidencing that she was thinking out loud. 'That murdered guy has this dodgy connection to Gina McQuarrie, then suddenly he turns out to be a Berrycloth? No *way* can that be a coincidence.'

Then suddenly, Maggie saw it too. Excitedly she said, 'Lori, if you want to prove that you are who you say you are, what do you need? If you want to open a bank account for example, or rent a flat or buy a car or get a job?'

'ID?' Lori offered. 'A passport or a driving licence?'

Maggie nodded. 'Good good. And what do you need to get a passport?'

Lori shrugged. 'A birth certificate I suppose.'

'Yes, good. But what else?'

The girl shrugged again. 'I don't know Maggie. I give up.'

'You need someone to vouch for you. Someone who's known you for a while.' Maggie paused then gave a knowing smile.

'Someone like a cousin or her husband for instance.'

Chapter 25

Twenty-four hours after his last trip up Braeriach, Jimmy's brain hadn't stopped spinning, and now he hoped the upcoming conference call with Maggie and Frank would either make everything click into place, or at least suggest a plan of action to make it do so. Before that visit, he'd been metaphorically lost in the dark as far as both killings had been concerned, but now, he at least had theories for both. Admittedly, they were little more than skeletons at the moment, but they were skeletons he hoped his colleagues would be able to put some flesh on. On cue, his phone rang, the video opening up with a familiar ding, which revealed Maggie and his brother sitting side-by-side, the venue evidently once again the Bikini Barista cafe. He greeted them warmly then said, laughing,

'Honestly Frank, I don't know why you didn't just buy the place off Stevie instead of wasting all that taxpayers' money on that new place up the town.

'The taxpayers are already paying for the other place, otherwise I would have,' his brother answered. 'Anyway, I hear you've been ranging across the mountains again in pursuit of justice, and with some success too. I got the gist of it from that last text of yours, but Maggie and I would like to hear it from the horse's mouth if you don't mind.'

'Yes sure,' Jimmy said. 'Coming to Gina first, what I found out has cemented my murder theory. It's not bollocks like your Police Scotland colleagues say it is, I'm sure of that now.'

'Something about a piece of fabric, is that right?' Maggie asked. 'That you found on the ledge?'

He nodded. 'That's right. It was red Gortex, and after I got back, I rang one of the mountain rescue guys who found her body. He confirmed that the jacket she was wearing was red and it was a Gortex fabric. It doesn't mean for sure that the piece is from her jacket of course, but we can ask her husband to show us it, see if it's got a tear in it. I assume he still has it.'

'I would think so,' Frank said. 'And he's fair game now, as far as questioning is concerned. You can leave that one with me, no problem.'

'The other thing though is even more significant I think,' Jimmy continued.

'You found footprints on the ledge, didn't you?' Maggie interjected.

He nodded again. 'That's right. And they looked quite fresh, although to be fair, I'm no expert. But what if they're the footprints of the murderer?'

'I'm not sure I'm quite with you here,' Frank said, looking puzzled. 'What's your theory?'

'My theory is that the murderer pushed Gina over the edge of the corrie, but with insufficient force to clear the ledge. He would have been worried that the fall might not have killed her, so he climbed down to the ledge, and then pushed her off to finish the job. And he wouldn't have wanted to hang about at the scene, which explains why he didn't spot the swatch of fabric caught on the jagged rock.'

'Yeah, I could see how that could happen,' Maggie said, 'And by the way, I assume we're not ruling out that the murderer might be a woman? It's just that you were using the word *he* all through your explanation.'

'No, you're right, it could be a woman, quite easily,' he conceded. 'But one thing that I did conclude was that since Gina's murder was premeditated, it needed to be done by someone who had access to the mountain rescue service's database. That's where she posted her detailed itinerary, and so anyone with access would have known in advance the route she planned to take.'

'Right,' Maggie said. 'And I assume they must keep logs of who accessed the system on a particular day? And when I say they, what I actually mean is the system must keep a log.' She paused for a moment. 'So how do we get access to that log? I assume they won't just dish it out to anyone.'

Jimmy grinned. 'That's where Frank comes in handy. He can get warrants and stuff like that to make them do it.'

Frank shrugged. 'That's true, but it'll be easier if I just get wee Lexy to ask them first. Most folks are happy to cooperate if they've got nothing to hide.'

'That's great,' Jimmy said. 'And just so you know, there's one guy in particular I'm interested in.'

'What, you've found a suspect too?' Maggie said, surprised. 'That's fast work.'

'I don't know if I'd go as far as calling him a suspect,' he said, 'but one of the guys who was in the rescue party that found Gina's body, a guy by the name of Craig Lochlan, well he was weirdly obsessed by Gina. I only met him the one time when the team were explaining what happened that day, but he was going on about how much he loved her music and how much he fancied her. It turned my stomach to be honest.'

'Doesn't mean he killed her, just because he's a fan,' Frank said, 'but we'll go and have a wee chat with this lad, definitely.'

'That would be great,' Jimmy said. 'But what about the bootprints? They could be evidence too, couldn't they?'

Frank sighed. 'Aye maybe, which is a bit of a bugger actually. The thing is, we've got specialist scene-of-crime officers who deal with that subject, but I don't know how many of them are mountaineers too.' He paused and sighed again. 'That's going to be an interesting conversation with ACC White, isn't it? *Excuse me ma'am but new evidence has come to light about the death of Gina McQuarrie, so I've got a wee request for you. Can I borrow a helicopter to drop one of our scene-of-crime specialists on to a dodgy ledge at the top of a mountain? We can fly him in from Inverness, it'll only cost about fifteen grand.*'

'Aye, very funny,' Jimmy said sarcastically. 'But I told you, I'm more certain than ever that Gina's death was murder, so you need to look at these prints. Definitely.'

Frank smiled. 'Calm down wee Jimmy. You're right, but we need to take this one step at a time. Step one, we ascertain that the swatch of fabric definitely came from Gina's walking jacket. Step two, if it did, then we can get the scene-of-crime guys involved.'

'And there's something else to consider, isn't there?' Maggie interjected. 'Because if Andrew McQuarrie has got *rid* of his wife's jacket, then that might be construed as suspicious.'

'Good point Maggie,' Frank agreed. 'And in fact, if either of these possibilities turns out to be true, then that would give me the ammunition I need to persuade the Assistant Chief Constable to parachute a boot-print guru onto that wee ledge.'

Maggie laughed. 'You never know, you might get lucky. You might find a boot-print guru who's a mountain goat as well.'

'Aye, and pigs might fly,' Frank said, 'if you'll excuse the terrible old cliché. But being serious, the situation regarding that red jacket will dictate where we can go next in the investigation. I'm not holding my breath mind, because it could have come from anybody's jacket'

'It's Gina's, I just know it is,' Maggie said firmly. 'One hundred percent.'

'Is that your woman's intuition thing kicking in again?' Frank said with a cautious grin.

She gave him a playful punch on the shoulder. 'Laugh if you like Frank Stewart, and okay, there is some intuition involved I admit. But look at it logically. She was wearing a red jacket, and it would have been a top-of the-range one given that walking was her passion. Then Jimmy's theory is that the murderer didn't push her hard enough to clear the ledge, so had to climb down to finish the job. It all fits, doesn't it?'

'A fair cop,' Frank conceded. 'Which hopefully will all become clearer after my wee conversation with Andrew

McQuarrie.' He paused for a moment. 'You know young Jimmy, this swatch-and-footprint thing could be quite a breakthrough. And now I'm hoping you've got something equally impressive to report on the Gordon Baird killing. In fact I'm kind of expecting you'll actually have solved it for us.'

'I think I have, as it happens,' Jimmy said, and he could tell from the sudden change to Maggie and Frank's expression this wasn't at all what they had been expecting.

'So tell us,' Maggie said. 'Don't keep us in suspense. Who did it, and how, and why?'

Jimmy smiled. 'To tell you all of that I just need the answer to one simple question. A question, I think, that only Sir Andrew McQuarrie can answer.'

Frank gave him a perplexed look, which quickly broke into a smile. 'Well that's handy, because me and a cop from Cambridge are seeing him tomorrow.'

Chapter 26

The Cambridgeshire murder squad had evidently decided that Sir Andrew McQuarrie was an interesting enough prospect to send the SIO himself up to Glasgow to conduct the interview. DCI Jeremy Black seemed a decent enough fella, Frank thought, having met him briefly to provide an update on what Ronnie and Eleanor had uncovered, but the guy had made it clear that it was his show and so it would be him who'd be asking the questions. Frank wasn't bothered, because he was only interested in the answers and was pleased enough that Black - *call me Jezzer mate, please*- had consented to him being in on the session, even if he suspected it was only to save the expense of sending someone else up from Cambridgeshire. McQuarrie would have worked out that it was serious too, having been instructed to present himself at New Gorbals police station in order to help the police with their enquiries, to do with a murder that had recently occurred down south.

DCI Black had driven up that morning for the two o'clock interview, and over a quick lunch in the station's canteen, had updated Frank on the progress they had made so far. In Frank's eyes, if he was to be critical, it wasn't overly impressive, with no motive yet uncovered, nor had any credible suspects been identified. They had however discovered that Peter Berrycloth owned a popular music venue in the city called the Cambridge Musician, and that was *very* interesting to Frank, because he recognised it as the place where Rhona Fraser had gone to a gig before her disappearance, and where Olivia Cranston had gone to see the folk singer Dan Jackson. Berrycloth had lived with his girlfriend in the Cherry Hinton suburb of the city, and they had been together just over two years. On interview, it turned out the girlfriend didn't know much about his background, other than he'd told her he was from Dundee – that assertion almost certainly a lie, Frank thought – and that he'd spent much of his twenties and early thirties bumming around South-East Asia. An unexpected inheritance from an aunt had brought him back to the UK, where he had used the money to set up the music venue. She didn't know why he had chosen Cambridge as his base, though speculated that he could have gone anywhere but saw that there was a gap in the market for such a venue in the city. Something else interesting had emerged from Jezzer's early investigations, and that was that the Cambridge Musician was owned by a company called Gregory & Clark.

The interview was not being recorded since McQuarrie was not under caution, but it was obvious that in all other respects DCI Black intended to treat it as if he was. He'd taken off his jacket, loosened his tie and rolled up his sleeves, and now sat with his elbows on the small table and his chin resting on his thumbs.

'Right then Andrew,' he said, glancing down at the bound file he had opened in front of him. 'It's alright if we call you that? Because I don't really want to be bothering with all that *sir* stuff all through these proceedings.'

McQuarrie gave the detective a cagey look. 'Fine, if you want.' He looked tense, resting his forearms on the table and craning forward, chin slightly raised.

'Good,' Black continued. 'So, I'm DCI Black of the Cambridgeshire Police Force and this is DCI Stewart with the Met but temporarily assigned to Police Scotland.' He paused to shoot McQuarrie a smile that radiated insincerity. 'And just to make it clear Andrew, you're not under arrest and we're not intending to charge you with any crime today. We just need to ask you some questions in connection with a murder enquiry that's ongoing at the moment.' The DCI looked down and sifted through some papers in the pile he had placed in front of him. Without looking up, he said, 'By the way, I see from my notes that you're planning to leave the country. To the US, is that right?'

McQuarrie gave him a wary look. 'That's right. With everything that's happened, I just feel my family need a fresh start.'

'Twins isn't it?' the policeman said. 'And teenagers too. They must be upset to be leaving all their friends behind? Have you not considered the effect on their mental health?'

'They're having a farewell party on Friday afternoon. We've hired the Guide hall in Milngavie. It's their fourteenth birthday too.'

'Milngavie? Never heard of it,' Black said. 'Is that in Glasgow?'

'Certainly not,' Frank said, grinning. 'It's where me and my Maggie live. Very select.'

'I'll take your word for that,' the Cambridge DCI said. 'So no other reason for the sudden move then Andrew? You wouldn't be running away from something, would you? Like justice for instance?'

Frank winced at the directness of his colleague's line of questioning, but he recognised what the detective was trying to do. It was the hoary old good-cop, bad-cop routine, with Frank involuntarily but pleasingly cast in the benign role for once.

'I resent that question,' McQuarrie said, anger evident in his expression. 'I've been offered a Chair at Stanford University and it's an opportunity that's too good to turn down. And by the way, I think I know what's best for my children. I don't think I need your advice, thank you very much.'

Black shrugged. 'Perhaps. Anyway, as I said, the reason we've asked you to come in is we want to question you about a murder that took place in Cambridge on the 16th of

July. The murder victim was a man called Peter Berrycloth, who we have reason to believe you had a close connection to. Can you confirm that's the case Andrew?'

'My wife has a cousin by that name, but I assume you can't mean him,' McQuarrie answered, looking surprised. 'Because the last time I checked, he was very much alive. In Kent, actually'

Black gave a sardonic smile. 'Come *on* Andrew, let's not waste your time or mine. This is a guy who was in receipt of substantial sums of money from you on at least two occasions, and by some miracle of coincidence, shares a name with your wife's cousin, and a very unusual name at that. Do you seriously expect me to believe you don't know what this is all about?'

McQuarrie shook his head. 'I'm sorry, but no, I honestly don't know who he is or what this is all about, as you put it.'

'Have you heard of the Cambridge Musician?' Frank asked. 'It's a pub or a club or something like that.'

'Of course I've heard of *that*,' McQuarrie said. 'It's a music venue. My wife played there once or twice with her folk band. It's a well-respected venue in that city.'

'And you're saying that's your only connection with the place?' Black said sharply. 'That your wife played there sometimes?'

He shrugged. 'Of course. I've never been there myself, but Gina always shared her gigging schedule with me. I remember the name, that's all.'

'So what about all the money?' Frank asked. 'And why the complicated trail of shell companies and the Cayman Island ownership?'

McQuarrie shrugged again. 'I don't know anything about any of that. Really, I don't.'

There was a silence as Black looked down at his file and read a few paragraphs. 'Okay, so eight years ago, a sum approaching four hundred thousand pounds was paid into the bank account of a company called Gregory & Clarke, a firm that just happened to be set up by the murder victim Peter Berrycloth. And then just nine or ten weeks ago, a sum amounting to half a million pounds was paid to - yes, you guessed it Andrew – to this self-same Gregory & Clarke outfit. So come on, stop pissing me about. What's your connection to all of this?'

'I told you, I don't know anything about any of this,' McQuarrie said, stony-faced. 'As I've said, I've never heard of this other Berryman guy and I certainly don't have any connection with him, business or otherwise.'

Black banged the table then laughed. 'Yes you *do* Andrew, yes you do. We have evidence of the amount of shuffling you and your wife had to do with your personal finances in order to make such a large sum of money available. There's no way that could have happened without your knowledge, is there?'

'Gina had access to all my accounts,' McQuarrie said. 'What was mine was hers and vice-versa. That was the way we organised our affairs.'

'That's nice,' Black said. 'So you're blaming your wife for all of this? Very gallant.'

'She was planning to leave me,' he answered sullenly. 'That's why she wanted the money. To buy a place of her own.'

Frank gave Black a slight nod to indicate this was something they knew about. 'Well, I'm sorry to hear about that,' the Cambridgeshire detective said grudgingly. 'But that doesn't answer anything, quite frankly. So come on Andrew, let's have the truth, please. Why was all that money going to Berrycloth?'

'Look, I've *told* you the truth.' He spat out the words, his anger either real or very convincing, Frank wasn't sure which. 'And in case you haven't heard, my wife died tragically very recently. My children and I are still struggling to cope with her loss, and we probably never will.'

Black gave Frank a wry smile then said, 'Okay then Andrew, let me ask you this. Where were you on the night of the 16th of July? Can you tell us that?'

'Where was I? Where was I?' McQuarrie's voice was raised now, his hands gripping the sides of his chair. 'I was at home of course, where do you bloody well think I was? With my twins. And yes, we would have been in the living room, and we would have been crying, because we've barely stopped crying since my wife died. Is that a good enough alibi for you Chief Inspector?'

'We're very sorry for your loss of course,' Black said, sounding anything but. 'I'm just doing my job. We need to ask these questions. It's what we do.' He paused for a moment. 'And I'm afraid I need to ask you if anyone can confirm that you were actually at home that night?'

Frank gave his colleague a brief look of sympathy, because it was a bugger of a question in the circumstances, but he knew as well as Black that it had to be asked.

'My children, of course,' McQuarrie said, calmer now, 'but I suspect you wouldn't accept their word for it. But my sister-in-law Laura is staying with me at the moment, with her two kids. By my calculation that's five people who can vouch for me. Is that good enough?' he repeated.

'Very well,' Black said with a brief nod and wearing an expression that failed to conceal his disappointment about the man's answer. 'So DCI Stewart, you've got a couple of questions to ask Mr McQuarrie, haven't you?'

Frank nodded. 'Aye, I have.' He had brought a slim transparent evidence bag into the interview room with him, and now he slid it across the table so that McQuarrie could get a closer look at the red material contained within.

'This swatch of material was found near where your wife's body was discovered,' he said. 'You can see it's from a walking jacket, and we wondered if it might have been from Mrs McQuarrie's, because we know that her's was a red one too . Is that something you might be able to confirm?'

McQuarrie looked at it for a brief second then shrugged. 'I couldn't say.'

'Fair enough,' Frank said. 'But maybe you could take a wee look at the jacket when you get back home. In fact, maybe we'll send a uniformed officer with you to help you out with that.'

'I'm afraid that won't be possible,' the man answered. 'I've disposed of all of Gina's walking gear.'

Frank gave him a searching look. 'So why did you do that sir?'

'Memories,' he said. 'She had a wardrobe full of the stuff and I just couldn't bear knowing that she wouldn't be using any of it again. I gave it away to a charity shop.'

'And which one would that be?' Frank asked.

'I don't know,' the man said, shrugging. 'I asked my sister-in-law Laura to do it because I couldn't face it myself. She bundled it all up in black bags and took it to a shop in Milngavie where I live. I'm sure you could check with them if you don't believe me,' he added churlishly. 'Laura will tell you which one it all went to.'

'I believe you,' Frank said. 'And that included the red walking jacket too, did it?'

He shrugged again. 'I assume so. But Laura would know.'

'We'd better ask her then,' Frank said. 'And as it happens, I've got another couple of quick questions for you too before we wrap up. Is that all right with you, DCI Black?'

His colleague gave a thumbs up. 'Yeah sure. Go ahead.'

Frank paused for a moment and drew breath. 'You probably won't like these very much Andrew, but they need to be asked I'm afraid. Just doing my job you understand.'

'So you two keep saying,' McQuarrie said sourly. 'So what is it now?'

'The first question is quite straightforward I think,' Frank said, smiling. 'It's a big police favourite, and the one you've heard already today. What I'm interested to know Andrew is where were you on the day that your wife had her terrible accident?'

'Why does that matter?' McQuarrie shot back.

'It's just a line of enquiry that's popped up in the last week or two, nothing to worry about, related to that wee swatch of material in fact. But where were you?' he repeated. 'I'm sure you must remember. It was such a horrible day for you and your family.'

The man was silent for a moment then said quietly, 'If you must know, I was in Aviemore. I was staying at the Cairngorm Hotel the night before Gina was due to set off on her walk. She was staying elsewhere in the village, and I wanted to surprise her. I'd booked a restaurant, and I was going to take her to dinner.'

'Really?' Frank said, surprised. 'And why did you decide to do that, can I ask?'

McQuarrie shuffled uncomfortably in his chair, then sighed. 'It's complicated. I was desperate to save our marriage and I was hoping I might be able to persuade her to change her mind. On top of that, I didn't want Gina to go on the damn expedition either. I was concerned about her mental state, with our breakup and everything, and I was worried she might come to harm. I remonstrated with her all through our dinner, but she just laughed and said she would be fine.'

'Does that mean you were worried about her *doing* herself harm?' Frank asked. 'Because as you know, that's been a subject of an investigation by the company who held your wife's life insurance policy. And as I understand it, when you spoke to Bainbridge Associates, who were working on behalf of that company, you failed to mention to them that you were concerned about Gina's mental state. Was that because you knew they wouldn't pay out if they found out she'd killed herself?'

'No no, of course not,' he said, raising his voice again. 'Gina would never have killed herself, no matter how badly she was feeling inside. But you need to be fully concentrating if you take on a challenge like she was planning, because any slip could prove fatal. And sadly, that's what happened, and I'll never forgive myself for not being more insistent.'

'So how did the evening end? Did you spend the night together? Because I think you both had hotels booked.'

'We had words,' he said bluntly. 'And things were said which I now bitterly regret. But I'm sure she would have felt the same, had she lived. And no, we didn't spend the night together. Gina made it crystal-clear that our carnal relationship was over for good,' he added bitterly.

'We all sometimes say things that we afterwards wish we hadn't,' Frank said, in what he intended to be a sympathetic tone. 'But coming back to these mental issues, were they something she always suffered with, or had something happened which caused her to be feeling bad at that particular time?'

'Gina was prone to depression,' McQuarrie said stiffly. 'It's nothing to be ashamed of, and she was quite open about it. But her episode at that time was particularly severe and therefore I was very worried about her.'

'Understand,' Frank said, nodding. He hesitated for a moment, considering where he should go next with this thread. The fact was, true or otherwise, it was a credible story that McQuarrie was spinning them, and he decided there would be little value right now in taking the line of enquiry any further. 'That's all good Andrew,' he continued, then paused again. 'So, just one final thing if I may. I want to take you back ten years, to the awful murder of Naomi Neilson up in Nethy Bridge. You'll remember that of course. I mean, how could anyone forget something like that?' He saw McQuarrie tense up, his brow furrowing and his eyes narrowing.

'I don't like to think about it,' he said, dropping his head. 'It was an awful time for everyone involved. But it wasn't ever proven that it was murder,' he added quickly. 'There was a very strong likelihood that it was a sex act that went terribly wrong.'

'And is that what you think happened Andrew? Were Gordon and Naomi so loved-up that they were into that kind of kinky stuff? Because one of my colleagues has looked at the files and the suggestion was that that night was the first time the pair of them had ever slept together. It was as if that was the reason they went on your expedition. You know, that it was some sort of pre-arranged assignation.'

'I don't know anything about that,' McQuarrie said. 'They were both keen members of our club and had been enthusiastic about joining the four thousand feet challenge. There wasn't anything more to it than that.'

'There was nearly a fifteen-year age gap between them, wasn't there?' Frank said. 'And Naomi was very beautiful, whereas Baird had a face that only a mother could love. Didn't you think it odd that they should end up in bed together?'

He shrugged. 'I don't see what it has to do with me. I was there with my wife, and I didn't pay any attention to what was going on with the rest of the party.'

'But Gordon Baird was a member of your staff, wasn't he?' Frank persisted. 'The University has very strict rules against its teaching staff having sexual relations with students. If that was what was taking place, you would have been bound to do something about it, wouldn't you?'

'Look, what's this all about?' McQuarrie said, suddenly angry. 'It was a bloody awful time for everybody involved, and Gina and I tried hard to put it behind us.'

Frank gave a wry smile. 'Aye, I bet it was awful for everybody. And I'll tell you what else is awful too, and that's the fact that everybody who was on that wee Cairngorm expedition of yours is either dead, or missing presumed dead. Obviously your wife's death is still very raw for you, but it's quite strange don't you think that Olivia Cranston disappeared at about the same time? And you're now the only one of the six who's still alive?'

McQuarrie, calmer now, shook his head slowly. 'It's a terrible terrible turn of fate, that's all. And Rhona and Gordon, they died years ago. Each in very different circumstances, but each tragic in their own way.' He paused for a moment then said. 'You think you've got the perfect life, and then fate comes along and ruins everything. The sad fact is, nobody knows what the future has in store for them.'

'I suppose that's true,' Frank said. 'But that wasn't really what I wanted to ask you about. As I said, my colleague DC McDonald has had recent cause to re-visit Naomi's case files and in the course of that review, something very interesting has cropped up. Something in fact prompted by my brother's investigatory work up at the Bhrochain corrie. He works with Bainbridge Associates, you might not know that.'

'I know of him. The woman Maggie Bainbridge came to see me at the Business School with her obnoxious little assistant.'

Frank laughed. 'Oh aye, that's wee Lorilynn Logan, and she's Maggie's associate, not her assistant if you want to be pedantic. And just so you know, that woman Maggie Bainbridge happens to be my wife. But that's by the by.' He paused, judging that the moment had now arrived to ask the massive question that his brother Jimmy was anxious for McQuarrie to answer.

'Anyway, as a result of my colleagues' excellent work, there's now something that's really bothering me, and I'm hoping that you can straighten it out for me.' He paused for a moment, looking McQuarrie straight in the eye.

'What I want to know Andrew, is why it was *you* that identified Gordon Baird's body?'

***

Afterwards, Frank reflected that he had come out of the interview with rather more to show for it than DCI Jezzer

Black. The Cambridgeshire detective had come to Glasgow with high hopes that Andrew McQuarrie would become the first proper name on his suspects list for the Peter Berrycloth murder. Instead, five family members were able to provide McQuarrie with as cast-iron an alibi as you'd ever see, proving he couldn't have been in Cambridge on the night in question. But it was a whole different story as far as Frank's investigations were concerned. He had discovered to his surprise that McQuarrie had been in Aviemore the night before his wife died and that the couple had had a row. He would have known his wife's plans, and as an experienced walker himself, would have had no trouble taking the western route up to Braeriach and lying in wait for his wife's approach from the north. Later Frank intended to call in on the Milngavie charity shop and see if anyone remembered a red walking jacket amongst the donations dropped off by Laura McColl, and if by chance they still had it, then he would examine it for a tear matching the swatch of cloth that Jimmy had found. The presence of a tear would seal the deal as far as Gina being murdered was concerned, and the absence of the jacket amongst the donations would put McQuarrie right in the frame for her murder.

> All of that was exciting enough, but that wasn't the biggest breakthrough of what had been a hugely eventful interrogation. And it wasn't the answer McQuarrie had given to Frank's final bombshell question, an answer he had only half-listened to, because he knew whatever the man

said it would have been complete bollocks. No, the reason Andrew McQuarrie had been so desperate to identify the body of Gordon Baird was exactly for the reason Jimmy had worked out.

The body wasn't Gordon Baird's.

Chapter 26

They'd gathered the Scottish-based team for a big brainstorming session, the objective being to consider the implications of the sensational developments of the past few days and to make some sense of it all. The venue once again was the familiar surroundings of the Bikini Barista cafe, and present were DC Lexy McDonald, Lori Logan, both Stewart brothers and of course Maggie herself. Down in London, Ronnie French and Eleanor Campbell were on standby in case they were needed to fill in any gaps in the team's collective knowledge or understanding. As she sipped on her pre-lunch coffee, Maggie could feel it in her bones, that sweet and familiar *frisson* that always swept over her when the solution to the crime started to crystallise in her brain. She recognised she wasn't *quite* there yet but was confident that with the input from the upcoming brainstorming session, followed by an hour or two of quiet contemplation, the remaining patches of fog would clear, causing everything to fall neatly into place. The only problem was, it seemed that opportunities for quiet contemplation would be in short supply, although since they were in the Barista on a busy Friday lunchtime, she had probably been optimistic in her expectations. But it wasn't the background hum of conversation in the eating-place that was going to be the problem, noise-wise. No, it was Frank, spouting off with his volume turned up to eleven, and showing no signs of moderating.

'Bloody hell,' she heard him exclaim for about the fifth time, his exasperation evidently caused by the phone call he had just hung up on. 'Talk about not being able to run a piss-up in a brewery? Honestly, you couldn't make it up. It's weapons-grade pathetic.'

'Something up sir?' Lexy said, failing to stifle a grin.

'Have you not heard Lexy? There's going to be a general election? A *snap* general election.'

'Aye, and it's come on so quick that I've no idea who to vote for,' Lori Logan interjected. 'I didn't bother the last time because I thought they were all a bunch of brainless morons, and that turned out to be true.'

'And they're not any better this time in my opinion,' Jimmy said. 'In fact, I think the moron factor has multiplied by about a thousand since then.' He sighed. 'The whole country's going to wrack and ruin. It's an absolute travesty.'

Frank gave them all a reprimanding look. 'Guys, why are we talking about the bloody election when my world's crumbling at my feet?' He saw Maggie raise an eyebrow and quickly corrected course. 'My *work* world I mean, obviously. But it's this damn snap election that's caused it all to go tits-up.'

'There there now darling, calm down,' Maggie said, laughing. 'We'll get Stevie to sort out our lunches and then you can tell us all what's happened.'

'Aye, all right then,' he said grudgingly. 'But I'm having chips with my pie and beans. I think that's the least I deserve. To sooth my nerves.'

Ever-efficient, proprietor Stevie arrived at their table with the lunches little more than five minutes after they had placed the order. 'Whose is the chips?' he enquired, holding up the plate, evidently surprised to see them on the order.

'His,' four voices shouted in unison.

'Help yourselves,' Frank said with an embarrassed smile, gesturing to the overloaded plate as Stevie placed it in front of him. 'I'll never eat all these anyway.'

Maggie raised a quizzical eyebrow but made no comment.

'So come on, tell us all your troubles,' Jimmy said. 'You know you want to.'

'Aye, so this bloody election,' Frank began. 'It turns out that my minister Miss Katherine Collins has only got a three thousand majority and so is odds-on to lose her seat. The outcome is, she's stepped down from the oversight of my new department to concentrate on her re-election campaign.' He paused for a moment and viciously stabbed an innocent chip with his fork. 'And then our CEO, who incidentally I've not even met yet...'

'Dame Helen somebody-or-other,' Maggie supplied.

'Aye, Dame Helen Dunbar. Turns out she's persona non grata with the opposition party, so *she's* resigned before she gets the push, which she says is inevitable if the other lot get in.'

'And it looks like they will,' Maggie said. 'Well, that's terribly bad luck Frank,' she added sympathetically, whilst suppressing another laugh.

'Wait, I'm not finished yet,' he said. 'You know my fancy new office on West Nile Street? Well, in a last-ditch attempt to win some support, the government have commandeered it for a fast-track asylum-seeker processing centre. It's going to be stuffed to the gizzards with sour-faced civil service drones pushing paper. No room left for little Frank Stewart and his wee organisation.' He gave Lexy an apologetic look. 'I'm afraid DC McDonald that it looks like the National Independent Cold-Case Investigations Agency is finished before it's even got started. I'm really sorry about that.'

Lexy laughed. 'No worries sir, I can go back to my old job no problem. But I say we should make sure we go out in a blaze of glory, all guns firing. Let everybody see what they'll be missing if they close us down.'

'Hear hear,' Maggie said. 'So, to that end, let's get the brains engaged and see if we can nail this baby once and for all. And remember the rules of brainstorming. We chuck in every idea that comes into our heads, no matter how crazy it might seem, and we don't shoot down anybody's suggestion. Every idea has merit because we know how even the daftest ideas can set us off on the right path. So come on guys, let's go for it.'

'But just before we start, there's a bit of late breaking news,' Frank said. 'I pottered round to the charity shop in Milngavie and asked about the donations of Gina's walking gear. The old dear on the counter remembered Laura McColl bringing in three bags of the stuff, and what's more, the red Gortex jacket was amongst the haul.' He smiled. 'And better than that, they still had it, so I snaffled it myself. They wanted fifteen quid for it, but I told her it's vital evidence in a murder case...'

'Which it is,' Maggie pointed out.

'Aye it is,' he continued. 'And the question you'll all want answered is, does it have that little tear out of it like we were expecting.'

Maggie smiled. 'And the answer?'

'The answer is, it does,' he said with a broad smile. 'A perfect match, which in my book confirms Jimmy's murder theory one hundred percent. After this session I'll be straight on the blower to ACC White and we'll have a SOCO guy helicoptered onto that ridge by break of dawn.'

For the next forty minutes or so, the pertinent points of the matter were tossed around as all manner of theories were proposed as solutions to this most complex of cases. Maggie was only half-listening, her mind churning over the facts which had emerged and trying to put them into some sensible chronological order. As she did so, one phrase was continually grabbing her attention. *Cause and effect.* Because the more she considered it, the more certain she was that this whole matter was held together by a related chain of events, each one prompting the next link in the chain, starting, she now realised, *before* that fateful night in Nethy Bridge, ten years earlier, and continuing all the way through to the last few weeks, when Olivia Cranston had disappeared and Gina McQuarrie had been murdered and the mysterious Peter Berrycloth had been found dead in the river Cam. Yes, something was going on in the period before the group of six met in that country house hotel, something that meant Naomi Neilson had to be murdered. That terrible act of violence had triggered the tragic chain of events which continued to this day, but now Maggie thought she knew what that original *something* might be. Her thought process was momentarily interrupted by the realisation that her associate Lori was helpfully summarising that self-same chain of events, evidently thinking out loud to help clarify her own thoughts and that of her colleagues.

'Aye, so first poor Naomi Neilson gets murdered in her bed,' the girl said, 'then her lover Gordon Baird disappears, although whether we can call him her lover is debatable, because in my opinion it seems as if it was only a one-night shag. Then Baird gets found dead at the bottom of that corrie, and we now know that death was a murder. Afterwards, it's Andrew McQuarrie who identifies his body, although Frank and Jimmy now seem to think there's some doubt that it actually was the body of Baird. And then a couple of years after all this happens, Rhona Fraser disappears in Cambridge and her body is never found. Everyone assumes that she was murdered, but we can't say that for certain, because she might have just run off somewhere, or changed her identity or something like that. And then nothing happens for a whole eight years until Olivia Cranston – who was Rhona's partner or girlfriend or whatever you want to call her –disappears too, also in Cambridge, which obviously can't be just a coincidence. And then a week or two after that, Gina McQuarrie dies up in the Cairngorms, a death we now know was murder, using the same MO as that which killed Gordon Baird ten years earlier. And that, as far as we know, is the end of the story.'

'But it's not,' Maggie blurted out. 'It's far from the end, I'm sure of that. That was a very nice summary Lori, but I think whoever is behind this is not done yet.'

'But who is behind all this Maggie?' Jimmy asked. 'Who *is* our killer?'

She sighed. 'That's the problem. I've not worked it out *fully* right now, but I feel I'm getting bloody close. First, I need to try and figure out what it was that triggered the whole chain of events, back before that group went on that fateful Cairngorm expedition ten years ago.' She gave a wry smile. 'But I have a working hypothesis, and in that I think we're in fact looking at *four* killers, not just one.'

'What?' Frank exclaimed, open-mouthed. 'What the bloody hell are you talking about Mrs Stewart? *Four* killers?'

She gave him a serious look. 'I know, it's sounds nuts, and I might be talking complete rubbish, but right now my bonkers theory is the only one that fits the facts. And I mean *all* the facts, not just the murders and disappearances. The money, Naomi's aversion to studying, Rhona and Olivia's late-night bus rides in Cambridge, everything.'

Frank grinned. 'I can see one of those Greta Garbo moments coming on. Am I right?'

'Who's Greta Garbo?' Lori asked, furrow-browed.

'Yes, who is she?' Lexy repeated. 'I've never heard of her.'

'Google her,' Frank said. 'But it means our Maggie needs to be left alone for her big brain to work its magic.'

Maggie nodded. 'I know it's a bit rude, but I'm just going to go and sit in the corner over there, if you all don't mind. Give me half an hour and a couple of strong americanos and I'm sure I'll have it all worked out.'

Frank stood up and snapped his fingers with a theatrical flourish. 'Stevie-boy, get your arse over here and sharpish. And bring your wee order pad.'

***

Maggie had brought a fresh A4 notebook with her to the cafe, and for the next thirty minutes she filled it with names and ideas, scrawling connecting lines between them, then erasing them with the rubber at the end of her pencil as she had second thoughts. Turning the book sideways, she selected a blank page, drew a timeline starting more than ten years earlier, then tried to slot each event in the matter into its appropriate place. With the discovery of Naomi Neilson's research thesis, she knew exactly what had kicked off the whole saga; now she had to work out how this continuing narrative was destined to end. So far, Maggie calculated, there had already been four murders, and she feared there were to be several more, murders she knew could not be prevented unless she solved this most intricate of puzzles. She rested her head on her cupped hands, closed her eyes and took a sharp intake of breath. *Come on woman*, she scolded herself, *think!* For several minutes nothing came to her, and then suddenly something struck her. *Don't just think about motive and opportunity, think about means too. Of course!* Because the more she thought about it, the more certain she was that this continuing drama would be played out not in Cambridge or in the majestic Cairngorms, but right here in Glasgow. So, of the potential actors, who would have the means to carry out a murder or murders in the city, that was the question? And where? Where would this terrible drama take place, and when? And then, in a rush, it came to her. Excitedly, she leapt to her feet and shouted over to the others.

'Milngavie! We've got to get to Milngavie right away!' But before they left, she had to make an urgent phone call to Sir Andrew McQuarrie.

Chapter 27

All five of them had piled into Frank's police BMW, and now they were powering up Bearsden Road with the siren blaring and blue lights flashing.

'That's ten red lights you've jumped by my calculation,' Jimmy said, grinning. 'And I've no idea how you got through Anniesland Cross without killing us all. Do you think you're Steve McQueen or something?'

'You mean Steve McQueen, my look-alike?' Frank shot back. 'Anyway, where is it we're going Maggie? You've been very tight-lipped about all of this I must say, and that always worries me.'

'I'm not sure exactly,' she said, frowning and not looking up from her phone, which she had been studying intensely since they left Byres Road.

Frank gave her a look. 'What do you mean, you're not sure exactly?'

'It's all about line of sight,' she responded. 'I'm trying to work out how many locations have a clear line of sight to the front door of the hall. The Girl Guide hall I mean. It's located on a street called Oakburn Avenue. I think I know where it is. I've taken Ollie to the little swing park beside it.'

'It's the leaving party, isn't it?' Jimmy said, cottoning on. 'The McQuarrie twins are having their leaving do today.'

She nodded. 'They are. And someone is intent in spoiling their day. That's what we need to stop. But if you don't mind, could everyone shut up for the next few minutes, please? There's five of us, and we'll need to spread out to cover all the possible locations where a sniper could be located. I need to plot their possible locations on the map.'

'Bloody hell,' Frank said. 'Are we talking about guns? Because if we are, we need to get an armed response squad up here, and pronto.'

'There won't actually be any shooting. Because I've told Sir Andrew to cancel the party. It's not due to start for another hour, so most of the guests should know by now. But I expect our shooter will be already in place, waiting for the hosts to arrive. Thank God he's going to be disappointed, because his targets are not going to turn up.'

'You say shooter, singular?' Lexy said. 'So there's just one of them then?'

'I hope so,' Maggie answered. 'I'm not one hundred percent sure of that, but I'd say it's the most likely scenario. But please, just give me a minute to plot out those possible sniper locations.'

'We will,' Frank said, 'but I'm getting the armed boys and girls in just in case.' He punched a couple of buttons on the steering wheel, connecting him to a Police Scotland response centre.

'This is DCI Frank Stewart,' he barked. *'I've reason to believe there's an armed suspect at large and we need a response team mobilised. The location is the vicinity of Oakburn Avenue, Milngavie, centred around the Guide Hall, and sorry, but I don't have the postcode off hand. I'll dial in further details when I have them. Over and out.'* From the absence of further interrogation by the telephone operator, Maggie assumed they had been trained to act first and ask questions later in matters of this type. Now they were approaching their destination, and accordingly a few minutes earlier, Frank had switched off the siren and light so as not to attract attention. 'We'd better not park anywhere near the hall I suppose?' Lexy said. 'Because I assume the suspects will be watching it.'

'Absolutely,' Frank said. 'I'm going to pull into one of the wee side streets a couple of hundred yards away. In fact, here's one right here that'll do nicely.' Without indicating, he suddenly swung the car left, attracting a blare of the horn from the motorist following. 'Sorry mate,' he mouthed, glancing in the mirror before parking outside one of the neat bungalows that lined the residential street. 'Right then,' he said as his colleagues got out of the car. 'No bloody heroics, okay? And that goes especially for you, Miss Maggie Bainbridge.'

She laughed. 'I'm not Mrs Maggie Stewart now? Make up your mind. But no, we're just here to reconnoitre, nothing else. Lori, I want you to go to the hall and make sure that anyone who didn't get the message about the party being cancelled is ushered inside with as little fuss as possible, but quickly. Are you okay with that?'

Lori nodded. 'Sure boss, I'll sprint round there right now.'

'Great. The rest of us will go in pairs. Me and Jimmy, and Lexy and Frank. Here, take a look.' She held her phone horizontally in her palm and pointed at the map. 'We have to assume that the sniper needs a little bit of elevation to get a clear shot, but also needs to find a location that's quiet so that they won't be observed.'

'That's a bloody tall order in a residential area like this,' Frank said.

'Exactly,' Maggie said. 'Which is why there are only two locations where he could be.' She pointed again to the map, then switched it to streetview. 'This row of scruffy lock-up garages is in a lane behind some houses just opposite the hall, and I doubt if many people go there during the day. And someone lying on the roof of them would have a clear line of sight through to the front door of the hall, just through this little gap between these two houses.' She paused for a few moments then swiped a finger across the map. 'Then here, at the other side of the park. This is a day-care centre or maybe an old folks' home. The street outside is a short cul-de-sac so there won't be any passing traffic, so again, nice and quiet. And the building design is all higgledy-piggledy, with lots of nooks and crannies someone with a long-range rifle could hide behind.'

She noticed that Lexy was wearing a concerned look, and now the young DC was speaking directly to Frank. 'I'm sorry sir, but I'm not happy with this at all. I don't think we can allow civilians to do this, can we? We'd be in total breach of our duty of care to members of the public. And that's what Maggie and Jimmy are, aren't they?' Lexy looked at Maggie apologetically. 'I'm sorry, but it's a fact.'

Frank gave a wry smile. 'I was going to say the same thing Lexy, but I'm glad you said it first. What we'll do is, I'll go with Maggie, and you can go with Jimmy. And remember, if there's guns involved, I don't want anyone going anywhere near them, okay? We can do a bit of scouting, but more than that we leave to the armed response boys. So Jimmy-boy, you were trained in urban warfare when you were in the army. If you had a choice of these two locations, which one would you go for?'

Jimmy's reply was instant. 'You always choose the one with the easiest and most reliable exit, every time. Trouble is, there's not much to choose between these two, because they're both in cul-de-sacs. All it takes is an Amazon guy to park his white van in the middle of the road whilst he wanders off to find an address and you're blocked in. They're both ideal for quietness, but they're not so clever for getaways.'

'Then they wouldn't actually park in the cul-de-sacs, would they?' Lori said. 'That would be dumb.' She craned over to look at the map. 'Aye, for either location, you'd park about *here*, on Oakburn Avenue,' she added, jabbing a finger on the screen. 'See, to the left there's a jitty leading up to the lockup garages, and to the right you're just a few steps from the door of the day care centre. From either location it's just a wee sprint and you're in your motor and away.'

'Good thinking Lori,' Maggie said. 'Okay, what if Frank and I head along the road away from the hall until we come to the jitty, then we can take a right and shoot over to the day-care centre. On the way, we'll check out the parked vehicles and see if any of them look suspicious.'

'Aye, and I can get onto the Vehicle Licensing database and see who's the registered owner,' Frank added. 'It's available online, twenty-four-by-seven.'

'And you know how to work it?' Jimmy asked, grinning.

'Ha-bloody-ha,' Frank answered, adding a rude gesture with his finger. 'If me and Maggie handle the day care centre, you and Lexy can follow the back lane round to the garages and see if you see anything there. And I'll say it again, just so you're all clear. The flying squad should be here in a few minutes, so no bloody heroics.'

The plan agreed, the two pairs set off on their respective missions.

'We're a wee bit conspicuous, aren't we?' Frank said as they began their walk along Oakburn Avenue. 'If we're being watched by the killer I mean.'

'Their eyes will be on the door of the Guide Hall,' she answered. 'But no worries. Here, take my hand and then we'll just be an old married couple out for a stroll. Just keep the pace down so not to invite suspicion.'

'What, are you turning me into a doddery old git already?' he said, laughing. 'Do you want me to walk with a limp too? Because I can do that if you want.'

'No, I think that would be a step too far,' she grinned. 'But look, the cars along this road don't look too promising. Just little family cars in the main. I don't see them as getaway cars, do you?'

He nodded in agreement. 'The thing is, Jimmy's premise assumes these guys know what they're doing. But they might not.'

'What, do you mean they might have parked up that cul-de-sac after all?' Maggie asked. 'Because if that's the case, we should sprint back and get the car so we can block the exit.'

He laughed. 'Are you joking? You've no idea how many forms I'd have to fill in if I got my police car bashed up. No, we'll let the assault boys do all that action-man stuff. We're just the observer brigade, remember?'

Maggie nodded. 'Fair enough. Anyway, the cul-de-sac's just round this corner. Knowe Street. It's only about three hundred yards long according to the map, if that.' She paused for a moment. 'Probably best if just one of us goes in, in case one of the killers is sitting in the car looking along the street, because that would draw less attention. And it would be best if it was me. I can just stroll along casually, as if I'm a legitimate visitor to the day-care centre, you know, a daughter going to visit a mum or dad, or a social worker on her rounds.'

He shook his head and gave her a strong look. 'No way. This is a job for the police, one hundred percent.'

'Darling, it's very gallant of you,' she said, squeezing his hand. 'But unfortunately, you *look* like a policeman. I can't put my finger on exactly what it is that gives you away, but there's something, and I fear they would spot you right away. No, you can just stand at the corner and await further instructions.'

He sighed. 'All right, but I'll give you a thirty-second start and that's it. After that, I'm following you in, whatever happens.'

She nodded her assent just as she realised they had reached the corner of the cul-de-sac. 'Okay,' she said, steeling herself. 'I guess I need to look purposeful, as if time is tight and I'm head down, needing to get on with things.'

'Okay,' he said. 'And thirty seconds, no longer.'

She nodded again but made no reply. Then taking a deep breath, she set off around the corner. The important thing was to make it look as natural as possible, especially if, as they now expected, there would be a suspicious vehicle parked on the street, ready to make a rapid getaway. And almost as soon as she'd taken her first step, she saw it; a dark green SUV, which she vaguely thought might be a Land Rover Discovery, this useful ability to recognise makes and models one of the many delightful dividends from having a car-obsessed young son. Her heart pounding, she kept walking towards the vehicle and then as she was in line with the front panel, she allowed herself the briefest of upward glances. *There was a woman sitting in the driver's seat.*

Keep walking, she thought, you've got to keep walking. But then after just two or three strides, she suddenly stopped in her tracks and spun round. As she had hoped, there was a dealer's sticker on the back window. *Allister McNair For Land Rover in Inverness.* Now she knew for certain that her suppositions were correct, because if you were employed as a ghillie on a Cairngorm estate, this was exactly the kind of vehicle you would drive. With a gulp and another intake of breath, she leapt back towards the car, yanked open the passenger door and hauled herself into the front seat alongside the woman. Maggie smiled at her and said quietly, 'Hello Olivia, I'm Maggie, and I'm glad you're not dead. But I'm here to tell you it's all over.' Startled, Olivia Cranston moved to jab the starter button, but Maggie, anticipating the move, grabbed the bunch of keys that were lying in the central cubby-hole and threw them out her open door with as much force as she could muster.

'That's the downside of keyless ignition,' she said. 'Doesn't work if there's no key, obviously.' Frank had now arrived alongside them and made to say something, but Maggie raised a hand to indicate that he should not speak. Instead, she turned to the woman and said, 'You need to call your brother right now and tell him it's all over.'

Olivia Cranston gave a haughty toss of the head. 'I won't. That bastard McQuarrie ruined so many lives and he needs to feel the same pain that everyone else did. That's all we ever wanted, for him to feel the same pain that we did. He's going to get what's coming to him.'

Maggie reached across, took the woman's hand and said gently, 'The McQuarrie children aren't coming. The party's been cancelled. Go on, phone Robbie right now. Don't make it any worse. Tell him it's over.'

As she spoke, a police van screeched into the cul-de-sac, emitting a loud squeal from the brakes as the vehicle was brought to an abrupt halt. Almost instantaneously a squad of armed police officers in full riot gear tumbled out. Immediately. Frank ran over to intercept their commander then pointed towards the day-care centre, barking instructions.

'You see Olivia,' Maggie said, nodding towards the officers, 'you don't want it to end this way, do you?' She paused for a moment then gave the woman a half-smile. 'So go on, call Robbie, please. Because no-one else needs to die.'

***

Behind them, Robbie Cranston, the ghillie of Strathrothie Estate, emerged from the gate of the day-care centre, clad in camouflaged fatigues, his face straked with black warpaint. Across his chest he cradled a powerful rifle, a weapon responsible for the deaths of hundreds of Cairngorm deer, but a weapon that was yet to claim the life of a human. As he surveyed the scene, he reluctantly came to the conclusion that it should remain that way. Wearing a truculent expression, he raised the gun above his head in an act of surrender.

Chapter 28

However you looked at it, the McQuarrie affair had ended rather awkwardly for the Edinburgh & Glasgow Assurance Company. Firstly, Bainbridge Associates had established that far from killing herself, the beautiful Gina McQuarrie had been murdered in an act of revenge against her husband Sir Andrew, and despite that brutal act of violence, they were obliged to pay out the three million pounds owed under the policy to the famous economist. Secondly, the fact that Sir Andrew had himself been exposed as a cold-blooded murderer and was consequently about to spend the rest of his life in one of His Majesty's luxurious prison establishments, was not exactly brilliant publicity for the austere insurance giant. *Naomi Killer to Bag Multi-Million Payday* was just a sample of the type of headline the story was garnering, and the company's Head of Life Mr Charlie Wilson was desperate for the affair to melt away, whilst praying that their army of lawyers could find a loophole that would prevent them having to pay out. Fortunately, their travails had not prevented the company generously hosting a lavish lunch to celebrate the successful end of the matter. The whole gang had been invited; Jimmy and Frank of course, and Lori Logan, and DC Lexy McDonald, and Eleanor Campbell and DC Ronnie French who had both flown up from London that morning. Present too was the former government minister Katherine Collins, who had unexpectedly retained her seat and was now adjusting to life on the opposition benches, and Jimmy's beautiful new girlfriend Frida. The venue was one of Glasgow's most prestigious city-centre hotels, and the food and accompanying wine had been as spectacular and plentiful as anyone could wish for. Now a team of waiting staff was serving up coffees and liqueurs, and whilst they did so, Maggie took the opportunity to take a final nervous look at her notes. The truth was, she wasn't exactly feeling her best, this being the third morning in a row she had been quite violently sick. But the insurance company had brought along what seemed like hundreds of their senior staff to the event and there was an army of media representatives too, including Maggie and Jimmy's old pal Yash Patel, no doubt hoping to get an exclusive inside track on the story from Bainbridge Associates, so the thing had to be done. Fortunately too, it wouldn't just be her up on that little platform, because lovely Frank would be sitting alongside her, his remit being to give the official police slant on the matter. They would be starting in a minute or so, she estimated, once Charlie Wilson, currently standing on the platform and in full flow, had finished his generous and effusive praise of her little firm.

'This was a bloody tricky situation for our company,' he was saying, wearing a wry expression, 'if you'll excuse my French. We were facing a lose-lose outcome if the media got to know we were trying to hang on to Gina McQuarrie's life insurance money, especially with her husband being such a prominent public figure too. But luckily, I remembered reading about Maggie's firm and particularly about her colleague Jimmy Stewart's mountain expertise.' It was evident that his speech was aimed principally at his senior directors, and there was a hint of self-satisfaction about his tone, a nuance that said *haven't I been a clever boy?* 'It turned out to be a sensational story, didn't it?' he continued, 'and it was Bainbridge Associates -with help from the police of course...' He paused and gave Frank a nod of acknowledgment, which was met with a half-raised hand. '...who worked it all out.' A ripple of applause echoed round the room, Maggie responding with an embarrassed smile. 'So, without further ado, let's hear from the super-sleuths themselves. Ladies and gentlemen, please give a warm welcome to Maggie Bainbridge and DCI Frank Stewart.' There was further polite applause, which Maggie allowed to subside before she got to her feet, notes in hand.

'Thank you Charlie,' she said, smiling. 'Yes, as you said, this was a *very* tricky affair. In fact, I think I wouldn't be wrong in saying that it was the most complicated case we've ever had the privilege to work on.'

'Aye, and that's saying something for you,' Frank interjected, giving a wry grin.

Maggie smiled back at him. 'You're certainly right about that Frank. But as to this case, first we need to go back ten years, when a group of walking enthusiasts from a Glasgow

University Economics Department club met up at a Nethy Bridge hotel with the intention of tackling the Cairngorm four-thousand feet challenge. For those of you who haven't heard of this mad challenge, it involves climbing five mountains each over four thousand feet in height in one day. In the party was Sir Andrew McQuarrie – just plain old Mr back then – his wife Gina, under-graduate students Olivia Cranston and Naomi Neilson, Olivia's girlfriend Rhona Fraser, and finally Gordon Baird, a lecturer and tutor in the department. And as you all know, barely twelve hours after they successfully completed the challenge, Naomi was found strangled in her bed.' As Maggie had said, everyone present would have read extensively about the tragic murder of Naomi Neilson, but that didn't prevent a murmur of horror reverberating around the room. 'That evening, Naomi had gone to bed with Baird, and so he was of course the obvious suspect for the murder. Not surprisingly, he didn't hang around to be arrested. After the body was discovered – by Gina McQuarrie, incidentally – everyone realised that Baird had disappeared. When some twelve hours later his body was found at the bottom of a remote corrie near Braeriach, it was assumed he had taken his own life out of remorse for what he had done.'

'And that was the verdict of the Fiscal's inquest too,' Frank added.

'But then my excellent colleague Jimmy Stewart proved that Baird's death couldn't have been suicide,' Maggie said, 'which caused us to look at the Nethy Bridge episode in a completely different light. The first thing that struck me was the notable mismatch in both age and attractiveness between Baird and Naomi Neilson, which made me realise that this one-night stand was likely to have been a business transaction rather than a romantic liaison. By all accounts, Naomi was a brilliantly-talented student, but she was a girl who loved to party, and in her critical final year, partying had overtaken studying in her list of priorities, much to the despair of her parents. So as her final exams approached, she began to panic, realising she had left it too late to earn the first-class honours degree she needed to take up her coveted post-graduate research post at Oxford University.'

Frank nodded. 'And that gave our bad guy the opportunity he needed.'

'Yes, our bad guy,' Maggie mused. 'So who was our bad guy in this ten-year old murder mystery?' She paused for a moment. 'Not, it turns out, Gordon Baird, although his role in the affair does him no credit. No, the role of villain in this affair was filled without question by Andrew McQuarrie.'

'And it all stemmed from that thesis, didn't it?' Frank said. 'The one Naomi wrote for her Oxford submission.'

'It did,' Maggie said, nodding. 'I discovered it in a pile of stuff in Naomi's old bedroom and as soon as I skimmed it, all the pieces in this complicated jigsaw began to slot into place. In fact, all I had to do was read the title and I *knew*. And by the way, it's not exactly snappy, so I need to make sure I get this right.' She glanced down at her notes. 'Ah, here it is. *Money Supply and the Link to Inflation - An Algorithmic Theory for Governments*. You see, I told you it wasn't a snappy title. But when Andrew McQuarrie read it, which Naomi had asked him to do before she formally submitted it to Oxford, he recognised it as a work of pure genius. Instantly, he saw that if he could have it for himself, it would transform his languishing career and give him the fame and recognition he craved.' She paused again. 'You see, he loved his wife, but he was madly jealous of her success as a musician and the money and fame that it had brought her. More than anything, he wanted to be her equal, and he saw that Naomi's brilliant theory would give him the opportunity to achieve that same level of success if he could claim it as his own.'

Frank nodded again. 'But for that to happen, Naomi had to die. And so he hatched his terrible plan.'

'That's right,' Maggie said. 'And in Gordon Baird, he had the perfect patsy for his scheme. Despite having been formally warned against it, Baird was still trying to sleep with female undergraduates in return for marking their exam papers favourably. Previously, McQuarrie, who was his boss, had turned a blind eye to his carnal activities, but now he saw an opportunity. The party girl Naomi needed a first to claim her Oxford place, and Baird, who would be marking her papers, could deliver that. It was arranged that both would go on the four-thousand expedition, and Naomi would sleep with Baird in return for gaining her first-class honours.'

'I don't suppose Baird put up many objections,' Frank said. 'It might have briefly crossed his mind to ask why McQuarrie was so keen for the girl to get a first, but he would have quickly dismissed any scruples. I know it's very unsavoury to say this, but she was a very beautiful girl and not many unattached men would turn down that opportunity.'

'Even if Baird had objected, McQuarrie had a hold over him,' Maggie said. 'If he didn't agree to do it, then his continuing predilections would be revealed to the University authorities.' She paused for a moment. 'Whatever the inducement, we know that Baird agreed to the proposition. On the night of the murder, the group had a dinner which was accompanied by a lot of alcohol, and we now know that at some point in the evening, Andrew McQuarrie slipped a quantity of Rohypnol into both Baird and Naomi's drinks. Eventually, the pair disappeared off to Baird's bedroom to consummate their arrangement, but we know that the effect of the drug would mean they would have passed out before sex took place.'

Now Frank took up the story. 'And that was *exactly* what McQuarrie had planned. As Maggie said, everybody had been drinking heavily that evening, including his wife, but he himself had been careful to limit his intake, knowing he needed to keep a clear head for the iniquitous task that lay ahead of him. In the early hours, he slipped out of his room and along the corridor to Naomi's room. We're guessing in their drunk and drugged state the couple must have left the door unlocked, but whether that was true or not, McQuarrie was able to gain entry to the room. Once inside, it took him just a minute to remove Baird's belt from his discarded trousers and place it around Naomi's neck.' He broke off and gave the audience an apologetic look. 'And I'm afraid you can picture the rest.'

'All murder is awful, but this one was particularly callous,' Maggie said. 'It was a cold calculating act carried out purely for the benefit of Andrew McQuarrie's career. Then after he had strangled her, all he had to do was take the few steps back along the corridor and go back to bed. The next morning, Gordon Baird woke up to the most horrific scene. The woman whom he had arranged to sleep with was lying dead beside him, with his own trouser belt pulled tightly around her neck. In a panic, he threw on his walking gear, jumped in his car and drove up to Glen Einich, where he abandoned the vehicle then set off on foot towards Braeriach. We don't know why he did that, whether it was an attempt to clear his head or whether he intended to take his own life. We *do* know that on the climb up towards the summit, he encountered first a party of students from Aberdeen University, and then the Sheffield climber Robert Harrison, who was following the same route as he was. His head must have been spinning, and in fact we suspect because of his drugged and intoxicated state, he probably wouldn't have known himself whether he'd killed Naomi or not. But what he did know was that the girl had been found strangled in his bed with his belt, and no matter what had actually happened, he would be the prime suspect for the murder. And so on the spur of the moment, he hatched his crazy plan.'

'Aye, crazy's the word for it right enough,' Frank said. 'After they left the students behind, we think Baird and Harrison walked together and would have reached the edge of the Bhrochain corrie about twenty minutes later. I suspect the two would have struck up a friendly conversation, sharing stories of their past adventures and all that, as these mountain types do. But all the while Baird was just waiting for the right opportunity to carry out his mad scheme.'

Maggie nodded. 'As they traversed alongside the edge of the corrie, Baird pushed Harrison violently over the edge, causing the Sheffield man to fall to his death. Of course, the act was totally unexpected, so Harrison would have had no opportunity of reacting to save himself. We assume Baird watched him fall, then climbed down to where the body lay, where he carried out the switch.'

'The switch? What switch?' someone called out from the audience.

'The body of Robert Harrison became the body of Gordon Baird,' Frank said. 'Baird searched the man and removed anything that could identify him as Harrison, which was in fact nothing more than his phone, his wallet and his car keys. Baird simply placed his own corresponding items in Harrison's pockets and the first part of the switch was done.'

'By now, we expect Baird was exhausted, both physically and emotionally,' Maggie continued. 'We speculate that he must have found somewhere to sit and rest and think hard about the events of the previous terrible night, and here's how we believe that thinking process might have gone. Let's assume Baird didn't remember killing Naomi, and as his head began to clear in the crisp mountain air, he became more and more certain that no matter how drunk he had been, he would have been simply incapable of doing something so brutal. Which meant that someone else must have done it, and the only person with the remotest motive was Andrew McQuarrie. Baird was one of Naomi's tutors, so we assume he knew about her proposed post-graduate thesis, although presumably had not appreciated the significance of it.'

'No, but McQuarrie *had* appreciated the significance of it,' Frank interjected. 'What if he'd asked Baird his opinion of the piece of work on more than one occasion, enough to arouse Baird's suspicions about why he was so interested in a student thesis? So interested in fact that he was prepared to kill for it.'

'That's right,' Maggie agreed. 'With these suspicions, Baird phoned McQuarrie from the mountain and told him what he must do to buy his silence. *I won't tell anyone what I know about you if you help me disappear*, that was the gist of the message.'

'And I know what you're all thinking,' Frank said, nodding at the audience. 'That doesn't make sense. You're wondering why Baird didn't just come clean and allow justice to take its course.'

'I can answer that,' Maggie interjected. 'Firstly, he knew that at that point in time, McQuarrie could simply laugh off the story about Naomi's thesis, leaving himself as still the nailed-on prime suspect. But he knew too that it would be a risk for the other man, causing the police to ask awkward questions that Andrew McQuarrie might prefer not to answer. No, it would be safer all round for McQuarrie to support the story that Baird had murdered Naomi then took his own life on the mountain. All neat and tidy and a speedy end to the affair.' She paused for a moment. 'But for that to happen, McQuarrie must identify the body of Robert Harrison and lie that it was Baird's. And we don't need to speculate to know how that came about,' she added. 'That modus operandi was in the original police files. Andrew McQuarrie phoned Baird's parents and said he would be happy to spare them the agony of having to identify their son's badly mutilated body. Best to remember him as he was, we expect he said, and the distraught couple agreed.'

'And that was it, all done and dusted,' Frank said. 'Naomi Neilson's murderer was himself dead, and from the police viewpoint it was a terribly tragic affair, but an affair with no loose ends. So the file is closed and tucked away in the archives to gather cobwebs.'

'Exactly,' Maggie said. 'But now Gordon Baird needs to build a new life, and with the help of Andrew McQuarrie, Peter Berrycloth is born. Or to be more accurate, a *second* Peter Berrycloth takes the stage. The first and real Peter Berrycloth is Gina McQuarrie nee Berrycloth's cousin, a man severely disabled from birth, and most importantly, a man physically unable to travel abroad so not in possession of a passport. It's a simple matter for McQuarrie to obtain a duplicate birth certificate. I did some research on this myself, and it turns out it's ridiculously easy to get one. In fact, you can do it all online with just a few clicks.'

'And once you've got a birth certificate, you can apply for a passport,' Frank added. 'And it turns out if you were born before 1st January 1983, it's particularly easy, assuming you have access to the family background of the applicant, as McQuarrie had, and can vouch, as a relative, that you know that applicant. I'll spare you the full technical details but suffice to say a passport was duly delivered to Gordon Baird in the name of Peter Berrycloth.'

Maggie nodded. 'And once you have a passport you can open a bank account, you can rent a flat, you can get a driving licence etcetera, etcetera, etcetera. But of course, when you are suddenly born again at the age of forty-one, what you *don't* have is a CV with credible references, so getting a job is going to be rather difficult. You could simply make up a glittering career of course, but if you do that, the chances are that at some point you're going to get found out.'

'Aye, which means the only option for making a living as a born-again fella is to work for yourself, where you don't need a CV,' Frank said. 'Baird had always been a music fan, and when he finds out that in Cambridge the lease of a pub-cum-music venue is available, he grabs it with open arms, with the help of some money he had borrowed from McQuarrie. The venture is a success and in a couple of years he's got enough cash to put down a deposit on a wee house in the suburbs.' He gave a wry smile. 'And all the while he knows his own personal insurance policy is about to mature.'

'Yes, Gordon Baird was *very* cunning,' Maggie said. 'But before we go any further, I really need to apologise for how ridiculously complicated and long-winded this explanation is turning out to be. And the bad news is, we're barely halfway through, even although Frank and I are going as fast as we can. I'm beginning to think we should have issued a trigger warning before we started.' She smiled as a ripple of sympathetic laughter bounced around the room.

'I'm afraid there's no edited highlights on the telly later either,' Frank laughed. 'But I mentioned Gordon Baird had a wee insurance policy, and I'll explain what I mean by that. You see, Baird knew that as soon as Andrew McQuarrie published his paper, the one which he'd ripped off from Naomi, he had him by the you-know-what's. From that moment on, McQuarrie's burgeoning reputation was entirely dependent on Baird keeping his mouth shut about the economist stealing the contents of Naomi's thesis. Because with that out in the open, as well as being ruined, suddenly McQuarrie becomes the prime suspect for her murder. From Baird's point of view, now there's nothing McQuarrie can do to harm him. He's untouchable.'

Maggie nodded. 'We imagine that Baird might have considered coming clean at that point, but when he weighed it up, he could see the risks. A fiscal enquiry had already concluded that he was the murderer, and he wondered how keen the authorities would be to re-open the case. The chances are he would simply be arrested and banged up in prison. Besides, he was enjoying his new life running what had become Cambridge's hottest music venue. The city was overflowing with young women desperate to find a showcase for their music, and Baird was more than happy to offer them a slot in return for favours of a sexual nature. And with McQuarrie on the hook, there was always that nice blackmailing resource he could tap into when money was running short.'

'That's right,' Frank said. 'And everything continued hunky-dory for the next two years, that was until the day Rhona Fraser's band was booked to play in Cambridge. The night before the concert, she went along to the Cambridge Musician to see one of her favourite bands, and that's when she saw him. We can only imagine how Rhona felt, but shocked, stunned and confused all at the same time would just about sum it up I think. Because after all, Gordon Baird had died in the Cairngorms over two years earlier, hadn't he? Yet somehow, here he was in Cambridge, alive and kicking. But of course that couldn't be true, she must have thought. So instead of confronting him immediately, she decided to follow him and find out where he lived, which explains why she got on that late-night bus.'

'Obviously, with Rhona and Baird both now dead, we'll never know what happened next,' Maggie continued. 'We can only assume that Rhona somehow overcame her scruples and decided she would confront him after all. We imagine she knocked on his door, and in his shock and panic, he murdered her to stop his real identity coming out.'

Frank nodded sadly. 'We've got a scene-of-crime team digging up his garden, but that's a long shot. If you want to know the truth, I don't think we'll ever find her body. It's so sad for her family and loved ones, but at least we've been able to tell them what happened to her. Although whether that's going to be much comfort, I can't really say.'

'Yes, it's all too horrible,' Maggie said, 'and we know it must have really spooked Baird too. We think that explains why he suddenly demanded these huge sums of money from Andrew McQuarrie and given that the economist's career was really beginning to take off, he felt he had no option but to pay up or risk exposure as a fraud. And we mustn't forget the terrible toll the disappearance took on Olivia Cranston's mental health, which was already quite fragile. Rhona was the most precious thing in the world to her, and she would never recover from her loss. And as we are about to find out, it was that loss that drove the series of events that played out eight years later.'

'Exactly,' Frank said. 'So not much happened for those eight years, save for Baird making the occasional call on the bank of McQuarrie when he needed a wee top-up of funds. But then Olivia Cranston decides to return to Cambridge to take up a wonderful job opportunity at the University, and just like Rhona before her, she is stunned to see Gordon Baird at his music venue, very much alive. Just like Rhona did, she followed him back to his home on the bus, but unlike Rhona, she evidently decided to take no immediate action. But the *big* difference was that Olivia had left a calling card, an act which explains why Baird once again fell into a blind panic, prompting him to again demand a huge sum of money from Andrew McQuarrie to maintain his silence.'

Maggie nodded gravely. 'And now, albeit slowly, Olivia Cranston is able to piece together the dreadful story, You see, she herself had benefitted from Gordon Baird's sex-for-grades racket, which explains how she ended up with a first-class honours when her school results had been nothing to write home about. As a result, she had always known why Naomi had agreed to sleep with the repellent lecturer, nor had she ever questioned that it was he who had killed her, either deliberately or accidently. But now she knows differently. Horror-struck, she realises that it could only have been Andrew McQuarrie who murdered Naomi Neilson and who had facilitated the disappearance of Gordon Baird. She realises too that Baird must have killed her lovely Rhona to stop the subterfuge being revealed. Distraught and seething with rage, she plots a terrible revenge on the perpetrators, aided and abetted by her brother Robbie, to whom she has run to in the aftermath of her shocking discovery. Obviously, Baird must die in order to pay for what he has done. Robbie and Olivia travel to Cambridge where he is stabbed late at night as he walks from the bus-stop to his home, then his body is bundled into Robbie's Land Rover and dumped in the river. But death is too good for Andrew McQuarrie, she decides. No, he must suffer like she has had to, which means both Gina and his children must die.'

'Aye, that's right,' Frank said. 'Robbie Cranston was a member of the Cairngorm mountain rescue team which meant he had access to the database that walkers and climbers used to post their intended routes. He knew from her social media posts that Gina was planning a big walk up Braeriach and it was the easiest thing in the world for him to go online and find out what her plans were. On the day in question, he set off via the western route and intercepted her at the edge of the Bhrochain corrie. He would have taken her by surprise of course, but he obviously didn't push her hard enough because she landed on the protruding ledge sixty or seventy feet below. He wouldn't have been able to tell if she was dead or not, so he climbed down to finish the job. Unfortunately for him, he left behind footprints which we've subsequently been able to prove came from his walking boots, and he didn't spot the swatch of fabric from Gina's jacket either.'

'Their grand finale was to murder the McQuarrie children as they entered that Milngavie Guide hall, but of course you now know that we were able to thwart that, thank goodness. Because these innocent kids didn't deserve to die.' She made to continue but as she did so, Yash Patel of the Chronicle stood up and raised his hands above his head, applauding then slowly rotating as he encouraged the audience to join in. To a man and a woman, the assembly sprung up and joined him in the spontaneous and heartfelt show of appreciation.

'Thank you, thank you,' Maggie said, beaming, raising a hand in acknowledgement, 'but that's not quite the end of our story, is it Frank?'

He smiled back at her. 'No, it isn't. Because what every one of you must be wanting to know is, how much did Gina know? And Maggie here is going to tell us the answer to that question.'

She hesitated for a moment before answering. 'She knew everything. *Everything*.' There was a collective gasp from the audience as they took in what she had just said. 'Do we really think it's possible that Gina McQuarrie slept soundly in her bed as her husband got up in the middle of the night and went along the corridor to strangle Naomi Neilson? No, I think that is stretching credibility to its limits, don't you? And all that shuffling of the money that was done to pay off

Gordon Baird? There's no way that could have happened without her knowing about it.'

'And there's something else too,' Frank said. 'You see, Emma King her financial advisor told us that when she set up the business structures of the Flaming Fiddles, it was done in such a way that both Gina and Rhona Fraser had equal and full access to all the money that the band had accumulated.'

'Which was a very large amount,' Maggie continued, 'and because of the way these finances were structured, she took full control of all the money when her partner Rhona Fraser disappeared and was subsequently declared dead. Given that fact, it's not beyond the bounds of possibility that it was Gina who persuaded Gordon Baird to kill Rhona.'

'Aye, because there was a double benefit to her from Rhona's death,' Frank added. 'Obviously, it prevented her ex-musical partner from betraying Baird and thus exposing the whole subterfuge, and she got all the money as an added bonus.'

Maggie nodded. 'And it was all going so well until Olivia Cranston decided to pursue her dream job opportunity in Cambridge. And that, ladies and gentlemen, really is the end of our story.'

***

They concluded their presentation with a name check for all the excellent members of their team, and one-by-one Jimmy, Lori Logan, DC Lexy McDonald, DC Ronnie French and Eleanor Campbell were asked to stand up and acknowledge the applause of the audience. Some did so with modest reluctance, others– actually, only Miss Lorilynn Logan – soaked up the adulation like a footballer who had just scored the winning goal in a cup final. Afterwards, drinks were served from trays by the attentive waiting staff, and the audience huddled in small groups, marvelling at the brilliance of Maggie and her team in solving this most convoluted of cases. As for Patel, he had made a beeline for Maggie, his hand clutching a piece of paper that turned out to be a media contract, promising her an eye-watering sum of money in return for exclusive rights to the case. Fending him off with the promise that she would think about his offer most carefully, she wandered over to the side of the room where she had noticed a group of three women in animated conversation. On the face of it, ex-minister Katherine Collins, forensic wizard Eleanor Campbell and Jimmy's beautiful Nordic girlfriend Frida Larsen would not seem to have much in common, but as Maggie came into earshot, the connection became clear.

'It's going to be our first, and I'm *so* excited,' Collins was gushing. 'Rupert and I had been trying for *years* and we'd began to give up hope. But then we had our little holiday in St Lucia, and well, it's embarrassing to say this, but it was *so* romantic, and we hardly left the bedroom if you know what I mean. And it just *happened*. It's too early to know of course, but I'm convinced it's a girl. I don't know how, but I just *know*.'

'I know mine's a boy,' Eleanor said. 'I found out last week and Lloyd is so pleased. He's desperate to buy him a little Chelsea shirt with his name on the back but we've not decided what to call him yet.' She gave a proud laugh. 'But he's not going to be a footballer. He's going to be an IT genius and he'll start a company that will like change the world.'

'That's fantastic news Eleanor,' Maggie said. 'I'm very pleased for you.' She paused for a moment then said. 'Actually, I think I have some news too. I took a test this morning and it was positive. But I didn't need to,' she added. 'The sickness gave it away and I remember it *so* well from when I was pregnant with Ollie.' She smiled at Katherine. 'And I don't have any feeling whether it's a boy or a girl, but I know Frank and Ollie won't mind which.'

Unexpectedly, Frida spoke.

'I think mine will be a boy and he'll be big and strong and handsome like his father, and he'll be a famous explorer or a naturalist,' she said, gently patting her tummy.

Maggie gave her a look of astonishment. 'Frida, you're pregnant? That's amazing news. Does Jimmy know yet?'

Frida beamed a huge smile. 'No. I bought a test yesterday because I was late, and I had been sick every morning for the last few days. I jumped for joy when it was positive. I'm going to tell him tonight.'

***

So there was to be two little Stewart babies, two wonderful little cousins to join Ollie in a wonderful extended family, a family bursting with joy and happiness. And for about the millionth time, Maggie thanked the heavens for bringing the Stewart brothers into her life.

A BIG THANK YOU FROM AUTHOR ROB WYLLIE

Dear Reader,

A huge thank you for reading *Murder in the Cairngorms* and I do hope you enjoyed it! For indie authors like me, star ratings are our lifeblood so it would be great if you could take the trouble to post a star rating on Amazon when prompted.

If you did enjoy this book, I'm sure you would also like the other books in the series -you can find them all (at very reasonable prices!) on Amazon. Search 'Rob Wyllie' or 'Maggie Bainbridge' and you'll find them.

You can also get a brilliant Maggie short story, Murder of the Unknown Woman, free for your Kindle by visiting my website - that's https://robwyllie.com

Thank you for your support!

Regards
Rob

Printed in Great Britain
by Amazon